A Lodging Place in the Wilderness

A Lodging Place in the Wilderness

Gilit Chomski

TRANSLATED BY
Ira Moskowitz

KTAV PUBLISHING HOUSE

A Lodging Place in the Wilderness

Published by

KTAV PUBLISHING HOUSE
527 Empire Blvd
Brooklyn, NY 11225
www.ktav.com
orders@ktav.com
Ph: (718) 972-5449 / Fax: (718) 972-6307

Typeset by Raphaël Freeman, Renana Typesetting
Cover design by Shira Atwood

ISBN 978-1-60280-335-0

Manufactured in the United States of America

That what there is
shall go to those
who are good for it

Bertolt Brecht

A SCREAM WAS HEARD WHEN I WAS BORN. I ASSUME IT WAS me screaming, though it's hard to say I was surprised. The sensation was familiar to me. I had experienced it for the first time eight months earlier, when I was conceived on the first floor of the same building, in the room with the flickering light bulb. About five years later, it would vaguely resurface in me when I slid down a water slide for the first time – a wet déjà vu of panic and a sense of victory and wild bliss.

I was born on the fourth floor of a hotel, and before my time. Two dazed volunteers and a woman named Teresa worked hard on my birth. The window was a thin brown frame around a picture of a tranquil sea and arid, wintry mountains. What else could I do but scream?

The sea, of course, was the Dead Sea, the sea my mother loves. Mother can't remember even one of my previous incarnations. She thinks the fact I was born at the Dead Sea is why I love burritos.

What does the future portend for someone who was born by the Dead Sea? I remember at least my last three incarnations (though it could be that I invented the old Indian woman). I'm less clear about the future. I assume I'll die someday, but for this I could've been born anywhere. As of the moment of my birth, my foggy future included only one promise I could count on – a birthday celebration each year at the same hotel. The hotel manager was so excited by my birth that he immediately awarded me a three-day stay, free of charge, every year on my birthday. He didn't know my mother.

My birthday was not my first visit to the Pomegranate Branches Hotel. Eight months earlier, Mother had come to the very same hotel for the regular annual workshop of a guru named Trip. At the time, she wasn't called "Mother" yet, just Darya, and this also wasn't her real name. Her real name was too boring and was incongruent with the white dresses and moon dance circles; they belonged to someone else. Dorit (Doris) Cohen was destined to pursue desirable jobs and a solid husband and home in the suburbs of Baltimore. Darya was born to dance.

On that moonlit night, she danced herself senseless around the most handsome man in the group. A primeval instinct of survival drew her to his strong body, his healthy hair and his white teeth that would save her a lot of money on dental treatment in another ten, fifteen years. Trip, who quietly observed the budding romance, was very dissatisfied. From the moment she emerged from the bus, he saw that it wasn't the same Darya who joined his circle each and every year: Her eyes did not focus on him, full of veneration and longing. Instead, they sparkled with a mature and strange light. To his great frustration, this vague feeling became a reality in front of his very eyes. The man who would soon become my father alighted from the bus a moment later and his eyes met her eyes. Like someone helplessly watching a traffic accident occur under his window, Trip knew a moment before the encounter that the blaze was inevitable.

What brought them together? A connection of souls in the previous incarnation, a prophetic revelation, the touch of a wand by a yet-to-be-revealed god? For whatever reason, within minutes Darya and the stranger became inseparable. Century-old traditions of cafés and conversations and searching for hints with hand movements lightly peeled off of them like cancerous skin that becomes too thin and dry. The connection was woven at the speed of light.

That night, during the moon dance, Trip instructed the participants to divide into two groups – men on one side and women on the other. It was a surprising move that was incongruent with the spirit of the liberated group. The regulars complained, but Trip did not relent. "It will help us concentrate on what is truly important," he said. But Trip, who on numerous occasions was almost my father, remembered too late this time: Darya, in a white sleeveless dress, and the new fellow did not intend to part. The thought that there were truly important things other than this moment they shared made them giggle. They left the group and went up to his room on the first floor.

Wearing a white dress on a moonlit night in the Negev is sort of like wearing a kaffiya on a hike in the desert – too precise to be real. And still, the sight of the radiant young woman and the powerful stranger disappearing into the moonlight reminded all of the participants of the emptiness they had traveled for hours on the bus to forget, the hole in the wall they had tried to fill with straw. For one moment, everyone experienced a shared pang of loneliness.

Since Darya and my father never met again after the workshop, one could say that this was their honeymoon: They were excited, as required, and he carried her over the threshold – I assume this is close enough. When he switched on the light, a spark was heard, a sort of "Sssssss!" and it started to flicker, creating a small and inappropriate discotheque, walking distance from the Communing with the Moonlight workshop. Father-to-be said "ugh!" and reached his hand toward the switch. Soon-to-be-Mother pulled his hand back and said, "No, leave it this way." Anyway, the change in posture forced him to lay her on the bed. Under the flickering neon light, he pulled up the edges of the white dress, which looked, quite surprisingly, perfectly appropriate. The psychedelic atmosphere quickened their heartbeats, which were already racing. Her fingers lightly scanned his face, drew a faint profile and moved on to thick and generous layers of gouache paint. This was also the closest moment to their wedding proposal. Darya said, "Yes, yes, yes!" and her eyes sparkled. The flickering light bulb went out exactly at the moment when the heart calmed down from the twists and turns of the waterslide. She hoped I wouldn't be epileptic.

In fact, I was created several days earlier. The longing in her eyes, the words of love on her lips, the butterflies in her belly – it was me. A secret. Father, of course, didn't see any of this. In the reflection of her blue eyes, he only saw himself and was happy. Men don't understand such things. When I grow up, I'll also forget. Already I sometimes find myself forgetting something or making a mistake and telling myself: Here, it's about to begin.

The moonlight workshop lasted a week. When it was over, a process began that would culminate a year later with Father's final transformation into an envelope of money, regularly arriving once a month. His image faded in the dust of the South, leaving a scar of sweet-salty DNA. For three days every year, I tried to summon his image from there, a task that turned out to be nearly impossible. Like the management game I would see in a few years in Shlomo's room, crystals form in a random way. You need a lot of luck to precisely conjure up the picture you want. In most cases, another picture emerges and you're satisfied nonetheless.

I often thought that if she had just waited a bit, let's say a month or two, maybe even a year, he would have married her. The initial thought was undoubtedly planted in my consciousness on that night with the white dress and the flickering party light, and it could ultimately be cultivated and processed into the desired result. But Darya, who now could already be called Mother, never had patience. "I think I'm pregnant," she already informed him the next day with sparkling eyes. It was too early to know, of course. Nonetheless, an unmistakable certainty dwelled in her eyes. The heart of a mother foresees and does not err. The handsome young man, who just yesterday had enticed a beautiful young woman under the moonlight in a sort of serenade for boundless youth, was about to become a father. The drastic change was quick and sudden. It's hard to blame him. To his credit, it can also be said that he definitely promised that he would support her in whatever she decided to do, but. She did not cry when he left. My consoling arms caressed her from inside the belly. She looked at the sea, gleaming with salty wedding crystals, and placed her hand on top of me, comrades in a shared destiny.

I was supposed to be born nine months later and dance my first moon dance at my mother's breast at the age of three months. But, as fate would have it, the workshop the following year was held four months early in order to accommodate the constraints of one of the participants, a young woman with black hair and green eyes who had yet to participate in moonlight workshops but had met Trip on his latest trip to India and promised to bring new depth to the group. So it happened that only eight months after the night of the flickering light bulb, Trip extended a bored hand to a pregnant Darya standing at the door of the bus. "You're not going to give birth on us here, right?" he asked apprehensively. Mother would surely have answered something like "no, there's another month, don't worry," if she had not been forced to suddenly wince from a certain finger movement of mine, which protruded from the front of her belly. She watched way too much non-educational television; she'd have to stop this after my birth.

Why did she even come to that workshop? A habit of years and pleasant memories of blessed forgetfulness. Moon dances were part of an ancient deal of the moon's diminution – since the moon's heroic surrender of its size compared to the sun, people danced and fell in love under the moon without getting burned. Darya loved these nights. There were years when she thought she'd continue to dance like this forever, but something in the air around her changed. Now she was no longer the beautiful, sought-after Darya and, surprisingly, she also didn't want to be. Trip's lectures and the moon dances, which once had imbued her with a sense of realness, bored her. By then, our relationship had already developed to the point that we could simply be together without doing anything and feel satisfied. On the second day, even before the moon rose and the evening fell, she said she was tired and left with me to rest in the room. In fact, this was the last workshop she would participate in. No one would have believed this. The small group looked at us with relief.

At the entrance to the hotel, she stopped for a moment and sighed an undefined sigh about everything that was over and done with, and about everything that was yet to be. One of the chambermaids, who happened to be passing by, hurried up to her and asked whether everything was okay. The chambermaid looked very alarmed. The protruding belly seemed to portend a situation in which she would be clueless about what to do. Mother said, "Yes, everything is fine, thank you." In order to calm the chambermaid and illustrate how fine everything was, she entered the elevator and went up to the fourth floor. She left the door to the room open in order to enjoy a light breeze, sat on the chair near the window and looked out toward the sea, gleaming in the light of the sun, which was turning orange as the evening fell. She regretted not buying herself a facial mud mask – she could have devoted the free evening to a material cosmetic treatment instead of glowing from within. She thought about her parents (who remained in America) and about the new love (aborted precisely because of the fruits it bore) and about her good friend Mika (who was knitting me a small sweater – in pink, for some reason). Against the backdrop of the sunset by the sea, she was emotionally stirred by her melancholy thoughts and she felt moisture streaming down her legs for some reason instead of her cheeks. I'm sure it's nothing, she assured herself. There's another month. It couldn't be.

The hallway on the fourth floor of the Pomegranate Branches Hotel ends at a glass door overlooking the sea. At that hour, the floor was empty and very quiet. The sun seared its last burns in the salt when Darya's first scream shook the hallway. What a scene from a Hollywood thriller this must have been!

The second scream was more effective – Mother stumbled to the telephone, dialed numbers with blind fingers and shouted into it: "I'm in labor!" She had directly reached the reception desk, where the frantic receptionist tried to call two of the chambermaids and the manager to go up and calm down the woman in labor while she telephoned for an ambulance. For a reason that later became clear, she could not find any of the hotel personnel; it seemed like everyone had mysteriously disappeared. Luckily, the elevator stopped at the fourth floor and two of the hotel guests, a man and a pretty woman in a black dress, emerged from the elevator just before the second scream.

The man was certain that he was about to witness a murder. The woman understood immediately that a baby was about to be born. They entered through the open door, calmed the frightened mother-to-be, and after a short conversation with the receptionist, who told them she had already summoned an ambulance, they simply sat next to her. The woman – we didn't know yet that her name was Teresa – held Mother's hand. We waited patiently.

When the Magen David Adom volunteers burst into the room, young and frightened and in high spirits (births and traffic accidents were not really supposed to happen during their shift), they immediately spread out the stretcher with exaggerated seriousness. This was the one thing they were sure they should do. But Mother didn't even have time to lie on it. "He's coming out, he's coming out!" she wailed. The thought of separating from me was difficult for her. I gave some thought to remaining, but the water slide had already embarked on its winding path, and there was no stopping. The hotel manager and the chambermaids entered the room just as I stuck out my head and stared at the upside-down woman in the black dress. I screamed. This scream granted me a free stay at the Pomegranate Branches Hotel for life.

In the ambulance on the way to the delivery room in the Southern city, we learned the reason why the receptionist was unable to find the manager: Amazingly, and contrary to all laws of probability, one of the chambermaids, who was also pregnant, began to experience contractions at the same time that Darya was parting forever from Trip and the moonlight group and I was starting to plan my entry into the world. So it happened that when the receptionist finally found the manager hurrying to the kitchen (he had seen in old British movies that you need to bring water) and told him that someone was giving birth, he replied to her: "I'm handling it." And he then returned to the room where the chambermaid was about to give birth, without imagining that there was another woman in labor.

The chambermaid's baby was less eager to set off into the world (for reasons that would turn out to be very justified). When this surprising twofold situation finally became evident, we crowded together in the rickety ambulance: a chambermaid in her work uniform moaning and groaning, another chambermaid holding her hand, the flustered hotel manager, the pretty woman in the black dress, Mother and I. The woman in black, Teresa, joined us on the spur of the moment after the manager asked Darya "should I call someone?" and Mother shook her head "no." Teresa was the first person I saw. I assume that this fact, as well as the fact that our shared secret was already beginning to take shape then, connected me to her forever. Outside the window, the weary fields of cotton that had yet to be redeemed from the *shmita** year were bending under the wild growth, much to the farmers' dismay. The chambermaid in labor screamed again, and though the road was empty, the ambulance driver turned on the siren. The Dead Sea road was never so full of life.

*   *   *

The Pomegranate Branches Hotel is situated right on the shore of the Dead Sea – a minor but significant victory over some of the more magnificent hotels located across the street, whose guests must cross it on their way back from the sea under a scorching sun. Like the other hotels in the area, it is not very new. But it is also not old enough to take pride in the title "historic." To its credit, it should be noted that the hotel was not tempted, like some of the

---

* Sabbatical year, when fields remain fallow.

others, to renovate parts of a pool or balcony, like those shapeless women who drag themselves once a week to the beauty salon to dye their hair with a color that lights up their face. Like many buildings, the secret of its charm lies ultimately in the eyes of the beholder. In order to discern its attraction, a thin layer of cataracts is needed. Nonetheless, and perhaps for this reason, it enjoys a considerable number of regular customers – elderly people who always take an annual vacation because of psoriasis, an annual conference of Qumran Caves researchers, the hotel's child and his mother, and a number of other couples. The hotel's permanent staff knows that not only many people tend to return to it, but also objects tend to return and visit, mainly before Yom Kippur.

Yom Kippur, the Day of Judgment and Forgiveness, is primarily known at the Pomegranate Branches Hotel as "Towel Day." On the third year of handling the Yom Kippur towels, Mimi truly believed that it would be her last Towel Day.

It was not only towels, they explained to her when she had just arrived, but mainly towels. Every year prior to the Day of Judgment, some of the hotel's guests – who in the meantime had become religiously observant, fallen ill or undergone another experience that led to soul-searching – felt pangs of guilt. They would carefully wrap the property they stole from the hotel a month, a year or two years earlier in a fit of uncontrolled greed (the record is five years) and mail it to the address on the Dead Sea shore. The envelopes would contain very small and usually worthless treasures – towels with the logo of two pomegranates and flowery writing, plates, cups, spoons or items stolen from other guests. Sometimes the senders would attach an anonymous note expressing remorse and asking forgiveness in the spirit of the reconciliation that Yom Kippur is supposed to foster, in their view. The phenomenon of returned objects is well-known in all hotels; for some reason, it seemed that the guests of the Pomegranate Branches Hotel were the most eager to atone for their sins. What was there in this hotel that filled them with remorse? Perhaps it was partly due to the fact that it was the smallest hotel. (It's a "boutique hotel" says Shlomo the manager, waxing poetic. Actually, its size derives from the fact that it's also the oldest hotel.) And in small places, feelings of guilt occupy a larger space. Or perhaps the objects themselves were the ones who were eager to return home. One way or another, every year the small packages heralded the start of the holiday season of the month of Tishri.

In Mimi's first year at the hotel, prior to her first Towel Day, she was sorting mail and found a padded envelope, signed with a name. Inside the envelope was a sewing kit with the hotel's logo and two letters. The following was written in the first letter:

My name is Sarah Wolf. On May 26, 1999, I stayed at the hotel with two of my granddaughters. Unfortunately, one of them did something that is forbidden and is contrary to our faith and took the sewing kit for no good reason. On her behalf and mine, as the Days of Awe approach, I ask for forgiveness and pardon.

The second letter was a small notebook page with two words – "I'm sorry" – written on it in childish, shaky handwriting.

Mimi remembered Sarah Wolf very well, an older and fervently religious woman, who was persuaded by a friendly official at the National Insurance Institute to exploit her eligibility for psoriasis treatment and go down to the Dead Sea. This was apparently her first vacation in a hotel, which explains her misunderstanding about the sewing kit. She arrived accompanied by two pale girls with braids who went down to the seashore with long-sleeved dresses and stockings. Mimi imagined the smaller of the two being repri-manded by the wrinkled Sarah Wolf, and her skin trembled. She immediately wrote a letter of response explaining that the sewing kit was placed in the room as a gift for guests, and she added two additional kits in appreciation of the nobility of Mrs. Wolf and her granddaughter. The story touched her heart. She had started working at Pomegranate Branches only a few weeks earlier, and the hotel guests seemed humane and very friendly. Mimi had planned to remain at the hotel only until she saved enough money to rent an apartment in Tel Aviv, but in the meantime she worked as both a chambermaid and a receptionist. Her salary was very high and, accordingly, she felt a great deal of responsibility. Her attitude toward the guests was almost maternal.

She heard about Towel Day from her chambermaid friends. They had worked at the hotel longer than the receptionist who worked alongside them, and were more privy to all of the hotel's secrets. Towel Day, they promised, never disappoints. And indeed, in addition to the original letter from Sarah Wolf and her granddaughter, two other envelopes arrived that week with the promised towels. The towels were old and worn out; short and anonymous letters were attached to them. Mimi tossed the towels in the trash and filed the letters in a folder.

This was, as noted, in the first year. A sewing kit and two towels. The yield on Mimi's second Towel Day, on the other hand, was boring and without surprises. The throngs of guests now appeared to her as a uniform and sunburned bloc of people with tagalongs in the form of children with salt in their eyes, and old women who did not receive their egg the way they ordered it, and people who wanted another chair, a view of the sea, or compensation for one sort of aggravation or another. It was hard to believe that these people were really once endearing infants, smiling in their strollers. She wholeheartedly regretted that she hadn't managed to save enough money to already get to Tel Aviv during the period of the holidays.

Mimi was not the only one who wanted to abandon the sleepy Southern city and move to Tel Aviv. Most of the young people in the region shared the same aspiration. The desire to leave is a law of nature, in the same way that mountains create valleys. The noisier the environment, the more people are attracted to the tranquil and silent places. The quieter the place, the faster the pulse of the residents becomes, particularly the young ones among them. In the Dead Sea area, the air stands still. Most of Mimi's contemporaries had left long ago to search for that elusive place named life. After all, what could the desolate city offer them? Here, take Mimi for example. No one doubted her qualifications. She was responsible and friendly, and could always be counted upon to come up with creative ideas. In a bigger city, she could be responsible for hosting important people such as singers and actors and prime ministers, a notion that appealed to her much more than tending to old ladies with psoriasis. With the experience she had already acquired, she could be a head receptionist, or maybe not even a head receptionist but something more impressive – an official hostess, let's say (though she wasn't sure there was such a position). And eventually, who knows. After all, here she was practically running the hotel herself. The salaries in central Israel were higher and the love life was hotter. She could count the number of young people her age remaining in the city on the fingers of her two hands. How was it that she was not yet in Tel Aviv?

It was her fault, of course. She needed a car for her work at the hotel and the battery had just died, and she had to buy a new refrigerator after the last one finally became sick and tired of the battle to preserve the food in the scorching weather ten months a year. This, in addition to the surprising weddings of two (!) chambermaids within two weeks, ruined her carefully calculated savings plan. Despite her double job, she would need the salaries of another few months at least.

Mimi was an optimistic person by nature, and there were also a number of advantages to the fact that she was ultimately forced to spend another Towel Day at the Southern hotel instead of in Tel Aviv: the pomegranate season, for example. During the intensive holiday period – Rosh Hashanah, Yom Kippur, Sukkot – dozens of fruit trees are in full bloom in the hotel's yard. Autumn clouds also find their way to the lowest place on earth and the oppressive summer heat becomes bearable. Besides, the recent period had been far from boring or uneventful – she had accompanied poor Kati and witnessed the birth of the first baby at the Pomegranate

Branches Hotel. All in all, she had accumulated a number of pleasant memories there. It was now the season when most of the hotel's regular guests arrived and she had already become connected to them – Elisha, Teresa, Darya. She listed their names quickly because, as sometimes happens, at a certain point of time we mistakenly think that the temporary is permanent and the permanent is short-term. She thought to herself that they would return next year too – older, different – and the pomegranates would be ripe. She would already be in central Israel, in Tel Aviv. She would not see how the hotel's baby learned to walk. The holiday atmosphere and the end of summer put her in a sentimental mood and she felt a pang in her heart.

*

As her third Towel Day at the Pomegranate Branches Hotel approached, Mimi was already irritable. Even before she noticed that another year had passed, she felt anger mounting in her, looking for a target. There was no shortage of reasons for anger – Ophira, for example, the new girl who just a minute ago pointed with a hesitant finger at a pile of letters resting on the table. "The mailman brought this," she said. "I didn't know what to do with it." She was ungainly and plain-looking in a way that infuriated Mimi.

"It needs to go into the mail drawer. But leave it, I'll take care of it," Mimi said, taking the package away from her demonstratively. In order to calm down, she called Ola on the internal telephone. "Are you busy?"

"She's driving you crazy, huh?"

She could count on Ola to understand. Ola was in charge of the range of cosmetic and spa treatments at the hotel, including body wraps of Dead Sea mud, hot salt massages, and facials using various creams also made from mud. Due to the large number of guests at this season, Ola also received reinforcement in the form of a young woman with dyed hair and dark roots. "Not a bit of class, that one," she grumbled from time to time. The weather in the hot season intensified Ola's bitterness. She imagined snow-covered hotels and frozen rivers and well-groomed women (whose roots never show) complimenting her on the massage in her mother tongue.

Mimi let out a sigh of frustration, rolling her eyes. Ophira moved toward the end of the reception desk.

"Actually, I have a treatment in a minute," Ola said. "But I finish at two. Want to go out and walk around a bit?"

"I'll call you."

Mimi hung up, feeling calmer now. The possible outing was a point of light she could look forward to, despite the fact that there were really no places to walk around in the area of the hotel – just a small and neglected commercial center, and the seashore. The guests spent most of the hours of the day floating on their backs in the saltwater, sprinkling salt on wounds and breathing mountain air. The sea itself was mucous and thick, a faded negative of the Sea of Galilee, located four to five hours from there by car. While the guests of the Sea of Galilee in the north sprinkled bread crumbs and watched the fish gather or, alternatively, yelled in anger when the fish nibbled on their feet in drought years, the guests of the Dead Sea could be certain that they were the only form of life in the water. The fishes' absence was what gave the sea its morbid name, the Dead Sea. There was considerable injustice in the name – one of the advantages of the lowest place on earth is that it is impossible to drown in it. The salt sets the bathers afloat, as if they were bread crumbs; the sun nibbles at them, drowning them in heat.

The commercial center is a few minutes by foot from the hotel. The sea and the mud on the beach across the street, free of charge to all, are the best-selling products at the center – guests at the Dead Sea like packages very much. In addition to a range of Dead Sea products, there are also a few stores selling bathing suits and sandals, and a small kiosk with several benches next to it. Mimi and Ola sometimes came and sat there. Mimi enjoyed Ola's company –

they had something in common. Ola was saving money in order to flee from the terrible heat and from the rude people and to finally return to Russia, a serious and much more complicated plan than Mimi's anticipated move to Tel Aviv.

There was another half hour until two o'clock. Mimi opened the mail drawer and checked the new pile. One of the envelopes was particularly big. She guessed its soft touch, and even before she touched it she realized that the towel season had begun, her third holiday season. This realization filled her with frustration. Though her status at the hotel was very well-established and impressive, and the double salary enabled her to live a life that was certainly comfortable, the realization of her plan was taking much longer than she had anticipated. Rent in Tel Aviv was so high and her small 1998 Polo had just broken down. She opened the envelope in anger. There was no letter. The towel was actually in good condition, though it had the smell of home laundering. She placed it on the bottom shelf.

At two o'clock, Ola and Mimi set out together as planned on their lunch break. They ran their fingers over shirts of airy material and one-piece bathing suits with padded breasts. Later, they bought Diet Coke and sat on one of the benches near the kiosk. Ola usually stood out because of her manicured red fingernails and blond, almost albino, hair. Now, two Russian-speaking teenage girls with perfect fingernails and straight hair were roaming around the center. She examined them with hostility.

Mimi said: "That Ophira is driving me nuts. She's so slow. God knows how she'll manage here without me."

"Yes, that Ayelet too. They don't have energy to work, they just want to finish and leave." Ola studied her toenails. "I think we need to talk with Shlomo about raising our salaries. We have to be both workers and babysitters." There was something condescending in her words when she said "Shlomo" – perhaps some intimacy, as if she had said the name enough times for it to easily wear out between her lips. Mimi wondered, but didn't ask. Instead, she said: "Yes, I wish he would. I'm already dying to get the hell out of here."

"Have you saved enough?"

"Almost, maybe another two or three months."

"Poor Shlomo. What will he do without you?"

"Everyone has a replacement."

But this, of course, is incorrect. Usually, people have no replacement. Mimi knew that Shlomo would have a hard time finding a devoted and efficient worker like her. During the not-so-short period of her work at the hotel, she had become familiar with the range of problems, big and small, that receptionists and chambermaids face (stolen property, a guest giving birth). She had learned to adroitly handle all of the emergency cases as well as the routine affairs. Technically, in her view at least, she was managing the hotel almost on her own. She hoped, of course, that Shlomo would get along without her, like those young women who go to the trouble of putting on makeup and holding in their stomachs when explaining to their beloved that it would be best for him to move on and not waste any space in his memory for them.

*

Though Mimi was depressed by the first day of the third towel season, an uninvited landmark of another year spent at the Pomegranate Branches, a surprise awaited her the following day: One of the envelopes, a small and unstamped postal envelope addressed in handwriting, attracted her attention. It was not the envelope of a bill or advertisement; it looked more like a personal letter. And what attracted Mimi's attention was the little bulge indicating that there was something there bigger than a piece of paper. A key, perhaps. From the corner of her eye, she saw that Ophira, who as usual was trying to keep her distance from her, was receiving a new guest. The guest looked familiar to Mimi, apparently one of the regulars. His elusive identify hovered in her consciousness and disappeared. She tore open the envelope and pulled a letter from it:

To: The management of the Pomegranate Branches Hotel
Re: Returning a lost item
About a year ago, on October 3, 2000, I was at your hotel and stole
a necklace from one of the guests. In my defense, it could be noted
that I was in the midst of an emotional crisis, though this does not
justify the action.
As Yom Kippur approaches, and after the difficult year I've been
through, I decided to return the stolen object to its owner. I would
appreciate if you would find her and return the necklace to her. I
don't know her name, but she was staying in Room 412.
Wishing you a good year,

The letter was not signed, of course. The style was clearly that
of newly devout Jews. Regardless of how the thief looked when
he stayed at the Pomegranate Branches Hotel, today he surely has
a thick beard, large white yarmulke and a fiery messianic look in
his eyes. But at that moment, she was not interested in his identity.
She looked at the chain and the pendant attached to it, and her
eyes sparkled.

The chain itself was pretty, but not really anything extraordinary – three fine strands of gold intertwined. What made Mimi's
lower lip drop was the pendant: a gold circle set with jewels (she
was sure they were precious gems); engraved on the back was
an octopus-like image with rectangular tentacles. The pendant
gleamed in her hand like a salt crystal in the sun. She was afraid
that the light would shine from the reception desk and catch the
attention of the guests sitting in the lobby. It did not really shine
so brightly, of course, and the guests sitting in the lobby continued
to focus on their affairs, but Mimi knew, with a primordial female
sense, that she had never held such expensive jewelry so closely.

As in the case of the first towel letter (from the eccentric Sarah
Wolf and her pale granddaughter), Mimi was certain about the correct course of action. The hotel has a procedure for lost and found
objects – it stores them in the hotel safe and tries to locate their

owners. The object remains in the safe until someone comes and asks for it, and so far no item had remained abandoned. She could, of course, stuff the necklace in her bag and destroy the letter, but she did not even consider this for a moment. Mimi was the most responsible person at the hotel. Who could be trusted if not Mimi? And besides, she was sure that the pendant would glow inside her bag like a sharp object in an X-ray and the alarm in the hotel would go off.

But what happens to lost objects if no one comes to claim them? That is, what would happen if she was unable to locate the woman from Room 412? She was not sure what the procedure would be in such a case. Perhaps there was none and she would have to invent it. In any case, there was no law in the world prohibiting her from checking for a moment how the necklace looks on her neck. She told Ophira, "I'm going out for a moment," and took the envelope and entered the ladies' room. There, in front of the large mirror with the reflection of the fragrant and fake orchids, she reverently put on the necklace and looked.

The necklace was perfect for the cocktail parties held in Tel Aviv in the 1970s and Mimi still hoped to attend them. She expected to see her image in the mirror in a short black dress and matching pearls and a drink in her hand. But instead of feeling the cheerfulness expected at prestigious events, the pendant filled her with a strange sensation of serenity. The image in the mirror did not change; it was still Mimi in her receptionist outfit. She stared at it. A long stare in the mirror, without blinking, conjured up strange and pale images. The necklace continued to shine. When tears filled her eyes, she finally blinked. The mirage faded.

The hotel was very quiet that day. Only a few guests were roaming around the lobby, and none of them requested the services of the reception desk. New guests would only arrive at noon. Nothing was stopping her from doing what she should do. She took the letter and went to the computer, opened the database of hotel guests and entered the desired date.

If Mimi had expected the hand of fate to actively prevent her from returning the necklace to its rightful owner, she was immediately proven wrong. No fatal virus had mysteriously deleted the records of the desired date, and Room 412 had not disappeared from the records. The name of the single guest who stayed in the room flickered on the screen: Teresa Holstein. Teresa was one of the hotel's regular guests. In the past, she had come to the hotel with her husband, Ephraim, but in recent years she came alone. Mimi clearly remembered a middle-aged woman, with pale skin and shiny black hair, tied back.

But Teresa was not the subject. (She didn't even bother to complain about the loss of the jewelry, Mimi noted to herself. Was it possible that she didn't notice it was gone?) Okay, Teresa would get her necklace back, but the real question was: Who among the hotel's guests was the thief? She pulled up the list of all of the guests who stayed at the hotel on October 3, 2000, feeling more efficient and important than ever – after all, it was a real mystery. Admittedly, the answer, as interesting as it might be, was unimportant because the lost object would be returned to its owner. But now, with the list of names spread out before her, she studied it meticulously.

Who stayed at the Pomegranate Branches Hotel a year ago? Among the regulars, she identified Darya Cohen (and of course her infant son, the hotel's child, if one insists on counting the minutes that passed from his birth until he was taken to the hospital with Teresa and poor Kati). Someone had exploited Teresa's good-heartedness and broke into her room while she was holding Darya's hand and helping her give birth. What audacity! Who would believe that one of her guests was capable of this? Another regular guest was Elisha Nathan – that's the date his vacation unit was available. Elisha was a researcher at the nearby Qumran Caves. He came to the hotel every year for his regular vacation and sometimes even gave lectures for a fee at the hotel. The list of non-regular guests included four couples and a single man. The fact that he was alone immediately makes him suspect in her eyes. She considered calling him on the phone, but what could she actually say to him?

And who said that the thief was even a guest at the hotel? She read the letter again. "I was at your hotel," the letter says. That is, any of the people who came on vacation or for health reasons to float on the doughy water could have entered the hotel, gone up to Teresa's room and coveted the jewelry. Something inside of her (she wasn't sure whether it was the chambermaid or the receptionist) was angry about how easy it is for an intruder to enter a room in the hotel. She made a note to herself to tell Shlomo to review the security arrangements again, perhaps to change the keys. After all, this could have been much worse in the end. I have to do everything here myself, she thought, not dissatisfied.

She placed the envelope inside the towel with the home fragrance and walked to the safe. The safe was also intended for the deposit of jewelry by the few hotel guests who are not satisfied with the room safe. It was nearly the exclusive responsibility of Mimi, and Mimi preferred for the jewelry to remain wrapped.

She went over the guest list again. Actually, what she should do is to reconvene all of the guests from that day and lock them in a room. Like in Agatha Christie books. Someone would step out for a moment, there would be a power outage and someone would be murdered. But there was not much chance that the guests would reserve a vacation at the hotel merely at the receptionist's request. And also, she reminded herself, she had discovered that a thief was present only after he had repented and returned the jewelry. So, only one thing remained to be done. She compliantly picked up the phone and called Teresa Holstein.

She assumed that Teresa would not be home or that the line would be busy (what are the chances of catching someone on the phone the first time?), so she did not plan the conversation. After two rings, she was surprised to hear a feminine voice emerge from the telephone. "Hello?"

The voice was very elegant. Mimi pulled out her official voice. "Hello, is this Mrs. Holstein?" Teresa Holstein?"

"That's right," the woman's voice wondered. Why would someone call and ask if her name is Teresa?

Mimi regained her composure. "This is Mimi speaking from the Pomegranate Branches Hotel."

"Yes, yes," Teresa said, as if recalling an old acquaintance. After all, Teresa and Mimi spent that long night together with Darya and poor Kati. One could hardly consider them strangers. "Can I help you?"

"Listen, umm … something a bit strange happened. You stayed with us last year on October 3rd?"

Teresa said: "Yes, correct. I come to the hotel every year around this date."

"So, yes … perhaps you remember whether you lost jewelry with us? A necklace?"

"Not that I'm aware of."

Mimi sent an unconscious hand to her bare neck. If this necklace were hers, she would never, never lose it in such a shameful way.

"Are you sure?"

"I'm sure."

"Because we received a letter from a person who claims that he stole a necklace from you. You know, prior to Yom Kippur people start to feel guilty…" (No, no that's not the subject. Focus.) "He would like to return it to you. Perhaps you'd like to check whether you're missing something?"

"No problem, wait a moment."

Teresa disappeared with short quick steps and Mimi waited. Would she hear a shriek? A moment later she returned. "Okay, I don't bring a lot of jewelry with me to the hotel. As far as I know, I just had one necklace with me…"

"And…"

"And I still have it."

"Are you sure?" The surprise prevented Mimi from thinking of a more original sentence.

Teresa sounded decisive. "Yes, I'm sure. One necklace, that's all I had. And here, it's in front of me now."

The detective in Mimi finally emerged, even if belatedly. She switched to an ingratiating voice. "I think I remember you wearing it. A shiny pendant, like an octopus, right?"

"Right."

"And you still have it?"

"Yes."

"And it's not possible, that is … that perhaps someone made a fake copy of it?" Mimi sounded contemplative now.

Teresa Holstein laughed. There was no doubt: She doesn't read Agatha Christie.

"No, it's okay. I have it. It's my necklace."

"It's not possible that someone else has exactly the same necklace, right? Mimi accentuates the "else" and the "exactly" to emphasize how absurd the idea is. Nonetheless, Teresa says: "He apparently stole someone else's necklace."

Mimi considered whether to say that the necklace was in the hotel safe at this very moment, and that the thief specifically cited her room number. After all, Teresa said that she was not missing anything, right? No damage was caused. But if the pendant were ultimately to come into Mimi's possession, she would prefer that it not be accompanied by guilt feelings of any sort. Teresa relieved her of further indecision.

"Fine, so we'll see you at the usual time, in October. Thanks anyway for calling," she said.

After a sentence like this, the only option was to end the conversation. Mimi took leave of her with an official "we look forward to seeing you" and put the phone back its place.

Strange. As long as the necklace wasn't found, it didn't bother anyone. But precisely when the lost object was returned, it raised so many questions. Mimi reviewed the facts time and again, and finally reached the only possible conclusion: The necklace that Teresa has is a fake. She simply knew it. That is, either it was fake or Teresa was lying. And what woman in the world, she thought passionately, would not want to have such jewelry returned to her? The month of October was situated a few pages away in the calendar. Considering the fact that she needed to inform Shlomo of her resignation at least (at least!) a month in advance, she would apparently not be in Tel Aviv yet in October. Teresa would arrive at the hotel, and perhaps would even bring the strange, fake necklace with her. Mimi would take the real one from the safe and justice would come to light. She imagined a pathetic pendant made of plastic, paling beside the shiny, true pendant. Yes, she would wait until Teresa arrives. With her own hands, she would bring the story to a close.

Ophira asked, "Are you busy?" and Mimi turned, surprised, to attend to the first person in the swarm of guests in line at the reception desk.

*

During the following weeks, necklace madness swept through the small staff of the Pomegranate Branches Hotel. The person who was personally responsible for this was Mimi, who in a moment of weakness succumbed to the temptation to show Ola the pendant that was in the safe.

"Wow, glamorous." Unlike Teresa, Ola knew how to appreciate the quality of the jewelry. Her excitement was reverent and quiet, as befit the grandeur of the occasion. "It's such a beautiful pendant! How did they steal such a thing from her?"

The jewelry was stolen, of course, precisely because it was beautiful, but Mimi completely identified with the question. To her, the pendant looked pure, almost sacred. How was it possible to imagine taking pleasure in stealing it?

"What does this symbol mean?" Ola asked, running a manicured finger over the octopus with the rectangular tentacles.

"I don't know. When she comes to take it, we'll ask her." Mimi told Ola about the letter and the jewelry, but for some reason chose to omit Teresa's sweeping denial. There would be time for everything, she reassured herself. But in light of Ola's enthusiasm, in a rare moment of closeness and mentoring, she showed the pendant to Ophira too. This spurred a renewed interest in jewelry by the three women– Ola coveted a new necklace she saw in one of the stores in the city center and persuaded Boris, her husband, to buy it for her as an early birthday present; in her jewelry box, Ophira found a necklace she had always liked, but whose broken clasp she had never found the time to fix. The compliments and mutual excitement induced the girls on the staff, receptionists and chambermaids, to resurrect more and more of their forgotten treasures. It reached the point that even Shlomo decided to buy his wife a necklace for their anniversary. ("She should buy him a necklace" was the new malicious joke among the staff.) He asked Ophira to help him choose the gift from the jewelry store in the lobby. Mimi noted to herself, with a sort of sadness, that on this particular matter he did not seek her assistance. He apparently viewed her as efficient and dedicated, but not as someone who knew much about expensive jewelry. And Mimi earned twice as much as Ophira – and no one knew this better than Shlomo. As the feeling of insult began to well up, she hurried as usual to drown it in very tangible imaginings: Mimi enters the lobby of a fancy hotel in Tel Aviv with the shining pendant on her neck. The other guests and the receptionist gasp in astonishment. What style, what class! Two daydreams combined in her head and she saw herself wearing the pendant while dressed in the chambermaid's uniform she saw on the Sheraton Hotel's website. Even so, the thought released pleasant currents in her body and the insult faded away.

* * *

On my first birthday, I arrived at the Pomegranate Branches Hotel waving my hands like a successful actress returning to her home town. After all, I was born right here, on the fourth floor, just a year before. At least among our small family unit, it was a particularly exciting event.

Held in a baby carrier on my mother's back, all I could do from the moment we passed through the revolving door was to wave my two hands and observe the people sitting in the lobby while she spoke with the receptionist. During this first year of my life, watching people sit was a sufficiently interesting activity. One of the seated people on the purple couches even looked familiar to me. I smiled. An older woman, delighted, smiled back at me. (For some reason, people get very excited when a baby smiles at them, though a smiling adult is clearly a phenomenon that is much more exciting.)

None of the guests recognized me, but when Mother explained to the receptionist (her name was Ophira, Mother read her name from the badge attached to her clothing) that we came to celebrate my birthday at the hotel, free of charge, (from the tone of her voice, one could understand that we would also come the next year, and the year after too), Ophira said "R-right! I heard about this story. You went with Teresa and poor Kati. So, can we have a look?" Since I was placed in the carrier back-to-back with my mother (a strange choice for a single mother, which somehow never ended in disaster), she had to turn around and look at the lobby while the receptionist made me laugh with very nice faces. "Hi there sweetie! What's your name?" I laughed at her with all my dimples and awarded her the only word I knew to say at that time: "Mama!" The word did not make her happy, contrary to my expectations. Instead, a shadow flashed across her eyes that would ripen in another two years into a chubby baby from a random husband. I wouldn't meet him because Ophira would no longer be here. The hourglass of her numbered hours at the hotel would already be flipped over. But, of course, she didn't know this yet. At that moment, she appeared very present.

Unlike Ophira, the hotel manager did indeed remember us. Mother didn't intend to call for him (unless the receptionist caused problems), but a well-groomed woman appeared out of nowhere by the reception desk and Ophira pinched my cheeks and said to the woman, "Hi! Just a moment, I'll call him right away." In the chunks of my developing world, I had come to understand that when people said "him" they were always referring to me. But Ophira, of course, did not intend to call me. She picked up the phone, dialed just one number and said: "Shlomo, your wife is here." A moment later, he emerged from the room. Mother was standing with her back to him, surveying the people sitting in the lobby (did she also recognize the bearded man?) and, still, he took one glance at our strange two-sided structure and his eyes sparkled: "It seems to me that we have special guests, right? Darya? Darya Cohen? And you, the hotel's first child? What's your name?" I smiled and stuck a fist in my mouth in embarrassment. Mother turned around, smiled and said: "Yes. A year has passed. We have a birthday." Someone who didn't know her was liable to mistakenly think that it was her new motherhood that imbued her with that joyful and graceful confidence. Shlomo clearly remembered the night when I was born. After a brief reminder of the events for his wife's benefit, he turned to Ophira and asked: "She has a room with a playpen, hot water and everything?" Ophira nodded and Shlomo said: "Come, come, I'll go with you to see that everything's okay." To his wife, he said: "A few minutes, okay?" and indicated to Mother with a gentlemanly gesture to walk in front of him so that he could be behind her and make faces for me.

Waving my hands, I took my leave from the denizens of the lobby and we went up to the room. This time we were located on the third floor, at the end of a picture-less hallway whose walls were covered with furry, light-blue wallpaper. The room did indeed include a playpen and hot water. Shlomo asked over and over whether we needed anything and insisted that we should not hesitate to call him. Before leaving, he volunteered to take me out of the baby carrier. The touch of his strong hands, at least relatively strong, stirred in me a memory of a father-mother-child triangle for a moment, though of course I could not remember such a triangle, not from my current incarnation at least. The beginning of gender distinction began to sprout. Shlomo was not like Mother.

Birthday presents: packages. "This is from Mother," Mother sang as she pulled tempting packages from the suitcase one after another, "and this is from Father, and this is from Grandpa and Grandma." The "Father" was a lie, of course. The entity named Father until now had been derelict in greater duties than sending a gift packaged in shiny paper, though the gift could be indirectly associated with the sum of money that arrived once a month enclosed in an envelope. The "Grandpa and Grandma" was also only partly accurate – Darya's parents did indeed send a check for my birthday from a post office in Baltimore in the United States, but immediately upon receiving it she called them and noted that a one-year-old would probably prefer a toy. Bracha Cohen responded by saying that someone had to look after this child's future and if she, Darya, was unable to do this, she and Father would fulfill their obligation and it was just a shame that she didn't make it easier on them and come back home. Darya replied that she was already home, and that it would be nice if the grandfather and grandmother of this child would come to visit and allow him to feel like he has a family.

Here it should be noted that in those days I knew in the clearest way, with unconscious absoluteness that had yet to be sullied with words, that I did have a family. I imbibed this information from my mother's breasts unaware; I felt it on her skin and absorbed it from the smell of her shirt. In addition to us being mother and child, Darya believed in the simple triumph of things that were destined to happen, and this was without the need for terms like "flow" or "providence" or "the law of nature" that were expropriated from the hands of those who truly believed in them. I was a child whose father had abandoned him, and whose grandfather and grandmother were far away. Nonetheless, Mother and I did not feel that we lacked anything and we harbored no anger. We were us and we were happy. Everything else had its time and season. So why did she insert that barbed comment? Not because of me. Apparently, she was defending the honor of another girl.

Telephone conversations of this type were conducted frequently, far from my range of hearing. This specific conversation ended with a check deposited in the bank and a box of push buttons purchased at Toy World for the Child – that's from Grandpa and Grandma. And in any case, there wasn't a big difference between the beetle you could pull on a string, a music-playing clown and the box of push buttons.

The torn wrapping paper surrounded us in joyful disorder. I grabbed it in my hands, tossed and tasted it, and sang happily. Mother pulled out a camera from her bag and with a "click" captured for eternity the moment I would likely forget. The internal camera made its own "click," capturing for eternity the smell of the nylon and a blurry picture of the legs of the bed.

After a few minutes, my game with wrapping paper already began to bore Mother. She took me in her arms and stood by the window. I didn't protest – at that time, I had yet to imagine there could be a truth other than hers. We looked outside. The sea was there, green and thick and much less cheerful than the torn wrapping paper. Perhaps "soothing" is the right word. I became serious in her arms and her voice was also quiet when she said: "There's still plenty of time, we'll go down to the beach soon."

About twenty minutes later, we were already covered from head to toe in our mother-and-child-on-the-seashore look: She was in sandals, shorts, a white shirt and sunglasses; I was in overalls, leaning on her shoulder and sucking on the shoulder strap of her bathing suit. The taste was old and salty, apparently a souvenir from previous years.

After Mother selected a distant chair for herself, a familiar song began to play on a radio belonging to a group of vacationers, monsters with black masks of mud. I bounced in the carrier impatiently until Mother pulled me out, laughing, swinging me in the air and dancing. The memory of a primeval dance sent a pleasant night breeze through me, but there was no moon or stars here and there was no trace of longing in Mother's eyes.

A group of young female tourists from a country where all of the women have light-colored hair and eyes was walking from the beach toward sea. Conscious of their relative advantage, they playfully stepped into the sea with legs that were smoothed earlier that morning in the hotel bathtub. The Dead Sea has no patience for this type of deception, and their stinging skin drove them screaming out of the water.

I had yet to discover the water's trickery – bathing in the Dead Sea is not recommended for infants. Instead, I discovered the trickery of the salt on land. After Mother spread white sunscreen on me and a black mud mask on herself, turning us into yin and yang, black and white, I slipped out of her sight, crawling toward the water, in a place where the sand was still wet but the sea was not yet sparking with salt crystals, radiant and tempting. I grabbed a handful and sang softly with delight that suddenly changed into the taste of betrayal and insult in my mouth. I must have looked very comical – an infant screaming with a mouth full of evidence of the innocent sin. People were smiling as Mother rushed toward me. An older woman declared, "So, you see, everything that glitters is not gold," and looked around with satisfaction. They say that our preferences and tastes are forged during the first year of life. To this very day, I love salt and hate clichés.

We came to dinner tired and sunstruck. The manager, Shlomo, mingled among the guests and looked happy. Before long, actually the next day in the afternoon, he was going to do something that would affect the rest of his life as he knew it, and he was excited and completely unaware of the impending disaster. When he saw us, he rejoiced: "Darya! Come, come, there's a guest who will be really happy to meet you," and he led us between the tables and waiters until we reached a table for two, where a bearded man and a black-haired woman were sitting. I immediately recognized her and applauded her: How wonderful to see you, it's already been a year since we met! Shlomo said: "Teresa, do you recognize this fellow?" But even before he asked, Teresa's eyes glowed. "Hey," she called. "This is the baby who was born on the fourth floor! How you've grown! What a beautiful boy you are!" he smiled at Mother a meaningful smile, hinting that their connection would last beyond the night I was born – another one of those layers of life that existed far from my existence.

A mustached waiter emerged from behind her back. Again that gender – not like Mother, not like Mika, not like Teresa. The other one. I burst into tears. Mother said, "He's tired," and rocked me a bit. And Teresa suggested, "Why don't you put him to sleep in the stroller next to you and join us?" By "us," she meant her and the bearded man I had seen in the lobby and who was looking at us now from his seat with great interest. I immediately decided to remain awake and to make sure that Mother's finger would not slip out of my hand. When I woke up, I discovered that the conversation had already ended and that we were no longer in the dining room. My hands were empty and clenched. It's no surprise that I started screaming. I'll never know what they talked about there.

On the second day of my first birthday vacation, I was very alert. Breakfast was devoted to aimless searches driven by a dim memory. On the day I was born, one of the chambermaids also gave birth. That is, there should be another child there of exactly the same age. Eventually, I would discover that Kati the chambermaid did not return to the Pomegranates Branches Hotel after that wretched night. She disappeared without leaving a trace. Since it wasn't clear what I was looking for, my failure to find it was meaningless. I opened and closed my hands and looked at their emptiness with great interest.

Still, it was a very significant day: I took my first step. This occurred on the way from the lobby to the beach. In the lobby, Mother ran into Teresa again. They appeared to be good friends. They chatted up the leftovers of the conversation they had conducted at night without me. No one was trying to make me laugh or fascinate me, and I quickly lost interest. Fortunately, the bearded man who was with Teresa at dinner was sitting on the couch in the lobby. His tangled, goat-like beard looked very promising. He saw me looking and reached out his arms to me. "Do you want to come to Elisha?" "He's not walking yet," Mother smiled at him. I experienced an early taste of adolescence: I wanted to go to Elisha. Not just one step, not two, but three. Three steps until I fell on the padded diaper and sat on the ground in amazement. Why didn't I do this earlier?

Mother hurried toward me. "Way to go, my sweetie!" she called. She turned to Teresa: "This boy is really the child of the hotel. Not only was he born here, he also took his first step here." She didn't mention the additional steps. She placed me on the floor and I crawled to Elisha. His beard was very disappointing, but the skin on his cheek was pleasant. It had the texture of an oft-worn sock that had been laundered at least once with non-matching colors.

And on that day, I also ventured into the water. This happened because Teresa joined us on the beach. She was taking care of me while Mother was floating on her back in the sea water. I watched her and I didn't like what I was seeing. I turned and looked at two sparrows frolicking around us. I was fascinated by the sight, but for some reason Teresa got the impression that I was bored. (Sparrows are too common and too drab; they are almost the exclusive purview of one-year-olds.) She took me in her arms and we walked around the small beach, Teresa softly singing a song that belonged to another child. Still, it calmed me. I leaned on her shoulder and mumbled. The internal camera came out, click, a memory of a small kiosk on the beach, a woman in an airy dress dancing in movements that appeared crazy or devoid of any logic. Actually, she had small earphones on her ears playing music that made the dance reasonable and even essential. Later, I would recall this when realizing in astonishment that some people saw my mother in this way. Teresa's eyes sparkled with joy when she discovered a small sea mattress. She bought it. When Mother finally came out, Teresa said, "What do you think, can I take him into the water a bit?" She had a sort of claim on me – after all, she was my godmother and confidante; she was there almost from the beginning. Mother did not object.

She held me while Teresa inflated the small mattress, and soon I was joyously being carried on her arms toward the sea.

They say that water remembers. If you freeze water and examine the ice with a microscope, you'll discover all of the water's secrets. All of the words whispered upon it line up in orderly and identifiable forms. Is it because I was conceived and also born near the water that dormant memories awaken in me? Or perhaps the intrinsic memory was seared within me from other water, from that primeval sea in which I was deposited as a direct result of an act of love? In wordless knowledge, I clearly remembered that behind this entire sea was that man who was my father, waiting patiently like the biblical Leviathan.

I bounced with excitement between the two arms skillfully holding me (was it possible that Teresa has children?) and was then placed on the mattress, like Moses sailing safely in his basket, knowing he would be found. I quickly discovered the water's deceit – my hand reaching out from the mattress did not encounter the pleasant bathwater I was familiar with. It had none of that pleasant flow. I put my finger in my mouth and was flooded with the taste of yesterday's salt. I considered crying, but Teresa sang to me, "Ein Gedi, Ein Gedi, how the furrows are plowed in the wilderness," and her arms were warm. Next to us a man was floating who saw the advertisements in the hotel showing that it's possible to float on your back and read a newspaper. He held the wet edges of the newspaper and turned the pages persistently forward and backward. I watched him and the tears quickly waned in the dry air.

One person's treasure is often the unwanted leftovers of another person – just a few feet from us, in the hotel, a young woman was sitting whose alert curiosity was entirely focused on a particular incident whose details were seared in me from the day of my birth as an insignificant memory. I would have given so much to change places, even for a moment, with all of those unfamiliar people who sat on a bus, in a café, in a train next to the man who is my father, yet didn't pay any particular attention to this.

Teresa wore a shiny piece of jewelry on her chest. It really glowed. Despite the knowledge that I was risking the taste of salt again, I reached my hand toward it and hummed.

*   *   *

When Teresa Holstein called to reserve her usual vacation in the regular room, at the last moment and after a month and a half of waiting, Mimi felt as if God Himself were calling to confirm the commencement of Judgment Day. Not that the necklace troubled her – she was quite busy in general. As both the chief receptionist and chief chambermaid, her hands were full of reservations and cleaning and arranging. She almost had no time to even take the pendant out of the envelope under the towel and look at it. But even when she was engaged in her busy routine, the pendant was not forgotten. It was positioned solidly on the periphery of her mind. There must be order. If a hotel guest had fallen victim to a forgery scheme, she, Mimi, was responsible for making sure that the stolen property was returned to its owner. And besides, was it possible for some reason that Teresa was lying? This was already a matter of principle. All in all, it seemed that the legal owner of the pendant was quite eager to get rid of it. Maybe it was even stolen property? But Teresa did not deny that she had a piece of jewelry like this and had even worn it at the hotel. This would make it harder for Mimi to rationalize keeping the jewelry by thinking it was simply a matter of stealing something from a thief.

The day on which Teresa Holstein arrived as scheduled in the hotel lobby was a surprisingly busy day. At noon, the dining room was swarming with people. They looked like they had slept all night outside the hotel and had waited for the gong to sound that would allow them to enter and claim all of the rooms at once. Of course, this was not the case. Their bleary eyes, the stretching of limbs and the traces of tears on the children's cheeks testified to the long trip on the monotonous road winding down from the hilly landscape of Mitzpe Ramon to the area of the Dead Sea hotels. Those who stopped on the way to see the ibexes would arrive later.

The swarm of people formed a single line for some reason instead of dividing itself between Ophira and Mimi, even though it was possible to clearly see that both of them were checking in the guests. The dumb centipede branched out at its head, one time in Ophira's direction and one time in Mimi's direction. As if to spite Mimi, when Teresa Holstein's turn came, Ophira was the one to receive her. And as if to spite Mimi, Teresa was wearing a white shirt with a high Mandarin collar. Mimi smiled happily at her, even though she was busy and exploited the three minutes she had until the guest in front of her would start to clear her throat impatiently. "Ms. Holstein, welcome!" she turned her head toward her and tried to check whether a twin pendant was gleaming on her neck. It seemed to her that something was there, but the shirt didn't allow her to be certain. Still, one had to admit that it was a very beautiful shirt and definitely suited Teresa, who generally wore black, as far as Mimi remembered. Did the white shirt signify the end of a period of mourning? And if so, mourning for what? Teresa's straight black hair did not budge when she moved her head elegantly and said. "Hello, it's nice to come on vacation finally. It's the best part of the year."

Mimi really wanted to say something like, "And we hope that this time no one will steal anything from your room, right?" but Teresa, she reminded herself, claimed that the previous time no one had stolen anything from her either. She wanted to ask, "Did you bring jewelry with you this time?" but the question sounded shamefully suspect. Mimi thought feverishly, but the sentence that would lead to a chance to compare the pendants and a victory for her (her?) pendant was slipping away from her, and her smile soured.

The guest standing in front of her cleared her throat. She tended to her courteously and efficiently. Of course, she managed to check in **two** customers in the time it took Ophira to look for the guest register and key and credit card approval. Teresa waited politely. When Mimi glanced toward Ophira again, she discovered that Teresa Holstein had already disappeared.

In fact, it was to be a short and disastrous career for Ophira. The countdown had already started. In a few hours, she would do something hasty that would end her days as a receptionist at the Pomegranate Branches Hotel. But at this point, neither she nor Mimi was aware of this. Ophira strutted slowly behind the desk, and when all the guests had finally gone off to their rooms, she grew bored and began drawing faces and lines on her forearm with a blue pen and ruined the vacation of an elderly man with psoriasis who approached the reception desk.

Throughout the next day, Mimi's eyes searched out Teresa Holstein, hoping to find a way to initiate a conversation that would set things straight. But it was as if Teresa, who always seemed to be tranquil and pleasant, was surrounded by an impervious glass wall. No moment was the right moment. The vacationing Teresa was always busy with something: conversing with the guest Elisha (are they having an affair?), dining in the company of one of the regular guests, going down to the swimming pool in a terry cloth robe that hugged her neck. No fruitful opportunities occurred the following day either. And thus, on the fourth day of Teresa Holstein's stay in her regular room on the fourth floor, Mimi did something forbidden, in fragrant violation of the global chambermaid convention: When she saw Teresa going out to the beach with the hotel's child and his mother, she hurried to her room, dragging behind her the innocent cart of cleaning materials, which suddenly became an accomplice in crime. After locking the door, she rummaged through Teresa's belongings, searching for jewelry. She herself was shocked at how easy it would be for a dishonest chambermaid to steal objects from a guest, though the act of theft itself surprised her to a lesser extent. However, Teresa's personal items made the trespassing detective blush with shame: Teresa turned out to be a simple woman. Her possessions in the room included several books (in various languages, Mimi noticed with admiration), minimal cosmetics, clothing (more than one black dress) and a booklet of crossword puzzles. For a moment, Mimi's heart fluttered with excitement when she saw what looked like a pendant on the table, but it was not shiny. It appeared to be made of simple and inexpensive silver, and when she opened it a child smiled from it. She was not even certain whether it was a picture or perhaps the same photographed child who comes with all of the pendants in the world, though his black hair was similar to that of Teresa. The room safe was locked and Mimi had no way of opening it. If the matching pendant was hiding there, no beams of light were escaping to reveal its existence. She cleaned the room more thoroughly than usual.

When her shift was over, she put on her regular clothes again and called the spa on the house phone to invite Ola to have a drink together before leaving work for the day. Ola did not answer. Mimi intended to go down to her, but ultimately changed her mind and drove home. In this way, she missed the whole incident. If she had gone down to the spa, she would have witnessed a very colorful sight: Shlomo's wife was fuming at Ola. At first, Ola was also shouting, but she gradually became very small, shrinking like a fading dream of returning to a forsaken land.

Here, in fact, the trajectory of Ophira's career came to an end. She was about to pay a steep price for her dedication. The beginning of the end already happened a week earlier. Shlomo's wife was waiting for him one day by the reception desk. Ophira, who was not very busy, started a conversation with her about the upcoming wedding anniversary of the hotel manager and his wife. Out of mischievous and giggly sisterhood, she decided to show the surprised wife the gold necklace that had been purchased for her and was waiting in the hotel safe. One could understand the surprise of Daniela, Shlomo's wife, when she went down to receive free treatment at the spa and encountered the reckless Ola wearing the exact same necklace around her neck. This, plus the fact that three whole months remained until their anniversary, definitely was about to change some things at the Pomegranate Branches Hotel.

Ola did not call Mimi that evening. This fact was not unusual in itself, but the next too, Ola did not call Mimi on the house phone to complain about the new girl. Mimi felt a growing sense of calm (Ola will call soon), discomfort (strange), vengeance (she'll call Ola herself!) and concern. The last emotion turned out to be most precise. When she finally called the spa, the new girl answered and told her that Ola would not be coming anymore. The girl did not know the details, nor was she interested in them. Only during Mimi's afternoon shift, in her chambermaid's uniform, did she learn the truth. The chambermaids giggled uneasily. Who would have believed it?

It was no wonder, therefore, that Mimi completely forgot about Teresa. She was completely focused on Ola now. Ola did not share her little secret with Mimi, but still, in a moment of graciousness, Mimi decided to call her and say a few words of encouragement. She planned to tell her that it could have ended up much worse. Clandestine romances at the Pomegranate Branches Hotel had already led to more serious problems. After all, Ola remembered poor Kati.

But Ola did not answer the telephone, not in the afternoon and not in the evening. Shlomo drifted past the staff like a rapid shadow and looked extremely tired. Ophira was also nowhere to be seen. Mimi decided to wait a few days and then go into Shlomo's office for a talk. She would explain to him that in her opinion it would be best for everyone concerned that she, Mimi, would only continue working as a receptionist and not as a chambermaid. Look what has happened recently, she preached to him in her mind, everything is falling apart. I can't keep an eye on everything with a remote control. This request meant that Mimi would be giving up the chambermaid's salary, but perhaps with a raise and additional shifts it would be okay. At this stage of her life, and in light of her seniority among the staff, Mimi felt that her days as a chambermaid were over.

She conducted the conversation in her head dozens of times in dozens of variations to her complete satisfaction. When Teresa Holstein approached the reception desk, with her suitcases and black hangers, Mimi realized that her annual vacation was over and the mystery of the necklace remained unsolved. Mimi was more determined now that in her mind's eye she was an official receptionist who had just received a raise. She would not allow this to happen. The time had come for a more direct approach.

"Ms. Holstein!" she tried to sound friendly to the proper extent. "Did you enjoy your stay?"

"As usual. It was excellent, thank you," Teresa replied with a pleasant smile.

"You know, a strange letter arrived a few months ago that pertained to you. I called you, do you remember? In regard to a necklace?"

"Yes, I remember," Teresa smiled. "The necklace was apparently stolen from someone else. I have just one necklace, and I didn't lose it." A very narrow window of opportunity opened a crack.

"Yes, apparently from someone else," Mimi agreed. "Even though no one complained. But tell me . . . your necklace, it's sort of jagged, right? With stones?"

"Yes, exactly. You liked it?" Teresa looked very maternal, with a type of alertness flashing in her eyes.

"Very much," Mimi nodded with raven-like enthusiasm. "Is it on you? Could I see it for a moment?" She could, of course, see through Teresa's shirt that she was only wearing a few new wrinkles on her neck. But Mimi thought the question befit the role of a naive receptionist. She hoped that Teresa would be unable to resist her pleading eyes and would agree to take the jewelry out of her suitcase. From here, the path to the hotel safe and the exposure of the fake pendant should be very easy. What a great moment it would be, what a story. They would have to discover, of course, who made the fake necklace. (And Mimi has already proven her ability to solve mysteries.) Teresa would thank her and the picture of the two of them holding the two pendants would appear in the local newspaper under the headline: "Mimi's Resourcefulness."

"I no longer have it," Teresa smiled innocently.

Mimi repeated the sentence to herself. I no longer have it. "What do you mean?"

"It's not here," Teresa slowed her speech and annunciated clearly: "The necklace. It's no longer in my possession."

"But . . . just a moment, so it was stolen from you?"

"Nothing was stolen from me. I had it, but I gave it away."

"When?" Mimi hoped that it was only in her head that the question sounded like a shout.

"Just yesterday."

"Okay," Mimi the gullible, Mimi the friendly, Mimi the curious, Mimi the alert – all merged into the real Mimi, who could barely stop herself from rolling her eyes. She could not, of course, confront a hotel guest and force her to take back a piece of jewelry she claimed she had never lost. But why for heaven's sake would someone refuse to take back a piece of jewelry that had been stolen from her, and even deny the fact that it had been stolen? Of course, she could have pulled out the letter and the necklace, but she did not do this. That darn Teresa and her necklace – if she doesn't want it, so be it, she contemplated in anger. As usual when feeling embittered, she used terms that distanced herself from the subject (such as "that Ophira" or "Ola's Russia"), but the term "her necklace" refused to settle down comfortably. Hers?

Teresa said, "It's simply not a necklace that stays with you. It's a necklace that you pass on."

That you pass on. Mimi was starting to feel sick and tired of this whole story. It seemed that Teresa felt this way too.

"Yes. Nothing was stolen from me. It's fine, really. I have no complaints," she said in summary and glanced toward the exit. "Oh, I think my taxi has arrived."

"Yes, yes. Right away." The efficient Mimi reemerged and took over. She hurried to take the room key from Teresa, who politely said goodbye and left. "See you next year!" Mimi called after her, as Teresa was swallowed up in the bright sunlight outside. She did not really think she would see Teresa Holstein again. Next year at this time she would already be in Tel Aviv. This thought did not sadden her. Until the story of the necklace, Teresa was one of her favorite guests, someone who did not make a sour face when asked "how was it?" and hope to receive compensation. Now she seemed dubious and unattractive in Mimi's eyes.

So, this story was over. There never were two pendants and no ceremony would ever be held to unveil the imposter. The necklace was probably stolen or something. She should call the police. Mimi went to the safe and removed the necklace from the towel. The pendant gleamed bashfully, a disappointed lead actor in a canceled play.

Still, the day was not a total waste. She had the talk with Shlomo that same day, and from Mimi's point of view it went very well. Shlomo was the one who asked her to come to his office, and when the meeting was over, her days of working as a chambermaid were also over. From now on, Mimi would be the chief receptionist and lobby manager of the Pomegranate Branches Hotel, and as such she would have the authority to approve or reject the hiring of new receptionists. Her salary increased nicely, though it was less than the total sum she had earned in her two positions. Shlomo seemed so exhausted that she didn't have the heart to ask him for more at this time. She also did not dare to ask about Ola's disappearance. People make mistakes, people pay. Nonetheless, before she left his office, she said: "You should know that the entire staff here, we think very highly of you."

Shlomo flashed a smile (bitter? appreciative?) and said, "Thank you. I also think very highly of you. What would I do without you, Mimi." The decisive period at the end of the sentence instead of a question mark flattered her.

"You would be fine," she said. "Every person is replaceable. Besides, we're capable of coping with much more than we think."

"I hope," he said. Before she went out, he remembered one other thing. "Tell me, why is there a towel in the safe?"

"Oh, that belongs to one of the guests," she replied assuredly. Shlomo nodded absent-mindedly.

When she returned to the reception desk, for the first time as the official boss and lobby manager, she found a red-winged beetle there tied with a string.

"One of the guests found it on the edge of the pool," the new receptionist informed her. "He said it was there for two days already." Mimi immediately recognized the plastic beetle (it was pointless to expect such alertness from the new receptionist). It belonged to the hotel's child. She saw it with Darya Cohen when they went down to the pool. It's no wonder that he forgot it. Who would even think of giving such a present to a child who can barely walk? The mother and the child left the day before. Mimi typed in their name in order to check their address and mail the beetle to them. Her heart softened as she recalled the night when the hotel's small child was born, and how she had accompanied him in the ambulance to the hospital exactly a year ago. Teresa Holstein also barged her way into this memory, though Mimi's heart was entirely devoted to poor Kati at the time. Unlucky Kati, young and beautiful, with brown eyes and brown curls tied back and a planned route for a great journey in India, in Thailand, in America, and then love. She worked at the hotel for at least six months and was an industrious chambermaid, though a bit scatterbrained. And in particular, she was full of the right type of joie de vivre. Mimi remembered the day she arrived. Her curiosity and young age were mixed then with a bit of bashfulness that quickly dissipated. If someone had told Kati then that a conference of an obscure government committee on the state of the Dead Sea would have a significant impact on her life, she would surely have burst into a fit of laughter. Kati had no interest in politics, not even the narrowest type of politics. Unfortunately for her, the gloomy state of the Dead Sea ultimately had a direct impact on her life – she was the chambermaid for the government minister who was in charge of this conference. He and his wife and their four children provided her with two rooms full of work.

What happened in the empty room when the minister's wife and children were floating with their arms spread on the warm water? Kati was a flighty young woman, but still, as time passed, the picture became a brutal one in black and white in Mimi's justice-seeking mind. Did she willingly enter the minister's outstretched arms, or were they forced upon her? Kati herself could not say for sure. How much the incident itself affected her – it was hard to know. Her appearance remained the same until about three months later, when she discovered that she was pregnant. A telephone call to the minister made it clear that he had no intention of supporting another child in addition to the four he already had; the minister denied knowing her and refused to take a paternity test. Another telephone call from a man who identified himself as "a close friend of the minister" strongly advised her to have an abortion. Kati herself had no interest in having a child. At this stage of her life, she wanted mainly to travel and study and fall in love. But the late discovery, her lack of seriousness, and the objection of her traditional family to an abortion ultimately made it impossible. It was decided that the baby would be given up for adoption. Mimi remembered Kati's screams in the ambulance, tormented screams of physical pain and emotional pain. For long hours, the unwanted baby fought with the tortuous umbilical cord, while his brother in the journey lay calm in the arms of his mother, wrapped in love. Kati, herself still an infant, screamed: "Take him out of me! Take him out!" and Mimi didn't know whether she meant the baby or the minister or both of them. After a long night, the scream gave way to a sorrowful mumbling: "Take him from me." The baby was taken to the nursery, where there were also two other babies at the time: the hotel's child and the first child of a very famous and very affluent couple who had spent the past few years in fertility treatments. The two babies encompassed by love accentuated the bitter fate of Kati's baby. His was a short life, whose beginning and end were without maternal warmth. After a few hours, the baby died. Kati did not return to the Pomegranate Branches Hotel. She returned to her parents' home and with firm politeness refused to take telephone calls or condolence visits. She seemed determined to put her short period at the hotel behind her, to let it shrink, rot and fade away. Some said that she found work at the King Solomon Hotel in Eilat; some said that she flew to America, that she got married. All of these were good endings. It is hard to say whether they had any authoritative source other than wishful thinking.

The day after the talk with Shlomo and the appointment of Mimi as chief receptionist and lobby manager, an unfamiliar young man appeared at the hotel and introduced himself as Michael, the new manager of the spa. The moment Mimi saw him, she knew she would fall in love with him, that he was one of those natives of central Israel who finds tranquility in the desert hills of the distant South, and that he was going to ruin all of her plans. Not even two minutes had passed in their relationship and she was already angry with him. It's not a big deal, she thought, the time will come to think about all this. In the meantime, she shook his hand in a friendly way. "Nice to meet you, I'm Mimi."

After directing him to Shlomo's office, Mimi took a small square piece of paper from the notepad and wrote on it with the hotel pen, attached with a chain to the desk. Perhaps Teresa's secret could be found in these letters she was writing, but who could tell her what they symbolized? They looked biblical to her, even kabbalistic. Mimi defined herself as someone who believes in God, but she had no clue about Kabbalah. There were not many people in the hotel who could understand the secrets of Jewish mysticism. The only religious person on the staff at the hotel was the *kashrut* supervisor, a nervous man with a black yarmulke and insipid jokes. She recoiled at the thought of consulting with him. And there was, of course, Elisha, the regular guest with the beard and the white knitted hat (was it a yarmulke?). Elisha would be staying at the hotel through the end of the week. He appeared to her to be a logical choice. She placed the note on the top of a pile of memos in order to remind her to ask him at the first opportunity.

The opportunity came an hour later. The guest Elisha came down to the lobby alone. He was wrapped in a bathrobe and held a book under his arm. She assumed he was going down to the pool. Mimi had envisioned meeting with him when he was a bit more dressed. She considered whether to wait for another opportunity, but for some unknown reason (which became known a moment later: he wanted to request a wakeup call), Elisha walked straight to the reception desk. The die was cast. She would ask him.

When he approached her, she patiently wrote down his wakeup request and flashed a friendly smile. "Excuse me, Mr. Natan. Can I ask you something?"

"Please, go ahead," Elisha replied agreeably and smiling, or perhaps it was just that the boredom in his eyes was no longer there.

"I have here ... some sort of symbol." She turned her head from him for a moment and took out the note on which she had earlier copied the symbol of the octopus from Teresa's necklace. "Maybe you can tell me what this means?"

Elisha examined the paper. Contrary to her expectation, he did not seem surprised. In fact, amused would be a more precise word. "It appears to be a combination of some kabbalistic letters. Where did you see it?"

"I saw it on someone's jewelry and I became curious."

"Mmm..." Elisha pretended to be engrossed in studying the note. "Yes, yes. It also looks familiar to me. One of the guests here wore a piece of jewelry like this, right?"

"Yes, Teresa Holstein." The moment Mimi uttered the name, she realized she had fallen into a trap. Of course, why hadn't she thought of this earlier? Hadn't she often seen Elisha and Teresa sitting together and chatting in the lobby, or eating dinner together? It was clear that Elisha was familiar with the necklace, just as he was familiar with Teresa Holstein. He and Teresa could be partners in crime, relatives, lovers. What was certain was that they knew each other.

"Right, Teresa," Elisha mumbled. "A very special woman."

"Yes," Mimi agreed, disappointedly. If Teresa stole a piece of jewelry, Elisha would be the last person to turn her in. "So you don't know what it says?"

"Hmm," Elisha furrowed his brow. Was he trying to remember? It seemed to Mimi that he was considering whether to share the answer with her. Unfortunately for her, his conclusion was apparently negative. "Listen," he said, "maybe you should consult with someone who understands more about this than I do."

"With whom, for example?" Sarcasm did not befit Mimi. It distorted her facial features, though she was not aware of this. Elisha mumbled again.

"Perhaps try Rabbi Elias. He's very knowledgeable about Kabbalah."

*

On Friday night, Mimi covered her hair with a black kerchief and went to meet Rabbi Elias. While she was arranging her hair in the kerchief, she asked herself whether only married woman cover their heads in the synagogue or all women. She decided not to take a chance. Besides, she liked the kerchief. She looked like a dramatic widow from a film whose name she couldn't recall.

Rabbi Elias served as the rabbi for the five hotels on the beach. Every Shabbat, guests from the five hotels who were interested in Shabbat services gathered together at the neighboring Royal Crown Hotel. They barely constituted a *minyan*.** Mimi specifically assigned herself the Shabbat shift in order to meet him (though there was also a benefit to this sacrifice – the Shabbat shift paid 150%). The fact that it was Shabbat confused her – she knew it was customary to give money to charity when visiting the rabbi, but contributing money is prohibited on Shabbat. Should she promise him that she would come back later?

* A quorum of ten worshippers.

Shabbat candles, lit by hotel guests, were flickering on a table covered with a white tablecloth at the entrance to the Royal Crown Hotel. It was a very beautiful sight – the warmly dancing candlelight, mirrored by the glass door at the entrance, creating an inviting and homey atmosphere, almost sacred, against the dark landscape outside the hotel. The nights were already cold at the Dead Sea. Mimi pulled her scarf tighter around her shoulders and felt modest and pure. With the onset of Shabbat, the sense of urgency that pursued her in regard to Teresa's pendant receded a bit. After all, she contemplated, why should she care if Teresa lied? If Teresa didn't want it, so be it. What difference did it make what the symbol says? The pendant would remain in the safe until some use was found for it. But nonetheless, the calm and consoled mood that swept over her did not persuade her to decide to hand it over to the police.

When she found the small synagogue on the ground floor, she saw that the service had just ended, and she recognized Rabbi Elias folding his *talit* by the ark. She had only seen him a few times (on the rare occasions when he stayed at their hotel), but his appearance was unmistakable – a suit, a shiny black yarmulke, a white shirt. A real rabbi. The sight of him flooded her with a sense of relief – she was definitely in the right place this time. Unlike Elisha in his terry cloth robe, Rabbi Elias looked like a person you could rely upon in matters concerning the Kabbalah. She approached him with a decisive gait. "Shalom rabbi, could I perhaps ask you a question?"

Hearing her voice, Rabbi Elias turned around. She discerned good eyes. Was it possible that the Shabbat candles were dancing in them?

"Please, go ahead."

Mimi was bashful for a moment, and then regained her composure. "I have a piece of paper . . . I was told you are well-versed in the Kabbalah (wait a moment, shouldn't she be using some honorific when addressing him?), that the honorable rabbi is well-versed in the Kabbalah . . . perhaps you could explain to me what this writing means?"

"I could try. Where did you get this piece of paper, if I might ask?"

Mimi fumbled through her pockets. Her purse decided for some reason to pop out and she quickly pushed it back in. "I saw it somewhere ... here it is." She handed him the square piece of paper.

Rabbi studied it closely, and then turned his eyes again to Mimi. He asked, "What's your name, if I might ask?"

Mimi identified herself by her full name. It seemed to her that he felt relieved in some way. He smiled and said, "Nice to meet you."

Mimi waited patiently.

"Okay. You're a bit early, aren't you?" he asked. Was he reprimanding her for arriving at the end of the service? She didn't know how to respond, so she remained silent. A moment later, the rabbi said, "Oh well, there's no great secret here. What does it look like to you?"

"Like an octopus."

"Not exactly," the rabbi smiled. He turned the paper around. "It's the Hebrew letter *shin*, a kabbalistic *shin*. It has four sides instead of three. It's a combination that was used by a certain rabbi, Rabbi Jonathan Eybeschütz. Rabbi Eybeschütz was a great rabbi and expert in Jewish law and Kabbalah, though at some point he was suspected of Sabbateanism and there was a big controversy about him. He gave out amulets to pregnant women and engaged in a major dispute with Rabbi Yaakov Emden ..."

The rabbi's voice was pleasant and caressing and monotonic. Mimi was conscious of the synagogue and the ark covered with an impressive curtain of red velvet. (Does the Pomegranate Branches Hotel also have an ark curtain like this? She must check when she has the chance and, if the hotel has none, she must tell Shlomo to get one.) She was also aware of the black kerchief on her head and the special nature of this occasion, but she only vaguely heard the rabbi's words. Even though it was difficult to concentrate, she actually loved when people explained things to her. Fortunately, she remembered exactly on time to refocus her attention on Rabbi Elias. The rabbi finished telling the story of Rabbi Eybeschütz and he was now turning his attention again to Mimi's piece of paper.

"I guess you saw this symbol on a piece of jewelry," he said, examining it from the corner of his eye.

"Correct," Mimi confirmed.

"Well then, I can tell you that the jewelry you saw is a type of amulet, apparently from Rabbi Eybeschütz. According to the Kabbalah, each letter symbolizes a particular attribute."

"Which attribute?" Mimi asked, and in order to steer the conversation back to familiar territory, she added: "I found this neckla... amulet and I don't know where to return it. I saw it on a guest at the hotel, but she insists it's not hers."

"It's actually a combination of several attributes," Rabbi Elias responded. He did not appear to be surprised. "It's a bit complicated to explain, but it's not a great secret. If you'd like, I could give you the name and address of the person who is probably responsible for the piece of jewelry you saw. He's a direct descendant of Rabbi Eybeschütz and is in charge of the estate and everything pertaining to him. If it's very important to you, you could contact him and check who owns the amulet you found. He could also explain to you anything you'd like to know about it. But it would demand quite a bit of effort from you."

She didn't realize they were walking while speaking until they arrived in the lobby again, opposite the glow of the waning candles. The rabbi's face, the aromas of the Shabbat dinner and the members of an ultra-Orthodox family – father, mother and four children – walking calmly and festively to the dining room in Shabbat clothes filled her with a sense of mission. She was ready to do whatever was needed. But what would she need to do in order to return the jewelry to its owner? To promise to observe Shabbat for the rest of her life? To wear a wig? She nodded in reverence when the rabbi said, "I'm sure he'll be happy to meet with you, but you'll certainly want to show him the amulet and the problem is," and here he paused in order to give greater emphasis to the tidings he was about to drop on Mimi, "he's in Tel Aviv."

* * *

What did Elisha mean when he said to Mimi that Teresa Holstein is a special woman? There was some injustice in a statement like this – Teresa Holstein is indeed special, but people who are well-known to us also appear special to us in the same way. That is, there is nothing special about her in the eyes of people who don't know her. That's the way of the world.

Mimi's original assumption was correct: The relationship between Elisha and Teresa went beyond drinking coffee together in the lobby, and this was the result of an earlier exception from the laws of history in the chronicles of Teresa – as a scion of a rich and aristocratic family from Germany, she was never supposed to have met Elisha, who was of pure Sephardic descent. According to the original plan, she should have been in America now. Abraham Epstein was a Jew who – fortunately, in retrospect – was apprehensive enough to decide on the eve of World War II to scatter his children among relatives outside of Europe. His daughter, Estella, Teresa's mother, was assigned to be sent to a relative who had achieved great success as the owner of a sewing shop in New York. But it turned out that Estella found herself trading in her ticket for a ticket to the same destination as that of a blonde and tanned Zionist emissary. On the ship en route to Israel, when it was already too late, her European soul began to doubt her ability to fit in with the idea of the kibbutz. She changed her mind when little Teresa was born. The Zionist emissary disappeared from her life and the kibbutz turned out to be the only possible way to cope with the new baby. And in any case, it was only a way station. Because even though rumors were circulating in Israel at that time about what was happening in Germany, Estella sealed her ears. The everyday difficulties made Europe her longed-for homeland, a continent full of delights, with culture and without this sun. She had no doubt that at the first possible opportunity, she and Teresa would board a plane back to Germany, homeward.

Therefore, there was historic injustice in the fact that the child Teresa, who was slated to return to Europe in the near future, was photographed on the shoulders of a soldier dancing in a *hora* circle during the first days of the state. She starred in all of the newspapers and entered all of the encyclopedias. Her innocent smile won countless headlines throughout the world.

But eventually the facts conformed and adapted themselves to the pictures – the trip to Germany never took place and Teresa grew up as a *sabra* in Israel. That is, Estella left Teresa in the children's house and traveled to Germany at the first possible opportunity, only to discover that the horrible rumors were nothing compared to what was really happening. She collected the remnants of the sundered family and returned to Israel. Abraham Epstein was murdered just before the end of the war and the connection with the relative in America was buried with him. The only ones who remained were her mother's elderly sister and the 16-year-old son of her mother's brother. The shocked Estella returned with them to Israel and left the kibbutz forever.

Instead of the purely Israeli experience at the kibbutz, Estella bought a home in Haifa in installment payments. She found occasional sewing jobs for herself and for her aunt, which eventually led to a fashionable and branded line of women's wear – Rocco Fashion. Driven by her childhood memories, Estella turned the home in Haifa into a small island of European nostalgia. Every designed coffee mug or butter cookie was accorded the significance of the home of yesteryear. Estella and the aunt shed many tears there.

The child Teresa grew up surrounded by books in three languages and became an intellectual, fond of poetry. "Like a child in Europe," her aunt would proudly say. She studied literature, specializing in political poetry, and married a young biology student, whose great dream was to achieve a scientific breakthrough and succeed in symbiotically combining two particular cells. Ephraim Holstein, the student, suffered from minor symptoms of obsessive compulsion (a fact that Teresa only recognized in retrospect). He worked as a lecturer and laboratory supervisor during the day and devoted most of his nights to trial and error in combining cells. He wanted to achieve a sudden breakthrough and amaze the world of science, so he told no one about his experiments. Thus, when he died at the age of fifty-five before completing his mission, neither the world of science nor his close family was shattered by his absence. Their only son, Nati, was impossible to reach at the time, as always. He heard about the death of his father two weeks later, mourned as appropriate, and even came to Israel for a month-long visit. When he resumed his wanderings, Teresa harbored no anger. Nati was a *sabra*, the first generation in an existing state, and had no need to long for it. He was scientific proof of the fact that more than one generation is required to extract the gene of wandering. She and Ephraim were not surprised when at age twenty-two he packed a backpack and set off to see the world. He settled in various places for short periods of time and declared that as a matter of principle he would not marry or raise a family. But one could never know. The principles of youth are as eternal as they are. And besides, Nati was a young man and handsome and Teresa did not rule out the possibility that one day a Japanese or Chinese or Indian child would arrive in Israel and seek to explore his roots and meet his grandmother.

The fact that she was a woman and a mother was special for several people in our world, but the reason that Elisha and other people defined her as special and admired her was actually a traffic accident. The accident in which Ephraim Holstein and another woman were killed was the fault of the other driver. No one ever doubted this, including the driver himself, who sustained moderate injuries and whose conscience was mortally wounded and impossible to heal. For a brief moment, he took his eyes off the road to switch the radio station, and for this he would be punished in both earthly and heavenly courts, he told the newly widowed Teresa while she fed him with a spoon.

Teresa herself was also in the car. What happened to her? She did not remember anything about the moment of the accident. Instead, all of the assumptions the doctors and insurance inves-

tigators shared with her crystallized into images in her memory:
When the crash occurred, the window broke and Teresa started to
fly. She flew to the flowering bushes at the side of the road, landed
softly and came away with just a few scratches.

After she was widowed, Teresa was invited to return to the small
home in Haifa where her elderly bachelor uncle still lived. At least
for awhile, he was like a brother to her. But all of the things she
had experienced since leaving this home – her studies, the wedding, parenthood, the loss – blurred its traces and her heart was
no longer drawn (had she ever been drawn?) to this sanctuary of a
lost homeland of the past. Instead, she returned home, to Tel Aviv.

The accident stirred within her a need she had stored away with
Nati's childhood clothes – to feel compassion and care for and
remain awake and worried at night. But without anyone to care
for – Ephraim was dead and Nati had returned to China or India
or Thailand – her nights were devoid of worry. She exchanged the
worry for pity – she pitied poor Ephraim, who all in all was a good
husband and good partner and good father, though perhaps not
particularly alert. And even more than she pitied Ephraim, she
pitied the guilty driver because, after all, as they say, Ephraim went
on to a better place, while the driver remained here, sprawled on
his bed and constantly exposed to the cruelty of that moment, a
small moment of a random movement that divided life into "before"
and "after."

So it happened that one evening, after she ate dinner and
browsed the newspaper a bit (two panda cubs were born in the
zoo, the police requests the public's assistance in identifying an
unknown person), she got into the car and drove to the hospital
where Ephraim had died and where that driver was still hospitalized.

At first, he did not recognize her. When he realized who she
was, his eyes became sorrowful and perhaps fearful too. (Did he
fear that she had come to avenge the death of her husband while
the murderer was still bedridden?) But Teresa did not come to
make demands on behalf of the dead, or to hear "how it exactly

happened" as grief-stricken people tend to do sometimes. "It looks uncomfortable," she said and gently lifted his leg, which was set in a cast and jutted partly off of the bed, back in place. Her voice was gentle and her eyes and hands were tender. He looked at her gratefully and his eyes filled with tears.

Even if the situation might appear strange to someone looking from the side (and besides one young nurse, no one bothered to look at her), a melancholy and comforting routine developed between Teresa and the driver. She fed him with conscious, almost mechanical, movements, as if she were the incarnation of a primeval nurse or perhaps her body quickly sprouted new caring cells. "You don't have to be embarrassed, I was once a nurse, I've already seen it all," she lied and claimed for herself the right to tend to his wounds. When his situation improved a little, she would read selected items from the newspaper to him, and they would converse and share life stories. Until the point where they met, their lives had been very different. The driver was from Tiberias, where his family of candle makers had lived for seven generations. While Teresa and Ephraim were driving to a play at the municipal theater (the absurd thing, she would later say, was that they didn't really feel like going, but their subscription was about to expire), the driver and his wife were on their way to a family get-together in Jerusalem. If he hadn't gotten bored with the commercials on the radio and taken his eyes off the road for a moment in order to change stations, the two cars would have continued in their opposite directions and never have met.

But, nonetheless, they met. And from the moment that metal was hurled against metal, it was no longer possible to separate the cars and send them back to their respective parking spots in Tel Aviv and Tiberias. Thus, it turned out that it was Teresa of all people who helped the driver pass his time with stories about Estella's old sanctuary and about her doctorate on the poetry of Natan Alterman, who in her opinion was the true national poet. And when he shared with her his fears about his fate in the afterlife, it was Teresa who suggested that he speak with someone who knew more about this than she did. She turned to the only rabbi she knew, Rabbi Elias, who had prepared Nati for reading the Torah on his bar mitzvah. Rabbi Elias, in the meantime, had received a job as a *kashrut* supervisor and *hazan* in hotels and had relocated to the South. Teresa's story moved him very much and he promised to meet with the injured driver.

After the telephone conversation with the rabbi, Teresa opened the bottom drawer of the storage cabinet, for the first time since the accident, and pulled out the photo albums produced by a photographer hired to document events. (The photographs that she and Ephraim took were still scattered in the drawer.) Among these albums, she picked out Nati's bar mitzvah album and started to leaf through it. Who was this family? A young boy with black hair and beautiful eyes, a proud father and loving mother in a dress ordered from a designer a month in advance. She touched the picture of Ephraim. Nothing, flat paper. Then she caressed the thick hair of Nati, who perhaps at that moment, somewhere in one of the countries of the world, was reaching out an unconscious hand to smooth down his wind-blown hair.

Nati and Rabbi Elias, her and Nati, her and Ephraim. The photos bored her, as if she were looking at a souvenir belonging to someone else. It suddenly occurred to her that cameras were the greatest fraud of the twentieth century, even more than television. It's impossible to really capture the moment; the only thing that exists is this moment. She reached out her hand and pulled a random handful of photos from the drawer. One of the photos was very early: Nati in a bathing suit and a Styrofoam float. Two others were photographed recently: the surprise party she organized for Ephraim's fiftieth birthday, and her and Ephraim on their annual vacation at the Dead Sea, under doctor's orders. She could frame one family picture, perhaps the one from the bar mitzvah, and still the present is the only thing that exists. She smiled at Nati and Ephraim, a smile of intimacy and acceptance of fate, and put them back into the drawer.

A month after Nati flew off – to China, he said, unless in the meantime a job he was promised as a tour guide in Nepal became available – that is, two and a half months after Ephraim's death, the widowed driver took two steps for the first time. Teresa was there, encouraging him and sharing his happiness. The wounds of the accident began to heal, the patient and the caregiver gradually got used to the idea of moving their scarred bodies outside of the hospital walls. A love story of the type featured in tabloids ("He Ran Over Her Husband – And She Married Him") did not develop here. Scabs would form over the wounds and fall off, and new skin would grow underneath them, stretched over the memories. Slowly, Teresa's visits became less and less frequent until finally coming to a complete halt.

Eventually, the story of the accident made its way to Rabbi Elias and Elisha Natan, and they both agreed that Teresa possessed qualities of compassion and humility, and acted as she did without any self-interest. The forgiveness she bestowed upon the accidental murderer and her ability to move onward led Elisha to believe that she was an exceptionally altruistic woman. But Teresa knew the truth. From her perspective, it was not altruism at all, but rather the body's natural demand to be merciful and let go. The far-off Nati, the dead Ephraim and the injured driver – all three of them touched her heart and left their imprint. The pure present was all that remained for her.

*　*　*

If one insists on identifying a single point as the source of the chain of events from Elisha's perspective, one could say that his path from central Israel to the Dead Sea was paved by a goat. This goat, tired of its regular grazing route, strayed from it and fled into a cave hidden by rocks. The young Bedouin shepherd, who was supposed to retrieve **all** of the goats from grazing, tried to coax the stray goat with various calls and clucking sounds, but to no avail. In a burst of resourcefulness mixed with anger, he then threw a large rock into the cave. What a rare angle of arched arm and trajectory, takeoff and landing, was needed to achieve such a result! The immediate and satisfying result was the goat's flight from the cave. The more significant result came a bit earlier – a muffled shattering sound in the cave, indicating that the rock had broken a clay vessel. The surprised Bedouin entered the cave, squatted over the shards and it contents, and uncovered what would turn out to be one of the most important archaeological discoveries in the world.

The lost Dead Sea Scrolls were immediately purchased by the State of Israel and stirred a tempest among scholars, religious figures and historians.

At that time, in 1955, Elisha Natan was a very young boy. He was oblivious to the importance of the Qumran Library and the Hebrew scrolls discovered in southern Israel. After all, at that time he barely knew the alphabet. If, nonetheless, some early connection was forged between him and the hidden scrolls through a meaty dinner of a certain goat, there is no one who can testify to this. His great interest in archaeology had yet to be unearthed at the time beneath the regular interest he displayed in childhood games. But forty years later, when he was surprisingly offered a much sought-after job as a researcher at the Qumran Institute, his excitement was so great that it very possibly may have transcended the boundaries of time and space and shattered the vessel itself.

One could understand him. As an archaeologist, even though he ostensibly lived in a country whose layers accumulated faster than they were studied, he did not have many options. Somewhere in his adolescence, he began to shed the fields of interest dictated by his age. The teenage Elisha discovered that the possibilities contained in a single fossil, in the history at the end of a stone, fascinated him. He was not endowed with the technological abilities that allowed his contemporaries to invent the future. He could uncover the past and shed a bit of light on the riddle of history that has made us who we are.

Or at least that's what he thought. As a teenager, he voraciously read the monthly *Tree and Stone* magazine, learned about the latest research and studied new methods for determining the age of a rock or earthenware plate. It was clear to him that only the barrier of age, something that is definitely reversible, prevented him from joining the best researchers in Israel and perhaps even leading them. (He was indeed still a teenager then.) His studies at the university also seemed auspicious – immediately upon completion of his army service, he signed up to study for a double major in Bible and Archeology. He was one of the few students who didn't choose these fields because they lacked the time or grades required to study in other departments of the university; his choice derived from pure love. As such, he was recognized almost immediately as an outstanding student, and from there his path to the world of academia was short and easy. Nonetheless, those accursed unwritten rules prevented him from touching upon what really interested him. His position as a lecturer in biblical archaeology at Tel Aviv University was very comfortable, but the real, exciting research somehow always eluded him. And now, after waiting for years, his turn had arrived.

Aya, his wife and the mother of his children, did not share his excitement. When they got married, Elisha was a promising student. His future at Tel Aviv University seemed limitless and they loved each other very much. Aya, then young and dreamy, believed that she wanted to live in a kibbutz or moshav, a good place for the children she would have. So for her, the move to Tel Aviv was a concession she made, happily and lovingly, for the brilliant man. Life on a kibbutz was exchanged for an average and ultimately satisfying life from her perspective – the vibrant city provided some slight cover for Elisha's lost silence. In Aya's eyes, the relocation to the South, "beyond the hills of darkness," as she described it, would brutally terminate the regular social life she enjoyed and was another concession she was being asked to make for him. Nonetheless, Aya understood very well that there are opportunities that must not be missed. How little Elisha understood the unseen stocktaking of life that would ultimately tip the scale. A few months later, their residence in the South was an established fact.

Elisha flourished in the caves of Qumran. His respiratory problems, which he was totally unaware of, disappeared in the dry air, and the brown-white mountains towering in front of every window in their new city made his heart pound with a vitality he had never known. A feeling of discomfort that had always simmered within him gave way to a present of sharp colors, as if till now he were a loose screw imprecisely screwed into place.

And, of course, there were the scrolls. Elisha was not the only one captivated by them – new researchers usually brimmed with enthusiasm over them like children discovering the tooth fairy. The scrolls were solid evidence of the real existence of legends. They contained parts of biblical books, as well as an ancient library of interpretations of Jewish law. Thus, they exposed the earliest known stage of the Book of Books. Two findings in particular enticed Elisha: the "commentary" literature, which offered solutions to the ancient prophesies of the Bible, and the *Community Rule Scroll* of the people of the Judean Desert sect. The *Community Rule Scroll* was nothing more than a collection of the sect's regulations and worldview. In Elisha's eyes, it constituted an entire world of its own. Who were the members of the sect? Essenes? Eccentrics? From his point of view, this was not the most important question. Their orderly way of conducting themselves, free of dissension, captivated him. Here, in these hills, people gathered from all parts of the country, united in the belief that the world was divided between the sons of light and the sons of darkness, and that when the great war comes, they would be able to win with the help of several simple rules.

Ah, the rules! The first rule: The fate of the sons of light and the sons of darkness (that is, all human beings) was sealed and known in advance and impossible to change. There was some relief in this. On the Day of Judgment, the sons of light would fight alongside the angels, living as people among them, against the sons of darkness and their allies. The fate of the war was also sealed and known. Elisha began to look at people and wonder whether they were sons of light.

Additional rules hermetically encompassed the members' lives and created a world with very tangible boundaries. Who was to be accepted into the sect and under which conditions? How did one behave during dinner and when did it take place? It seems that at every given moment the members knew their place.

In addition, he was enchanted by the power of a group. Not every group – Elisha was not good at participating in groups like the parents' committee or a group of childhood friends at a picnic or neighbors on Shabbat. The dim expectations of him always left a trail of disappointment in Aya's eyes. But the members of the Judean Desert sect conducted themselves according to simple and strict rules. They gave him a feeling of security. For the first time in his life, he understood how the laws he bitterly hated were capable of providing a complete mantle of security, like a baby enwrapped in a uterine universe. Ironically, this internalization of laws engendered an addictive sense of freedom.

He spent more and more hours at the institute, and did not feel how his usually shaven beard started to sprout. The library, the shards, the carved stone shelves discovered in the caves – all these told stories that he really saw in front of his very eyes.

The ones who eluded his probing eyes were his wife and two of his three children; their skin was seared by the sun in the meantime, while the reflection of the dusty hills in their eyes created a type of screen. Aya would dream colorful dreams about the life she had known, which suddenly seemed very lively, and then abruptly awaken to a barren reality. In her dreams, she would be strolling around a mall with two of her friends (knowing that they were continuing to have fun without her did not please her at all) or driving slowly along Dizengoff Street, drawing inspiration from the display windows. To her credit, it should be noted that, at least in the beginning, she tried to conceal her emotions. But like sugar mixed with salt, what was not visible on the surface popped up in the cooked food and cakes. Before long, a wide abyss gaped between them.

At this stage, the denouement was known. It only remained to fill the holes in the time they were stuck with until the denouement came, and they both played their roles faithfully. Occasionally, Aya would say, "Eli, I'm suffocating here." Elisha would then look at her in true sadness and say, "But such little time has passed. Maybe you can still give it a chance." But her sense of alienation intensified in the face of his unwillingness to take her back to the places that were clear and familiar to her. There, I was a fish in water, she told herself bitterly as they were driving alongside the Dead Sea once. Sometimes you simply know that a particular place does not want you to feel comfortable in it. For the first time in her life, she could understand her husband and perhaps identify with him. This offered no consolation.

The anticipated departure gaped like a crack in burnt ground. As it widened, Aya packed her few possessions and her two older children and rented an apartment on the outskirts of Ramat Gan. They had rented out their home in Tel Aviv instead of selling it, and only two months remained until she could return there. The children were happy to return to their previous school, their previous friends and their previous life, which had always existed in their mother's eyes and thus had never ended. The rest was very formal. Just one surprise climbed through the cracks: Elisha's youngest son, Nadav, declared that he actually liked the Dead Sea and wanted to stay with his father. His mother looked at him, surprised. The child who scampered in parks and gardens never seemed to her as the desert type. "I like it here," Nadav insisted. "I'm not going back."

This time too the denouement was predictable and known in advance: After a series of arguments about the separation of siblings, legal threats and each child's need for his mother (though Nadav had always been a child of his father), one separation scene was ultimately staged in which Elisha (his beard had already grown and extended beyond the boundaries of his face) and Nadav waved goodbye to a car as it faded into the distance on the dusty, twisting road. Yes, there were kisses and hugs and conversations about visiting arrangements. But, nonetheless, to some extent this was a last goodbye. That night, Elisha dreamed about Nadav standing on a piece of land, his feet straddling a crevice, underneath him a yawning abyss that threatened to rip his strong stand to smithereens.

It was the most beautiful year in Elisha's life. Actually, it lasted for a year and three months. During this time, he learned some things about himself – for example, how much he disliked the burdensome work in central Israel, full of its diversions; for example, that he truly loved his children and that visitation arrangements were not a bad idea after all. The children were very independent, Aya sounded happier and more serene, and he was happy for her without any sense of envy or missed opportunity.

And mainly, he was drawn to the scrolls, hidden secrets of the past that took shape in front of his very eyes. Elisha had already participated in archeological studies at the university. It was not particularly difficult – all that was required of him was to cast bits of information into research frameworks known in advance. Now, for the first time in his life, he was required to mount a real scientific effort, to give it his all. He contacted the new rabbi who came to the area, Rabbi Elias. They were two opposite poles, material and spirit, the biblical knowledge of one and the archeological knowledge of the other created a clear picture for both of them. They were full of enthusiasm. This was the period when a white, hat-like yarmulke appeared on Elisha's head. From afar, one could mistakenly think that he was covered with dust.

Nadav was then at that wonderful age – mature enough to demonstrate inquisitive curiosity, while young enough to idolize his father and want to be like him. He adjusted well to the new school, but most of all he enjoyed the hours he spent with Elisha at the institute. Together, they would go down to the caves and investigate the crevices. The cliché of father and son was sweet, very sweet.

And as in any beautiful period, Elisha was sometimes struck with fear. There were rules that were clear, even to him, and one of them was that life is not designed to be perfect. Elisha had indeed experienced a separation from his wife, and two of his children lived at a distance of several hours drive, but all this was not suitably severe punishment for his freedom and for Nadav and for the sparkle in his eyes and for the sense that he had arrived home. He feared illnesses, accidents, dismissal (his standing at the institute was strong, but one never knows). He feared the worst of all. Even though he was cautious, the complete realization of his fears was well-hidden among the hills and ultimately caught him by surprise.

If we ignore motives such as the age of adolescence, the wind direction and the depth of the water and focus solely on facts, the person who brought an end to this period was the representative of the "Vacation for Life" campaign who came to the Qumran Institute one morning. The representative promised a real pearl necklace to anyone who came to meet with him, with no obligation, to hear about an opportunity to buy vacation units in the area at a special price. Two of the female researchers decided to go and they convinced Elisha that he also had nothing to lose. At the end of the meeting, he was the legal owner of a pearl necklace, as well as a vacation unit in one of the adjacent hotels, which would be rented out by the company for eleven months a year and would yield handsome profits within about three years. For one month a year, Elisha would be eligible to stay in it himself. ("You're divorced? Excellent!" the representative rejoiced. "What could be better than to host the children in a hotel one month a year?")

In retrospect, there was something annoying about the need to spend his annual vacation in the same area where he spent the whole year, but since it was already a done deal, Elisha reported to the hotel on the date designated in advance. He arrived alone because Aya had asked to take her three children on a vacation to Greece. He was slated to stay in the hotel for a week and then they would join him. Elisha planned to pass the time reading research studies and perhaps some fiction too. The trigger to the end of the period was about to be pressed.

Because a strange thing happened on the way to the hotel: Elisha drove mindlessly in the empty car when suddenly a feeling of love swelled up within him, out of nowhere. Love for whom? Why? There was no apparent reason, but it was still so tangible! His heart overflowed. He felt an urge to say "I love you" to the empty air and it was true love. Until this moment, the separation from Aya had barely affected him – his work with the scrolls and the change in atmosphere provided him with emotional stimulation that left no room for longings. In fact, it seemed to him that there was no other path than the pursuit of scholarly passion in the desert air. Like people who become addicted to bread with butter or a particular snack, the moment they become convinced that they could suffice with it, with as much of it as possible for the rest of their days – marks the impending onset of revulsion to it. Suddenly, all at once, Elisha became sick and tired of being alone. His body and his heart stirred desires in him that he thought he had forgotten. He wanted love. Desire is the frame into which the picture sometimes walks. When he met a guest his age in the dining room, a refined woman in a black dress, who was eating by herself, it seemed to him that it was the continuation of a romance and not its beginning. (He also already knew that he would soon be giving her a pearl necklace.)

Pleasant Teresa, pearls suited her. Her confident smile, the magnanimous hand gesture she made when he bashfully asked if he could join her. How natural it was for him to sit down across the table from the handsome, mature woman, who gleamed in the dim light of the dining room. Her black dress and her manners were so foreign, yet so right. It seemed to him that she had been sitting there and waiting for him forever, and the most amazing thing was that he knew exactly what he had to do.

After their dinner together, they did not go their separate ways. Their meeting continued beyond the steamy curtain of darkness that fell, as is customary in such cases. The next day, they sat at the same table for breakfast, like a regular couple of many years – he poured water for her, she passed him a croissant – only the twinkle in their eyes indicated how much younger their love was than they were. Teresa seemed worthy to him, nearly holy. The story of her life touched his heart, which opened widely toward her. By the time Aya and the children arrived at the Pomegranate Branches Hotel, Elisha and Teresa were already a fact.

This was precisely the tragedy. Just when it seemed to Elisha that his life was finally being painted with the long-awaited hue, and just as he was beginning to believe that for the first time in his life he was doing exactly the right thing, the end of happiness chose to mount an assault.

The romance with Teresa was justified, pleasant, without any fear. Moreover, it was inevitable. If so, where was the mistake? It apparently was hiding beneath the belief that Nadav, Elisha's young son and the apple of his eye, who chose to remain in the desert, far from his mother and siblings, was the type of plant that acclimates and strikes roots. When Aya arrived with his three children, tanned and joyful, to continue the vacation at the hotel, Elisha introduced her to them: "I'd like you to meet Teresa." His two older children stared at her curiously and said, "Nice to meet you." Nadav remained silent. Both Elisha and Aya attributed his silence to fatigue and bashfulness, or perhaps the difficulty in accepting the fact that his father had a girlfriend. But they assumed this difficulty would pass as time went by. They were both wrong. The next day, Nadav refused to go down to the pool, claiming that he had a headache and sequestering himself in the room. When he emerged from there, he had suddenly changed from a growing boy to a sullen adolescent. "I hate you," he told Elisha quietly. "I hate you, and Mother, and this place."

From this point, the descent was as steep as the road leading to and from Tel Aviv. As long as his silence was drowned out by the voices of his two brothers, Elisha was able to persuade himself that it was only a case of temporary anger. He decided not to be in contact with Teresa in front of his children until Nadav's anger abated. At breakfast the next morning, they found her sitting by herself at a small table for two. A newspaper was spread out in front of her and her smile said: "Please continue, I won't bother you. I have time." This small gesture of consideration touched Elisha's heart. He decided not to glance at her and to focus on his children. Nadav was silent. His silence continued the whole week, except for essential sentences. His farewell from his mother and brothers was also restrained and quiet. On the way home, it was already clear that this angry silence would remain plastered on his face for a very long time, if not forever.

The days following that vacation were not pleasant – the summer came to an end and strange winds began to threaten. Teresa returned to her home and took with her the magic of dinners under the dim hotel lights. Of course, they planned to meet again many times before the next year, when both of them would return for the regular vacation at the hotel. But it was difficult to predict how long this magic would survive. Would it also appear in another place, in a different setting? In any case, Elisha thought that at least in the near future it would be best for him to devote his full attention to Nadav. It was a paternal decision whose rationale was never tested because Nadav never came to the Qumran Caves Research Institute even once after that vacation. The conversations with him were very short and pointless. Gradually, that adolescent contempt appeared on his face that signaled to Elisha: I won't be like you.

Elisha tried to understand, but to no avail. Could it be that Nadav had hoped to rescind the decree of his separation from Aya and had decided to remain at the Dead Sea only in order to serve as human glue for a disintegrating family? Or perhaps it was hard for Nadav to accept the fact that his father was also a human being who needed love? When parents separate, children are always the victim. Elisha did not deny this, but believed, justly, that children are victimized in one way or another in any case. And he, Elisha, would never sacrifice his son on the altar of his loves and longings, of this he was certain. He was even prepared to give up his job at the institute, which imbued his life with meaning, if he only knew this was needed. In fact, the son was the one who ultimately bade his father farewell, against the backdrop of Mount Sodom and under the autumn sun.

The end did not come immediately. At first, Elisha tried, in full agreement with Aya, to send him for a short time to his mother's home. But when he returned, feeling a sense of relief in leaving his foreign siblings behind, he was even surlier. Softened by Elisha's sorrow, Aya restrained herself from saying "I told you so." Surprisingly, the news of Elisha's new romance brought them closer together. It was easier now that there was parity in their emotions and shared hopes for love. Instead of "I told you this place would only bring trouble," she said "He's a difficult adolescent. He'll get over it." Elisha hoped she was right.

At age fifteen, a year and three months after forging the father-son alliance that slowly unraveled, Nadav appeared at the entrance of the house. "I'm going," he told Elisha, who was relaxing in the living room, reading a newspaper. The tone of his voice was as if he were continuing an argument or dispute that had never been conducted. 'I'm going and don't bother to look for me."

"You want to run away from home?" Elisha tried to sound amused. A moment later, he discovered that his son had grown up considerably and was also very serious in his intentions.

"No. I have no home. I'm simply leaving, that's all."

"But... what about your matriculation exams? Your friends? Your mother? Are you going to her? And what do you mean you have no home? You know that this is your home just as much as mine." The old age that was about to overcome Elisha in another few moments already reached out a hesitant hand. He suddenly felt weak.

"I'm not going to Mother, and I don't need matriculation exams."

"You're not happy here with me?"

The personal question stunned both of them. Nadav thought for a moment and then replied, a bit conciliatory, "I don't know. I can't find myself. I feel that I need to go. I saved a little money, I packed, and everything is already prepared."

"We can find a solution for everything. You don't need to run away. Maybe you can travel somewhere to clear your head. I'll pay for you. Maybe you do need a little vacation."

The words dripped, meaninglessly, and finally combined into one shapeless chunk. Later, the alliance was severed. The affiliation of the son to his father and his obligation to live in the home built for him were no longer self-evident.

"Where will you go?"

Silence.

"What will you live on?"

Silence.

"Don't go."

But this was really not a possibility. Even if Nadav felt like suddenly abandoning his backpack, which he had carefully packed, and staying at home, pride has its own ways of driving the world. The sadness in his eyes was real when he said, "I'm sorry. I have to. Don't try to stop me, I don't want to run away."

How long did they stand there incarcerating the air between them, the air that held many possibilities and actually only one? "Goodbye Father," Nadav said and walked to the door without looking back. Elisha went out after him and saw him walking toward the bus stop. And as if in collusion against him, the bus was already racing up the hill in the same direction.

The expression "his hair turned white overnight" is not precisely accurate. At that very moment, just one hair on the back of Elisha's head started to whiten. It's temporary he reassured himself. He must be heading to his mother's after all. He'll be back. He'll write. He'll calm down. He needs a little space. But as time passed, a clear and objective truth became evident – Nadav wrote farewell letters to his brothers and never arrived at his mother's home. The police were not very helpful – none of the passengers on the bus remembered a fifteen-year-old teenager. Who would have believed that a stolen life was hidden in his innocent backpack? Notices were published and a few people reported seeing him in Eilat, in Beersheba, in Tiberias at the Sea of Galilee. In the end, none of these tips led to finding him. One morning, Elisha woke up and discovered that his hair was white.

*   *   *

And here is the news: At a high school in a Southern city, a teenager stabbed his friend, seriously injuring him. The Knesset was about to vote on a no-confidence motion. A television star was convicted of possessing hard drugs. The wind was stagnant in the skies over the Dead Sea. Only a light breeze from the winds blowing in central Israel made its way to the isolated area of the hotels. Mimi was vaguely aware of all of these insignificant news items. She read the daily newspaper, but always started from the back page. She didn't always get to the front page. From her perspective, there was a lot more weather and puppies and fields of flowers in the world than news items. She did notice that next to the drawing of the sun, the logo for the weather forecast, a stubborn caption had recently appeared: "Neta, I love you." Still, it should be noted that she was following with great interest the adulterous affair of a particular government minister, which was receiving wide media coverage. In any case, the most burning local news for her was that she was traveling to Tel Aviv.

The previous evening, on Saturday night, she again made the five-minute trip to the Royal Crown Hotel so that Rabbi Elias could give her the exact address of her destination. The road connecting the two hotels was depressing in its uncharacteristic liveliness – a convoy of cars of Shabbat-observant families with ironed shirts hung on a hanger in the back of the car and tired children, together with families that are not Shabbat-observant with muddy bicycles tied to the roof and tired children, all streaming toward the exit from the city, from the hotels where they stayed to the roads leading homeward, and something in the air was being depleted. She did not stay long with the rabbi, perhaps five minutes, and the whole trip to Tel Aviv suddenly seemed dubious. But on Sunday morning, the road regained its usual demeanor and Mimi also woke up in her usual good mood, alert and energetic, propelled by a sense of freedom.

The official reason for her vacation without pay that she allowed herself was the necklace, of course. Mimi was a very responsible person. She would not rest until the lost item was returned to its rightful owner. The unofficial reason was that she wanted to travel. The time had come for her to start to get to know up close the area where she was going to live, to walk around a bit, perhaps she might even chance upon an apartment or job. Who knows, perhaps it was a sign from heaven that Rabbi Eybeschütz himself was the one who signaled to her that the time had come for her to leave. Her comfortable, non-binding religious faith mulled this thought with a sense of satisfaction.

As she got dressed, she realized how much the receptionist's uniform had become an inseparable part of her – almost none of her clothes looked suitable. Her everyday clothes maintained a very brief relationship with her body. She only wore them on the weekends when she wasn't working. The cloth material did not have enough time to learn (or had already forgotten) how to cling to her body in the correct way. In the end, she chose jeans and a button-down shirt, and when she looked in the mirror she was actually pleased.

Michael's generous offer to drive her was politely, but firmly, rejected. He has family in central Israel and would be glad to visit them, and in any case he planned to drive there soon. Still, Mimi preferred to travel there on her own. Underlying this resolute declaration of independence was a reasonable fear that people like her, who are smugly knowledgeable and confident in their natural locale, get lost in the big city. If this were indeed the situation, she would prefer to be alone when it happens.

This was not Mimi's first visit in Tel Aviv, of course. She had already visited a number of times in family circumstances such as a vacation or a funeral or a party in central Israel. The city itself did not attract her. Instead, it was the opportunities the city offered – to breathe colorful air, full of possibilities; to live in an area where people are young and businesses are flourishing and the air is polluted due to all of the activity, unlike the barren air of the desert. Prime ministers, actors, singers – some of them have perhaps vacationed on the beaches of the Dead Sea (a picture of Bill Clinton hangs in the lobby of the Royal Crown Hotel till this very day) – but all of them ultimately came to the pulsating heart of the country, to Tel Aviv.

Absurdly, the closer Mimi (or, more correctly, her car) got to Tel Aviv, her anticipated move to the big city faded further and further away. The gas was expensive and the drive was very long and, at this stage, she cautiously assumed that upon seeing the stores and designer clothes she would maybe feel like buying something too. When she arrived at King George Street, the words "feel like" were replaced by words of a higher urgency. Unwittingly, she would adopt a local lingo that would tell herself: "I need to have that." It could also be a good opportunity to buy some of the good type of underwear instead of the inexpensive three-packs stuffed in cardboard packaging. And of course, she planned to visit the Sheraton Hotel (in order to see what the competitors are doing, she noted to herself self-righteously). The radio was playing songs with a lively beat. She didn't know them, but still managed to hum along.

But before all this, she had a meeting to attend. The official purpose of the trip seemed very distant. When the green road signs signaled her proximity to Tel Aviv, she tried to stir renewed interest in Teresa Holstein's necklace. The note on which she had jotted down the address Rabbi Elias gave her was next to the gearshift. She followed the map she had cut out of the hotel's Yellow Pages and looked for the street she needed. (From a distance, she recognized Dizengoff Square. The meeting would be short, she promised herself.) After circling three times around the same street, she found the small corner street, parked her car and set out.

Mimi had no appreciation of the fact that she had violated the first and undisputed law of central Israel by finding a parking spot immediately. Within a few minutes, she arrived at the appointed building. She stopped for a moment by the entrance, pulled out a small mirror from her bag and covered her head with a kerchief, white this time. As she was doing this, she looked around her.

Not surprisingly, the building where Rabbi Elias had sent her was a synagogue. A stone path surrounded by greenery led to the synagogue, which was clearly very old. It radiated calm. The windows were half-closed and seemed almost bored. Inside, a very high ceiling came into view with a giant chandelier of imitation crystal in the middle. When it was purchased (in fact, according to a small sign attached to it, it was donated by Samuel Levy in memory of his mother), it must have been very shiny. The ensuing years had covered it with dust.

There were no worshippers in the synagogue at that hour (and she wasn't even sure whether it was an active synagogue at all). She walked inside; the silence wafting from the empty seats filled her with reverence. Mimi noticed another door at the back of the sanctuary, exactly opposite the entrance. Sounds of conversation could be heard behind the second door. She knocked one knock and entered. Four men turned to look at her all at once. (Four rabbis meet at a synagogue – that reminds me of the beginning of a joke, she thought to herself.) One of them had a large black yarmulke and a clean-shaven face. Two others were bareheaded, while the fourth one was bearded and reminded her of someone (Elijah the Prophet perhaps?) and suddenly she realized that maybe she should have worn a skirt instead of pants. But, she told herself, this is still Tel Aviv here. Just to be sure, she tightened the kerchief on her head. The man with the yarmulke asked her politely, "Shalom, can I help you?"

"Rabbi Elias sent me," Mimi said confidently.

"And who are you?"

When she introduced herself by name, the eyes of the yarmulke-wearer made a quick movement: For a split second, a spark of understanding ignited, which immediately transformed into a look of surprise. He was actually turning with a questioning look toward his three friends when he said to her, "Of course, the rabbi told us you'd be coming. You're a bit early, aren't you?"

"They didn't tell me to come at a particular hour," Mimi said, in a friendly yet official way. The yarmulke-wearer did not reply. Since the conversation seemed to her to be dying, Mimi added, "I simply found a necklace that appears to be expensive and I want to return the lost item to its owner. I consulted with Rabbi Elias and he sent me here and said that you'd know who owns it."

"And where did you see the necklace, if I might ask?"

"Someone sent it to our hotel. He claims that he stole it, but the guest who had a necklace like this insists that nothing was stolen from her and doesn't want it back."

"That is, you received it in the mail and you were simply curious about it? A necklace with a pendant with three letters engraved on it?" the yarmulke-wearer asked her. When Mimi nodded, he looked satisfied for some reason. "This is very nice, very nice indeed. Yes, I know what this is about. Rabbi Elias did not send you to us for no reason. You saw Rabbi Eybeschütz's amulet. A very special pendant. I'll be happy to explain to you about the necklace. Come, take a seat."

Mimi politely closed the door behind her and sat on a chair by the naked wood table. One of the bareheaded men got up from his seat, also politely, and opened the door again. "So there won't be *yichud*,"** he smiled at her apologetically and she nodded in understanding.

The bearded one (he reminded Mimi of someone, who?) took over now. His pleasant voice had a calming effect on her. "Actually,"

* A prohibited closed-door encounter of men and women.

he turned to Mimi, "you came to a meeting of our charitable organization, Food for the Disadvantaged. We collect donations before
every Shabbat and distribute hot meals to the needy in Tel Aviv." He
made a slight gesture with his hand and when she followed it, she
suddenly noticed a considerable quantity of closed cardboard boxes
stacked against the wall. Apparently, they contained food. There
were maybe fifty boxes there. How could she have failed to notice
them earlier? The bearded man continued: "But that's not what
interests you. The truth is that we also do something else. After all,
you traveled all the way from … (he was silent until Mimi said "from
the South") in order to understand the meaning of that necklace."
He took a key from his pocket and opened a small desk drawer and,
like a magician, he pulled out Teresa Holstein's necklace.

"But…" Mimi said, the four of them smiling at her surprised look,
as if they had guessed which card she had chosen or had amazed
her with a show of telepathy. Their moment of glory was very short.
Then, the bearded one said: "Surprised, huh? Don't worry, it's not
the same necklace you saw. There are several like it, though not
many. In fact, there are seven in the entire world." To Mimi, the
necklace looked exactly like the one hidden in the hotel safe at that
moment. It sparkled from his hand and made the participants of
the small meeting look dull. The man appeared to be weighing in
his mind how to proceed. She waited in patience that ultimately
paid off when he said: "Here, I'll show you something," and then
rummaged through the drawer again and pulled out a black and
white newspaper clipping that had almost disintegrated. "Do you
recognize this woman?"

The paper showed an elderly woman who was nearly bald. Mimi
did not recognize her, but she still knew who she was because under
the woman's wrinkled face in the newspaper was a caption revealing
her identity: "Mother Teresa Declared Saint by the Vatican." The
old woman, of course, was not the issue. Mimi immediately noticed
that a familiar pendant peeked from her cracked neck, only half of
which was photographed.

"It's a necklace for people named Teresa?" If so, it was a shame. Mimi's name was not Teresa. As she spoke, she realized that her question was ridiculous. Come on, really. The small group smiled. The bearded one said: "No, no. That is, perhaps by chance... but this is really not connected to the name Teresa."

"Actually," the man with the black yarmulke added, "a great many people with a great number of names have already received this amulet. I only remember these two Teresas. And they were not chosen according to their name."

"Then according to what?" Mimi asked, and the four smiled, as if she had asked exactly the right question. The men in the room were holding on to information that the guest lacked. Everyone felt comfortable in their places. The man with the black yarmulke was the one who quickly shared this information with Mimi, with the generosity of a person of status: "Okay, as we said, this is an amulet that Rabbi Eybeschütz wrote. Have you heard of him?"

None of them really thought that Mimi had heard of him. He continued without waiting for an answer. "Rabbi Jonathan Eybes-chütz was born in Poland more than two-hundred years ago. He was a very wise man and very sharp – at age twenty, he headed a yeshiva in Prague and had hundreds of pupils." Mimi made an impressed facial expression, the best one she could, and the bearded one continued: "Some people believe he was secretly a Sabbatean, that is, one of the followers of Shabbetai Tzvi. He had a major dispute with Rabbi Yaakov Emden, but this was never proven and this is not our subject. Rabbi Eybeschütz was a great *tzadik*, a saintly person. He delved into the Kabbalah and, among other things, wrote amulets. You know what an amulet is, right?" Mimi nodded her head. Of course she knew. And the bearded man continued: "Contrary to what people think today, an amulet is not a trivial matter. Not everyone can write an amulet. Only righteous and honest people are entitled to give amulets. And do you know why?" Without answering for a response, he continued: "An amulet written with a correct hand helps to draw abundance from the upper worlds. A written word creates reality. The world was created with a thought, an utterance and an action. A proper amulet combines all three of them. It's like a pipe in which there is a body and a soul. A person is also a body and a soul. If a worthy person writes certain letters with a certain intention, there are people who believe that these letters, together with the intention of this righteous person, have power. A lot of power. A word written by the right person can draw upper forces into our world. It's a very complex subject." He stared at Mimi with a serious expression and she nodded compliantly. "Rabbi Eybeschütz wrote amulets for all sorts of purposes, primarily for people who asked him for remedies for health, a spouse, success. His most famous amulet was an amulet for women who are giving birth. But the amulet you saw, he wrote on his own initiative." It seemed to her that he was expecting her to say something. She could not think of anything intelligent to say, so she just nodded her head. The bearded one sufficed with this. "In short, Rabbi Eybeschütz believed that you fan a fire with fire, a mighty waterfall with water, and people who bestow kindness on others are able to draw an abundance of kindness to this world. Do you understand?" (She nodded again, regretting that she had nodded earlier.) "This works for both sides. The rabbi believed that people who give from their soul to others without seeking anything in return deserve a spiritual boost, something to restore the energies they lost in their giving, something to strengthen them. Therefore, he wrote eight identical amulets for this purpose. The amulets were intended to be circulated among deserving people in the world, to draw the goodness and add it to our world. Rabbi Eybeschütz handed out the amulets himself the first time, and left detailed instructions about whom to pass it on to afterwards. Each amulet is given for a period of two years, then it returns to the rabbi or to his heirs and they pass it onward."

"So... it's actually like a prize? For good people?" Mimi asked. The bearded one smiled, "Not exactly. That is, it's also a sort of compensation. The amulet definitely has a good influence on anyone who wears it, but the person helps the amulet just as much as the amulet helps the person. And Rabbi Avram here," he pointed toward the man with the black yarmulke, who smiled with modest pride, "He's a direct descendant of Rabbi Eybeschütz. His grandfather had the privilege of giving one of the amulets to Mother Teresa. He passed away soon afterwards."

"But she wasn't even Jewish," Mimi protested.

"It doesn't matter. Kindness belongs to all human beings. Mother Teresa took care of thousands of poor people and lepers whom no one else agreed to touch. They say she also performed a type of healing miracle and for this was beatified by the Vatican. But this, of course, is nonsense that is not relevant to the matter at hand." Mimi thought this over for a moment. "So it's possible that the hotel guest who received the necklace didn't lie. She really didn't lose it, but returned it to you after two years."

"Not exactly to us, but indirectly, yes. It is very probable that the amulet moved on to the next person."

"And how do they know whom you're supposed to give the necklace to? And who passes it on?"

"As I said, the descendants of Rabbi Eybeschütz are responsible for the amulets. Sometimes they consult with other people. It is not easy to find truly kind people these days. Together, they make sure that only people who have done something for someone else without seeking anything in exchange will receive the amulet," he said, studying her closely. "This does not always have to be kindness of thousands, as in the case of Mother Teresa. Sometimes kindness toward one person is also big enough."

"And there's something else," Rabbi Avram interjected, "We prefer that the person who bestows the kindness does not know about the amulet when performing the action. For this reason, we try not to publicize it too much."

So, as good as she might be, the pendant was already lost for Mimi, who already knew of its existence. She was no longer so sure whether this saddened her. "We hear about people through word of mouth," the bearded one said. "Sometimes those who receive the pendant pass it on themselves. If they don't find a worthy person, they return it to us after two years, and here it awaits the next person. It's not simple, but there are still good people. The seven amulets have already made their way around the world with hundreds of people."

"You said there were eight."

"Mother Teresa asked to be buried with hers."

Any plans Mimi had to keep the beautiful pendant were now gone. To steal an amulet intended for good people – this was something that should not be done; she was sure this would incur divine punishment. No, she would have to give it up. She now regretted that she hadn't brought it with her. Wasn't this why Rabbi Elias sent her all the way to Tel Aviv? On the other hand, she thought resentfully, he didn't tell her to bring it. It was no big deal, she could send it by mail.

"Okay, if so, I must return the necklace I have to you," she said. The conversation suddenly became very down-to-earth. Surprisingly, after learning that the pendant was a religious item of great significance, it lost a bit of its luster in her eyes.

Rabbi Avram thought a moment. "You could send it by mail, but I'm not sure that's necessary. Is it stored in a good place?" Mimi nodded, thinking about the towel that was gently covering a pale light.

"So keep it that way for awhile. When the right person comes, we'll take it from you."

She nodded again, and then asked: "And this amulet really does something?"

"Look," the bearded man sighed, "ever since the cinema and television appeared, everyone expects miracles with stardust. It doesn't exactly work that way. A true amulet works in ways that are hidden from the eye. It's a type of reward for a good deed. In fact, it only intensifies the impact of the deed itself. Good is attracted to good, fire to fire, water to water. Do you know how to decide whether an amulet is a true one?"

"No, how?"

"If it proves itself three times."

The two bareheaded men and Rabbi Avram smiled knowingly, as if they wanted to say what the three times were that proved that Rabbi Eybeschütz's amulet was true. Then one of them said: "The delivery men will be here in another three-quarters of an hour. We should start working on the distribution." He shot a meaningful glance at the boxes, which suddenly seemed like they filled the entire room, and everyone nodded. For a moment, she did not understand what they were talking about, but then she quickly remembered – the reason they came here was to distribute food. She realized it was a signal for her to leave, but could not find parting words that were appropriate for this strange scene. Finally, she said: "Fine, then thank you … I'll keep the necklace – that is, the amulet – in a safe place, and good luck to you."

"Thank you very much, and good luck to you too," the bearded one answered on behalf of everyone. "Who knows, perhaps we'll meet again. In the meantime, take a brochure about our organization. Maybe you'll want to donate something," he said, thrusting a colorful brochure into her hand and smiling.

She slowly walked across the sanctuary of the synagogue, in contemplation. Who would believe it?

But the closer she got to the exit door and the rays of the sun shining through it, the amulet became more distant. When she blinked, she realized how dark it was in the synagogue. She had been there no longer that half an hour and it was already difficult for her eyes to adjust to the light. The mystery of the necklace had come to an end and it was now time to move on; there were still more plans for the day. According to all of the criteria the bearded man described to her, the amulet was not meant for her. On the other hand, the bustling streets of Tel Aviv were meant exactly for her.

After a ten-minute walk from the small synagogue, she finally came upon the real Tel Aviv. She walked among the stores, checking her reflection in the display windows and feeling very alive. Her happiness indicated that she fit in well – she did not look different than the dozens of other young people her age, scattered around her in stores and inside the cars on the street. None of them approached her, of course, and she couldn't just go up to one of them and say: "Shalom, I'm Mimi, nice to meet you. Next year I plan to rent an apartment here." It's natural, she said to herself, and did not feel disappointed. The reception rules in the street are more elusive than those of the hotel. For example, in the latter you just need to register and pay and you already receive a key and feel like you belong.

After a half an hour of roaming around (she was a bit disappointed that she had bought only a can of soda so far) and walking along the street, she discovered that she was standing exactly, but exactly, in front of the Sheraton Hotel. It was a sign from heaven, she thought with excitement. Who knows? Perhaps this was her reward for not coveting Rabbi Eybeschütz's amulet. Good is drawn to good, water to water – and Mimi is drawn to the Sheraton. Without hesitation, she marched across the street and entered the lobby.

The moment of entry surprised her. The reception desk and chairs looked similar to theirs, yet different, like entering a strange living room. The chairs in the lobby were upholstered in brown velvet, and the wall mirror made them look twice their actual size. In any case, this hotel was bigger than the Pomegranate Branches Hotel, but it was not as beautiful, she loyally thought. After surveying the lobby, she turned her attention to the receptionist, who appeared to be very busy and did not take notice of her. Mimi examined the chairs in the lobby and the buttery cakes in the showcase and suddenly she realized that she had already been working for two years at the Pomegranate Branches Hotel but had never sat in the hotel lobby. She walked past the indifferent receptionist with an air of importance, entered the sitting area and chose a seat.

A few minutes later, she was already situated comfortably on the other side of the mirror. Just past the mirror was a window overlooking the sea, a clever architectural idea that confused Mimi for a moment due to the different reflections in this space. It only took her a moment to get used to the new situation. After a few minutes, a waiter who didn't recognize her served her a tall cup of hot chocolate and she stretched out comfortably in front of the window. It was not the Dead Sea outside the window. Instead, she was looking at the Mediterranean Sea, with its waves and surfers, with a white and soft bed of sand stretched out before it. The water churned up heavy waves of froth. She had almost forgotten that water could move. This will be her backdrop for the next two or three years, when she is hired to work here, she thought, feeling satisfaction. And maybe she would win the lottery or find another job and come here as a guest? In a fashionable purple dress and sunglasses, she would sit by the same window.

She thought about looking for the manager and asking him if he needed employees immediately, but nobody who looked like a manager was anywhere in sight. And besides, for such an important meeting, it would be appropriate to prepare in advance. In the meantime, the busy receptionist would be able to keep her job. Instead, Mimi reflected back on her trip to Tel Aviv. At first, she imagined herself telling the story of her trip to Michael, but the fact that he was originally from Tel Aviv bothered her a bit. So she switched to telling the story to Doreen the chambermaid. Everyone there is young, alive, energetic, she tells her. Not like it is here. (Actually, the hotels at the Dead Sea are at least as big as those in Tel Aviv, but Doreen in her imagination, like the real-life Doreen, is an enthusiastic and not particularly critical listener.) In general, Tel Aviv is the center of activity, the business center of the country. There are many more possibilities to advance. Not like here, where the chief receptionist or spa manager is the top and there is nothing other than hotels in the entire area. There, if you're good, you become the manager of a large staff. When you gain experience, you can advance to other places. And Dizengoff (though she was still walking distance from Dizengoff, at this point Mimi longed for it). Oh, what stores! Expensive, but there's no alternative: For quality, you have to pay. And these are clothes that last too. Doreen nods her head, greatly impressed.

As Mimi left the Sheraton, the pleasant experience of sitting idly in the lobby was translated into the not-so-justified equation: Sheraton = a good place to work. (Isn't this how tastes and aspirations are determined? A favorite song or enjoyable film is etched in one's memory because of the girl sitting next to you when you first encountered them, or because of a pleasant breeze or good tidings at the beginning of that day.)

When she got into the car, the brochure she had received from this building two hours ago peeked out at her from her bag. (Strangely, she didn't remember seeing it when she took out her purse.) She started reading it. In addition to explanations about the organization's activities, there were a lot of pictures of people with their faces blurred, eating hungrily, and of Rabbi Avram in the company of various people and boxes full of food. One of the pictures finally made her remember, of course, whom the bearded man reminded her of. Smiling at her from the colorful brochure was the familiar face of Elisha.

She tossed it onto the seat next to her. The fact that the guest Elisha was connected to the strange bunch in the synagogue was not surprising in itself – after all, he was the one who sent her to Rabbi Elias. But the familiar face reminded her that, in fact, the question of the pendant remained unsolved. She felt as if she were in one of those maze riddles in children's magazines ("Help the dog reach the bone," "Help the cook reach the spoon"). Though she now knew that the necklace was in fact an amulet awarded to Teresa Holstein for some act she performed (Actually, what act? She was sorry she didn't ask), the story grew even more bizarre because if Teresa was such a good woman that she merited being one of the seven chosen ones, why did she lie and deny that the amulet was stolen from her? And why did she claim that she still had it at a time that Mimi knew with certainty that the amulet had been stolen from her room and was in her custody, wrapped in a towel in the hotel safe? And if Teresa did not lie and indeed returned the necklace after two years, from whom was the additional amulet stolen?

Strange, she thought, and turned on the radio. An unfamiliar singer performed an old Bob Dylan song. In front of her, and then above her and behind her, there were signs announcing the exit from Tel Aviv. Soon the route would become a winding chain of barren hills. The sun was already starting to set. By the time she returned, the southern part of the country would be dark and cold. It took such little time to cross over from one geographic region to another. Actually, what difference did it make? Still, it apparently did make a difference. She stifled a yawn. She planned to go right to sleep when she arrived. The stories of Tel Aviv for Michael and Doreen would have to wait till the morning. (All in all, she admitted to herself, the stories were not particularly exciting. Fortunately, Mimi was a good storyteller.)

*

The following weeks were uneventful. Mimi's routine was very easy during those days. At 7 o'clock every morning, she took her place behind the reception desk (except for Mondays and Wednesdays, when she worked the evening shift.) She checked the wakeup calls, sorted the mail, read a book and received the few guests who trickled up to the reception desk. There were very few guests during this period – several tourists who had purchased a book about the recommended places in the Holy Land but didn't heed the warnings about the recommended date for the trip; two elderly women from England who were staying at the hotel for a full month; a young woman who was writing a book about the Dead Sea; and a group of researchers who set out each morning for an irresponsible outing in the hot winds of the Judean Desert. They spent the afternoons basking in the illusion of weightlessness in the Dead Sea pool, their floating bellies in stark contrast to their eyes, which were closed in contentment. From the edge of the pool, the sight was amusing.

None of the regular guests stayed at the hotel during this season – the Morgenstern couple did reserve a room, but at the last
moment Avi Morgenstern had to fly to Europe and their annual
vacation was postponed to October. They would arrive together
with the hotel's child and his mother. Mimi correctly guessed that
this would make them happy. The lobby was empty for most of the
hours of the day. For breakfast, the bored cook would meticulously
prepare eggs, garnished with fried onion, green onion, rosemary
and idleness.

Though Mimi made an effort to appear active and busy, it was
undeniable that most of her hours behind the reception desk were
devoid of activity. The few guests hardly ever required her services.
They nodded at her politely on their way to the pool or to the lobby
to buy an exorbitantly priced soda or water draw from the nearby
Ein Gedi spring. She did crossword puzzles, nibbled on crackers
and slowly read an old book she had borrowed from the library.
It was precisely because of days like this that she had a lottery
subscription and was registered in the bone marrow database and
a number of other activities aimed at maintaining the chance of a
phone call that would suddenly come and change everything.

But, nonetheless, something had changed – the unit called
"MimiMichael" was now part of her daily routine. It was not the
kind of rapture one can sometimes talk about, but they could
comfortably be described as a couple. Every afternoon, after an
eight-hour shift that was usually without interruptions (one day
the smoke alarm went off, but fortunately the guests at the Pomegranate Branches Hotel during the slow season are not the type to
get excited about alarms; most of them probably didn't even hear
it), she would go down to the dining room and they would meet.
By virtue of Mimi's status, Mimi and Michael were "the" couple of
the hotel. Any waitress and waiter recognized as a couple would
automatically be ranked below them. When did they actually
become a couple? Already on Michael's first day of work, when he
came up from the spa floor, Michael parted from Mimi with a "see

you tomorrow" that embodied all of the possibilities of two young people who share a workplace. Mimi asked, "Did you eat already?" guessing correctly that he didn't know yet that all of the hotel employees were allowed to eat at any time in the dining room or in the kitchen. Mimi and Michael ate lunch together that day, and the next day too. At the end of the week, they already went out to dinner together.

Michael's rented apartment was not far from Mimi's, and both of the apartments were a twenty-minute drive from the hotel. Within this short distance between home and work, there were not many places to go out to. If they wanted to go out to a more significant place, it would entail a long and onerous drive on the hilly road. Perhaps that's why their routine almost immediately slid into a very pleasant, if not rapturous, mode – as if they had always been together. One night when she slept at his place, she poked him in the back with her elbow to stop his snoring and an old memory arose and scared her: She reminded herself of her mother.

What is there in an excessively pleasant routine that makes people want to slip out of its arms, only to long for its embrace again? It seems to be an inevitable process, just like an infant disembarking from his mother's arms, a declaration of independence that ultimately engenders a yearning to return to her breast. Did she fall in love with Michael? Not immediately, but gradually an emotion crept into her, an emotion she found hard to define. Her favorite hours of the day were the afternoon hours when she would go down to visit him at the spa. As he massaged her shoulders, she was at the Pomegranate Branches Hotel with Michael and dreaming about the Sheraton, and for a few moments a day she held onto both worlds and serenity encompassed her.

Michael himself found peace of mind in the desert, so he told Mimi when he took her to the Judean Desert and spoke with sparkling eyes about the charm of the desert wilderness. "There's so much power here," he said. "What strength, what quiet." Mimi nodded, but was actually impatient. She felt hot and was also a bit bored – she did not believe in the overly romantic interpretations of the barren land. In her eyes, the mountains were neither beautiful nor lacked beauty – they simply were. She found it hard to see how either side would benefit if she loved or hated them.

Perhaps that same mountain stillness was responsible for the fact that Mimi, busy with her work, failed to notice the changes in the faces of the children who were about to return to school and the heaviness that started to infiltrate the air. When she was walking through the hotel's backyard one day, she suddenly noticed that the pomegranate trees were already full of red fruits. Sadly, she realized that the aroma of the holidays had sprouted and ripened, another year had passed and she was still at the Pomegranate Branches Hotel without any practical plan to advance her toward moving to Tel Aviv. And, as if to prove this, when she returned to her place by the reception desk, she discovered to her chagrin that the mail had brought with it a letter heralding the start of the towel season.

*   *   *

In my previous incarnation, I was a kangaroo. Snuggling securely in my mother's pouch, I spryly hopped in the broad, green forests of Australia, my trusting heart leaning against her heart in a sort of strange, two-sided engine. I entered my second birthday with weightless leaps, a primeval memory from distant forests.

At this stage of our lives, if someone had asked Darya what I had done in my previous incarnation, her unimaginative reply would probably have been "a car mechanic." One could understand her. I could identify every vehicle, including those I had never seen. Riding in a moving car calmed me, as if it were not contrary to human nature. On my second birthday, the steep and long ride was an exhilarating gift in itself.

The rest of the birthday presents – cars. Mother bought be a fleet of cars with a remote control, the abstract nouns bought me a tiny garage (that was from Father) and simple and exciting wooden cars (that was from Grandfather and Grandmother). What joy! I drove all the way back home in three different cars, including repeated stops at the gas station. In the meantime, Mother changed clothes.

When she emerged from the bathroom, I immediately noticed my pregnancy dress and ran to greet her with a hug. The white, romantic dress had adapted well to the new conditions that time had engendered. She looked businesslike and tired. Mother sat on the edge of the bed and I hurried to climb onto her knees, snuggling in the familiar position and softly singing the water song. I enjoyed this position; there was also something familiar in the touch of her hand on my back. Still, the space between us refused to shrink and the blessed buoyancy was pushed aside again and again by the alert senses of the consciousness. Perhaps you once loved the chairs in kindergarten – try to squeeze into them now. At the age of two, I made my final exit from the womb.

According to the widespread legend, a baby is born with an invisible thread connecting him to his father and his mother. The thread gets longer and longer until the person finally severs it from his father and mother and attaches it to the heart of a spouse. This is a nice story. Darya never (as far as I know) connected any thread that would tie her to a partner for any period of time. (The leading candidate to receive it, my father, fled before she had a chance.) Her thread remained, therefore, with her parents in America. It was a type of aerial line to them. Birds rested from their flight on it, exchanging gossip from far corners of the earth. The stupid creatures were unaware of the fact that they were saved from a charred fate on the electric lines. But the ravages of time, the winters, the summers and airplane traffic must have damaged it until it finally broke. For me, she had a new thread. On my second birthday, it reached to the end of the dining room.

During breakfast, I checked my new space again and again. After several times, the results of the experiment were indisputable: I was allowed to go as far as the door; as long as I didn't go out of it, Mother ate quietly. Going out the door triggered a pull on the invisible thread that brought me back to her. She would retrieve me and I would be forced to set out again on the long journey toward the exit.

It was a shame. Outside the door, children who were bigger than me competed in running races. From the place where I stood, I could only watch. The competition was held in the space between the bathroom and the lobby. The two outstanding runners were twin brothers. One of them, the thinner one, was the undisputed winner. Since both of the brothers emerged from the same egg cell, the egg cell was actually the winner. The brother who lost the race did not think so. His face was sad and serious, and furrowed with thoughts. When they returned to their home in Ramat Gan, he would embark on a secret training program that included running at night around the house. And in another year, when then returned for their regular family vacation, he would fulfill a universal childhood fantasy and defeat his brother in a surprising and sweeping victory. I would be there, of course, like every year, but would only learn about it years later, when he became a successful CEO and would tell educational stories to an economic magazine about competition, determination and persistence.

A girl with a full head of curls, who as far as I could see was consistently losing in the competitions, dropped out. She noticed me by the door and responded to a female instinct that impelled her to smile at me graciously and ask "What's your name?" I fled back inside the dining room.

A surprise awaited me at the table: Mother was no longer eating by herself. Where did this couple, a man and a woman, come from? The man looked very familiar to me. He aroused in me an unexplained urge for milk. I dipped a finger in Mother's bowl of cornflakes and put it in my mouth, but remained unsatisfied. Not this kind of milk. Mother collected me in her arms and said: "Honey, do you know who they are? They are your friends. They have a child who was born together with you. Do you want to play with Daniel?" Daniel appeared as an extra arm protruding from behind the woman's back. She pulled him out of there. "Come sweetie, don't be bashful. After all, you're almost brothers!" Her advanced age and the fact that Mother was eating alone led her to assume that the two of them were members of the single-child club. But Mother was still young and beautiful, and the fact that she was eating alone did not prevent her from bringing me into the world. I never even considered the idea that I would remain an only child. It was evident that the woman did not know her. I was too young to be bothered by this. I reached out a hesitant hand to Daniel's face and, for the first time, felt the face of a child like me, of my height. The gesture led the grownups to plan a morning together by the pool.

By the pool, we were both rubbed with sunscreen in amounts reserved for only children. Danieli's father took both of us to what he called, for some reason, "the pool for the little ones." In our eyes, it was actually wonderful and very big. We slapped the water with our hands and laughed and cried and calmed down and laughed again. Danieli called him "Father." When we went back to meet Mother and the other woman on the grass, I also called the man by his name, Father. He pointed out my mistake. "Avi, sweetie. My name is Avi, okay?" Okay. I stood with my back to Mother and couldn't see her reaction. (Oh, if only I had a time machine and eyes in the back of my head.)

Sarah said quietly, "Children need a father." There was an almost religious devotion in her voice. Darya didn't hear, or pretended not to hear. The incident did not harm the warm relationship being forged in the heat of the sun.

We were a very happy fivesome: two women, a man and two almost-twin children. (I was blond at this stage of my life, with blue eyes; Danieli had black hair and green eyes. But we were about the same height. The similarity shocked both of us.) Danieli did not want Avi to feed him. "Only with Mother, only with Mother!" he screamed. For a moment I wondered how, for heaven's sake, Darya could feed him. She was feeding me! And then, like a song you've heard a thousand times, on the one thousand and first time the words began to sink in. The parts of the picture began to come

into focus. Mother. My long journey was about to begin. When
we returned to the hotel room, Mother tried to undress and bathe
me, and I fled to the other side of the room. "Only with Father," I
informed her.

This should have been a high and tear-jerking hurdle. But it
turned out to be a very short scene, almost insignificant. Mother
softened her look, smiled at me and said: "Father has left. Only
Mother is here now. And Mother loves you the most in the world.
We have fun the two of us, right? Come to Mother." At the age of
two and without any older siblings, I had yet to learn how to harden
my heart to outstretched arms and endearing words. I snuggled in
her arms and was then led to the bathtub, where I consoled myself
with calm splashing in the refreshing water. The scene was only
almost insignificant and definitely not completely marginal because
a simple truth was firmly fixed in my childish mind that day: Father
has left. That is, Father was supposed to return.

Did I enjoy my birthday vacation? It's hard to say. At age two, I
was not very choosy. At dinner, Shlomo the manager recognized
me. He took me into his arms, asked how I was doing ("kay") and
told Mother that I had grown since the previous year. Shlomo had
apparently gone through a longer period of time. The skin on his
face, which was taut, was now drooping, too big for his face. I tried
to help him and smooth it with two hands, but my hands on his
cheek only emphasized his older appearance. I took a toy car from
the pocket of my pants and drove it over the obstacle course of his
face, mountains and valleys, lips and cheeks. Shlomo gave me a
new and green plastic ball as a birthday gift. (Where did he get it?
It was probably forgotten by one of the guests.)

We sat and waited for our new friends: Avi, who wasn't Father,
and Sarah and Danieli Morgenstern. Meanwhile, the waiter brought
me a child's portion of hotdogs and French fries, but my attention
was diverted – at the table next to us, I recognized a face that
looked familiar, though from a different angle. In order to be sure,
I slid off my chair, stood with my back to this face and peeked at

it through the space between my two legs. The upside-down face immediately took on a form and name. Teresa! Teresa Holstein, my unbeknownst godmother and confidante, the woman who revealed to me the secret of salt water, was sitting with a familiar and older-looking man with a very tempting beard. She recognized me (or actually, she recognized Darya), smiled and came right over to our table. I was so excited that I fell when trying to return my head to its place.

This was the second birthday vacation for me and Darya at the Pomegranate Branches Hotel, and it was the first time that our small family unit enjoyed a sort of routine. The hotel staff and the regular guests filled the role in our lives that *seder*** guests fill in other families – we would meet on a regular basis, at sufficiently long intervals, and measure each other with a probing eye: who has grown, who has simply grown old, who has changed his status and was promoted or fired or married. There was something nice in this. Mother apparently also felt this way. She gave Teresa a "Shalom!" of surprised joy and pulled out a chair for her. Their relationship looked closer last year. Their connection seemed to have been severed. I had no idea why Mother was too busy and exhausted to cultivate and maintain friendships, just as the rain is oblivious to the fact that it is rain or what sprouts in its wake. In any case, they did not have time to converse for more than a minute before the Morgenstern family also entered the dining room. ("Danieli, say hello!") Our small table was replaced with a larger table. The meeting took on the form of a reunion photo.

The circumstances of Danieli's birth, which was also premature but did not occur in a hotel (he was born in the middle of a business meeting), did not entitle him to a free annual vacation at the Pomegranate Branches Hotel. ("Actually," Mother told her friend Mika on the telephone, "they could buy the hotel if they wanted to." But why would someone buy a hotel? It would turn it into

* The Passover ritual meal.

just an ordinary home.) After the birth, Sarah and her new baby were rushed to the same room where Mother and poor Kati had also been rushed. This was the first time the Morgenstern couple met Teresa and Mother since that triple night at the hospital. They spoke about births and epidurals and a bit about poor Kati. (As far as I could tell, Sarah and Teresa preferred to talk about epidurals.) Luckily, Danieli also brought a toy car of his own and both of us drove our cars on the floor, occasionally bumping into a piece of bread or an olive. Danieli's hidden thread was very short; it only reached to the end of the next table.

The next day, I witnessed another example of the sense of family that linked the regular guests of the Pomegranate Branches Hotel: We were sitting with the Morgenstern family on chairs at the beach. (At this stage, to go down to the beach without the Morgenstern family would be considered brazen.) I wandered for a moment out of Mother's sight. At the end of the small beach, the internal camera captured a smell of sweat mixed with salt and a young woman drying the upper part of her leg with a towel – an insignificant picture that would later emerge from the depths of my memory as a new one. The evolution of the mature person within me was interrupted when Mother got up and pulled me to her. On the way back to our piece of the beach, we heard the end of a sentence uttered by an old woman sitting near us, who was covered with a layer of gray mud. "Salt Lake City, Utah was so much nicer," she said in English to her twin, covered by an identical mask. The twin squinted, creating cracks in the mud mask. The first old woman, encouraged, continued in Hebrew: "Yes, yes, they also have a salt sea. And the people there are so nice. Believe me, I don't know why everyone insists on coming here." The arrogance in her voice bore fruit. A first volunteer stepped forward to defend the homeland: "Excuse me for butting in," said an older man I recognized from the dining room, "but the lake in Utah is really not similar to the Dead Sea. It lacks the same therapeutic qualities, and it's less saline and much shallower." His wife, who was lying on a towel with sunglasses and appeared to be sleeping or frozen, did not bother to turn her head. She spoke to the sun gods: "We didn't enjoy it there at all. The people here are nicer." My car was hard to drive on the granular sand and, as if wielding a magic wand, I turned it into a hovercraft. The old twin again squinted and a piece of mud fell from her forehead. A blond woman with a Russian accent, who was sitting near the woman in the sunglasses, asked: "What, there's another salt sea? I thought this was the only one." Before the old lady had a chance to market the Utah lake to her, so much nicer, the older man answered in a scholarly tone: "Not exactly. The lake in Utah is indeed saline, but only relative to regular sea water. It's really not similar to our Dead Sea. There is life in it!" he summarized, beaming in victory. Nothing was as low, salty and devoid of life as our Dead Sea. The vacationers who were listening to the conversation nodded in consent and the old lady shut her eyes in defiance. When it seemed like the matter was resolved, the discussion arose again in an unexpected way.

"Utah is indeed a very beautiful state," a familiar male voice said. "but I doubt they have a history like we have here." Whose voice was that? It was our Elisha, a bearded prophet of doom, wrapped in a towel. The fact that he had just arrived and was still standing gave him supremacy over us, who were lounging on the beach. "We're on a piece of land where the stories of the Bible took place. Sodom, Lot's wife, the hidden scrolls. Everything is here." True love wafted from Elisha's warm voice, but those sitting on the beach did not take note of it. Their love for the area was not as profound as Elisha's, which didn't mean it was any less true.

"Amazing," the woman in the sunglasses agreed, "this is really an enchanting area. We were at Ein Feshkha and we had a great time."

"Ein Feshkha? Is that nearby?" the one with the accent wondered. The couple immediately volunteered to explain the way to her. The old ladies with the masks pointedly removed themselves from the conversation.

Not far from us was Lot's wife, who looked back at the primeval sins and turned into a pillar of salt as Sodom burned. This story is actually very tragic. At the age of two, none of this concerned me. I loaded grains of sand onto my little car and drove it backwards. If Lot's wife had known Darya, perhaps she would have learned from her – there's no point in becoming frozen for the sake of past sins. It's best to move on. The past will eventually be forgotten or will race to catch up to you.

Faithful to her way, Darya never froze. I know, because the way she looked at me was always very warm. Did she ever regret that in exchange for several days of unripe love the path of her life had changed forever? That love, she believed, would ripen or wither. Her healthy nature protected her from the weakness that spreads through the limbs when thinking deeply about the structure of the skeleton, how these bones are able to carry us. As far as I know, she did not harbor even a bit of regret.

*　*　*

What reason is there for an older person's body to exist, for the cracked skin, for love that is not unique or perfect? Like many young people, the young Teresa also believed there was no reason. Only young women were designed to fall in love, to remove a shirt from a taut body. The choice of one path only seemed meaningful when a thousand paths were open before you. Who cared what a middle-aged woman did – if she cried from excitement or from a broken heart, whether she took off her dress in the wrong room?

This truth was ingrained in Teresa (though she never gave much thought to it), despite the fact that she was never particularly beautiful or desirable even as a young woman. She was simply herself, pale-skinned with dark hair and eyes. Her young age was an obvious asset that always gave her an advantage. Like all young women, Teresa believed that the great love awaiting her on the horizon, ready to sweep her off her feet, was the only love worthy of her attention. Her mother, her aunt, her cousin – they all could conduct relationships of one sort or another, wrinkled and unimportant. They were just the shadow of a young man and a young woman and great love. The young man was late in coming, but Teresa had patience.

But at some stage, all of her assets were no longer obvious. The taut skin and the future extending across the horizon began to blur – when exactly did the young woman Teresa reach her peak? It's difficult to say. After all, the peak is the beginning of a steep and slippery decline. It wasn't terrible like, let's say, the first time that a whistle in the street was not directed toward her – her plain appearance protected her from this particular trauma. Still, at some point, young women walking in the street started to give her pause.

This was not the only tragedy. As she grew older and began to recognize that her advantage was slipping away, she was also surprised to realize that, in fact, all of the women in her life – her mother, her aunt and school teachers – were merely girls trapped in a heavy and distorted body. This clear case of mass abduction filled her with horror. There were no grownups in the world to rely upon, only young men and young women in different bodies, waiting to be rescued. Was it possible, she wondered, that her mother was also still waiting for love that was yet to come? That her aunt was also secretly examining old, used and lusterless men, and coveting them? But she has a child! she said to herself in disbelief. From Teresa's perspective, this topped it all – who would believe that after this people would still be thirsty for love.

Falling in love with Ephraim was a momentary blunder. He was pleasant and smart and an academic, a quality held in very high esteem in the European-Haifa home where her mother and aunt lived. Their opinion was important to Teresa and she already realized that a momentous young love would not emerge from her, and she thought she had grown up. Make no mistake – she did truly love him. If not a boundless teenage love, at least a quiet love that sprouted like a weed that could not be uprooted. Their shared European background was the basis for many pleasant evenings with a newspaper and coffee and light conversation in the living room, and, in particular, there was a lot of calm that was worth embracing. Gradually, his body became so familiar, until any thought of another body became impossible. The two of them studied and worked and wrote articles, and tended a garden and a cat and a hedge of bougainvillea, which turned out to be a very forgiving plant – several times, it was neglected and dried out and looked like a hopeless case, but it was enough to water it once for it to begin a process of renewed flowering in full confidence.

Nonetheless, during the first year of their marriage, she would imagine, for example, a strange man entering their kitchen, opening the bread drawer and finding, to his great surprise, the disc of Tchaikovsky's Pathétique Symphony, the one that always made her cry. "Oh, leave that there. It makes Teresa cry, and she never goes into the bread drawer," the imaginary Ephraim would say while drying a rinsed cup. But the disc of the Pathétique never disappeared from the shelf into exile in the bread drawer. Therefore, Teresa was compelled to listen to it over and over, and tears would trickle from her eyes without her even knowing why. It was only after Nati was born and grew a bit, and after their unsuccessful attempts to bring him a brother or sister, that she woke up one morning and discovered that she was still waiting.

Her son was very smart. He never saw her as someone to lean on, as she pretended to be. Nati left with a light heart. "Everything will be fine, Mother. There's nothing to worry about," he said. When they returned from the airport, the car was empty of all the things that traveled with Nati – a backpack and jacket and food for the way, which she insisted on packing for him in a separate backpack, despite his protests. Instead of all this, a new recognition now crouched in the trunk of the car: Teresa, the trapped girl, wanted Nati to come back. Ephraim was a comfortable partner in life; Nati gave them the gusto in life. It wasn't worry, just yearning. Don't throw yourself on him, she said to herself. He's young, you need to look after him and not lean on him. All in all, it comes down to a decision. This thought was a formative moment of maturation.

It enabled Teresa to be relatively calm, and very practical, and also alone in a sort of existential and consoling way.

Thus, the year when she was widowed of Ephraim found her in an emotional situation that was forged within her nearly two years earlier. "She's a strong woman, the tongues whispered at the *shiva.** "She has an only son who is seldom in Israel; she copes with everything on her own." That was true. Eventually, despite the sorrow, life continued in its routine, more or less. She was sorry for Ephraim that he died before deciphering the secret of the cells, and something inside her died with him, but she continued to study political poetry at the Department of Political Science and to publish articles and hoped to receive tenure and all of the usual things. The sounds of the house consolidated themselves into a new and regular heartbeat that was much different than its predecessor – the keys tossed on the table every morning at a certain hour, the tea being stirred to the sounds of the radio program, the lemons with only a few drops remaining in them making the sounds of kissing. The new title of widowhood put a final end to her right to fall in love, to strip off her clothes, to quiver from excitement. A middle-aged widow, what rights did she still have? A happy ending became irrelevant; the peak had already passed or perhaps had been canceled. There was some serenity in this.

Since her life was conducted in lusterless equanimity, she needed foreign eyes to realize that the care she extended to the driver responsible for her tragedy was an extraordinary act. Without noticing, she had violated the laws of anger; in her new role, she was supposed to be poised for revenge. One time, a young journalist called her, a young woman whose heart thirsted for stories of self-sacrifice and Christian forgiveness and melodramas in general. "Please tell me your story. How did you forgive the driver who ruined your life, even taking care of him? It will inspire the readers, it will empower them. It will lead them to believe in the

* The seven-day period of mourning.

good," she told Teresa, waxing poetic. As they were conversing, a small spider crawled on Teresa's arm. She opened the window and tossed it outside. And just in this action, she thought in surprise, there was greater compassion than in staying by the driver, a stay that did not entail giving without recompense or true kindness. She refused to be interviewed, but several weeks later would still look for the name of the journalist, whose vision of empowering readers apparently failed: The newspapers were not overflowing with inspiration and the journalist's name appeared less and less frequently until it no longer appeared at all, or perhaps Teresa was the one who had stopped looking.

Still, and despite all this, fate has its own right to exist. In the second year of her widowhood, as her annual vacation from the university approached, she picked up the telephone and reserved a room for herself at the hotel where she and Ephraim had regularly stayed. The official reason they traveled there every year was an inexplicable rash on Ephraim's chest. This reason, of course, was no longer relevant, but time melts reasons and establishes facts. Now, she could not imagine going anywhere else. "A single room," she said, converting the speculation about divorce and death into a ten-percent discount. It was the first time she had set off on a vacation alone. Even before arriving, the mountain landscape had already filled her with a smothering and consoling serenity. The radio ungrudgingly played the regular station. During that vacation, she met Elisha.

It still required special courage to eat dinner alone, she thought to herself. When the hour came, she put on the black dress and perfume and combed her hair and was very nervous. When she was at dinner with Ephraim, the hotel was full of vacationing couples about their age. But now she noticed for the first time all of the people eating dinner alone. Gradually, calm spread through her limbs.

By the time Elisha entered the dining room, her eyes had already become accustomed to the world of the single person. She knew immediately that he was alone. His hair was black and his skin scorched by the sun. His eyes were still cheerful (and her heart would ache when she belatedly realized this). What happy event befell him that brought on this momentary cheerfulness that enables people to sit down opposite a strange woman and invite himself to a conversation? Elisha had no need for juvenile pickup lines (an advantage of age, which is never sufficiently appreciated). "Sorry to bother you. Are you dining alone?" he simply asked. ("Dining," he said. She would later smile at the choice of this particular word.) Teresa nodded, grown-up and mature. Her sweeping hand gesture led to a dinner for two.

After a meal and wine and a walk on the promenade outside of the hotel, a man and a woman in middle age went up to a room in a hotel. What they did there is their private business. The young receptionist, looking bored, bid them good night.

Nonetheless, on that very evening, to her surprise, Teresa discovered a renewed right to exist. Her new assets – the skill to insert a blanket in an inside-out blanket cover, indicating that a child had grown here, the chafed skin on her hands from washing dishes after meals that had simmered slowly, diffusing the aroma of home – were not immediately visible, but their presence was felt. And Elisha looked at these assets and loved them with a typical male love – that is, instinctively and without thinking too much. And that in itself, in Teresa's view, was no less than a miracle.

More than she was surprised that he desired her, she was surprised that she didn't flinch from his touch – at first glance, he was shriveled and bony, and the spirit of the girl trapped in Teresa was deterred, but only for a moment. There were a girl and a boy, a woman and a man, free of the fear of hasty juvenile decisions. It turned out that the body still knew how to become impassioned. But, it calmed down faster. There was something pleasant in this.

They talked so much that night! She told him about Nati and about Ephraim and his eyes teared up. She believed she had touched him with the solidarity of parents whose children are far away. Later, she would think that it was perhaps a prophetical sparkle in his eyes, because soon afterwards Elisha would unite with her in the sorrow of parents whose children were not spared the constant search for home.

In retrospect, the next three days were everything they had. Three meaningful days of existence that lacked nothing. And that's quite a bit – morning, afternoon and evening full of possibilities, an entire universe. After breakfast, they went down to the beach together and floated, side by side, devoting themselves to the quiet. Bathing in the Dead Sea has unique therapeutic qualities for the body and soul. At their age, contempt for such qualities is superfluous. As she looked out at the eternal mountains standing on the water line, she was aware of the fact that the other people sitting at the beach mistakenly believed that they had always been floating together like this.

When Elisha's boys arrived, tanned and happy, it was the end. Neither of them knew this yet. She saw it in the eyes of his youngest son. The two others appeared to be simple and healthy; Nadav scared her. How devoid of hope this child was, she thought to herself. It was not first time she had encountered the tortuous power of aspiration for the past.

Elisha warmly introduced her to them. The boy's eyes blazed. All that day, he avoided her, as if she would fade and disappear if he didn't look at her. In a way, he was not mistaken.

The next day was the last day of her vacation. She finished it as she had begun, alone.

On the way home, she already felt the memory of the vacation slipping away from her, grabbing the horns of the mountains. The sea vanished from the window of the car and then, to her surprise, reappeared after a few miles of wilderness. (The heart of the sea is concentrated in bottles and tubes sold in tourist shops in the area. A sort of baldness remained in their place.) Eventually, the landscape returned to its familiar track. When she returned home, Elisha was nothing more than a sweet memory belonging to a different part of the country. Still, she remembered him for another week or two – it was a silly thought, of course. A woman of her age, if her period is late it can only be for one reason – it has simply stopped coming. The waves of heat and cold turned out to have a purely emotional source – a familiar stomach ache and a very earthly bleeding immediately aborted any illogical thoughts of a baby with dark hair and eyes. The vacation from the university also finally came to an end. Life returned to its familiar course. She continued to wear the pendant she received from him before she left – not because she thought that her nursing of the driver was an extraordinary action, but simply as a keepsake.

Despite their promises to meet again, at least a year would pass before they found the right moment. Elisha's sorrow filled his world and then shrunk him, and Teresa's place was hidden between the folds like the writing on a deflated balloon.

They met again only a year later, during the annual vacation. She was shocked at how his hair had grayed. At the sight of him, her hair began to pale in shame, as if she did not long for Nati enough.

During the same vacation, her heart experienced another spurt of excitement, also unexpected – her soul became attached to that of poor Kati, a young chambermaid whom Teresa would never have met in an orderly world. The nocturnal, surreal encounter with Kati flooded Teresa with memories she had repressed for a good reason – for example, a small book Nati once bought her. It was not a particularly personal gift; it was entitled "To My Mother" and included childish drawings, and was sold in bookstores alongside similar titles: "To My Father," "To My Grandfather" and "To My Good Teacher." The book was a symbol of a lack of thoughtfulness, but she was still happy with it – Teresa the child, gathering attention. One of the poems stated: "If I had to choose a mother, I would choose only you." In her mind, she already wondered whether this was true. Would Nati choose her? Later, she would wonder whether Nadav would choose Elisha.

If the amulet of Rabbi Eybeschütz had any effect, it was hard for her to notice it. Life went on, full of small successes and small failures, no more than usual, as far as she knew. She received tenure at the university, which was expected in any case, students came and went, she read books and went with a friend to some concerts. (Nonetheless, one time a woman fixed a meaningful stare at her and smiled. Her hand on her exposed chest testified to an act of kindness in her past too, and for a moment Teresa felt as if she were part of a secret sect with rules of its own.)

If someone had asked her to point to a miracle elicited by the amulet she always wore on her chest, she would have found this difficult to do. However, if this anonymous questioner had insisted that she point to one, she most likely would have pointed to Elisha.

*   *   *

There is more than one way to show something to somebody. The overall picture received in the end must include the presenter, the audience, the thing itself and everything between them. If, for example, you are very familiar with the Ben Shemen Forest and take someone for a hike there who is unfamiliar with it, you become the forest's exclusive owner for at least a few hours. However, there can be a considerable degree of arrogance in this presentation of things. Another possibility is to deliberately conceal the specific place you once visited with someone else, or intentionally refrain from visiting the place with the most flowers blooming in season.

The barren southern region is less generous when it comes to places that are possible to conceal. The land spreads out in a single color and behind the rocks there are no flowers hiding that you can claim as your own. The hyrax and ibex move independently in any case. Still, when Elisha took Teresa on a tour of the Qumran caves, he showed them to her in the most generous way – that is, neither proud nor concealing, but sharing them with her. His enthusiasm was almost childlike, but the success of the tour was mainly due to the lack of anxiety between them, mature and self-sufficient. Teresa, an entrapped girl but also a woman in all of the known aspects, could give him what youth seldom is capable of giving – sharing without making a bored face or glancing over one's shoulder, interest that is not feigned and calm recognition of the beauty of the moment.

The caves themselves, it must be admitted, are not particularly impressive. Ultimately, it is a desert nature preserve. The fence surrounding it, the deserted souvenir shop, and the outdated theater combine to give it a meager appearance. It encompasses no more than a few miles of exposed land with hints of stairs, a table, a cold room and plates. These basic accessories served the Community Rule people in their everyday lives and were not something they had to think about particularly. The school children who are sometimes brought to trudge through the nature preserve tend to agree with them. The blazing sun above the heads of the visitors during most months of the year also contributes its part. At this stage, most of the tourists are already impatiently waiting to get to the second part of the tour – that is, the Dead Sea. Those who did not read the tour book or listen to the guide envision a cool beach, soft sand and children running around. A disappointment soon awaits them.

Elisha and Teresa came to the nature preserve on a weekday. Besides them, only two other couples were roaming around, after choosing not to join a guided tour scheduled to start an hour later. The Japanese couple examined the monotonous scenery through the eyepiece of a camera and clicked in boredom (in the northern region, with its plentiful flowers and birds and rivers, Japanese cameras tend to sound like three aces in a slot machine) and a bit of the desert's soul would soon be sent to the other part of the planet. The other couple was actually Israeli. The woman brought a book to be on the safe side – its back cover peeked from her cloth bag. The photographed author looked quite melancholy.

But under Elisha's enthusiastic explanations, the caves shook off their dust. He was completely focused on Teresa. Upon entering the fenced preserve, he told her how the scrolls were found. Elisha was accustomed to the oppressive heat. His eyes were alert and his voice did not sink from exhaustion as it occasionally does. The supportive audience, Teresa, completed the picture. The two couples noticed them inside the preserve and stopped to listen.

First of all, of course, there is the matter of the date. The scrolls discovered in the tracks of the miserable goat were composed just a bit after the composition of the books of the Bible themselves. It is the oldest evidence of the existence of the books, he said, the barren hills providing this information with a backdrop of authenticity.

The scrolls themselves are not at the site – they were acquired and preserved and are exhibited at the Shrine of the Book in Jerusalem. The Japanese man came up very close to them. He said "ah" in interest and they were surprised to discover that he understood Hebrew. His wife smiled politely. There was no need for the scrolls, an inanimate piece of history. They followed Elisha and the ancient community came to life.

"The scrolls of the Judean Desert sect include the Community Rule – a book of laws for members of the sect from the days of the Second Temple," he explained. "The laws were designed to prepare the members for a war of the children of light against the children of darkness. With the help of these laws, it would be possible to win. The course of history was determined in advance, including the apocalypse."

He continued, more slowly: "Until this war, the world would be ruled by the wicked, who would destroyed in the apocalypse. After the revolution, the Lord's chosen, the children of light, would be saved. For this purpose, they must be united. The members of the community lived their lives in declared readiness for the Day of Judgment, the final day," Elisha thundered. It was clear from his voice that this was a terrible tragedy. Teresa noted pleasantly that this was not necessarily bad. The last bite of the cake is always sweeter. When you know it's the last one, you chew it slowly.

The Israeli couple also approached. The woman was very beautiful and wore a fluttering white dress. On her wrist, a gentle and nearly perfect bracelet gleamed in the sun. The only thing detracting from her appearance was the thought that she had bothered to wear it. The melancholy author was stuffed deep into her bag and the man next to her said, "Oh, here, there's someone who knows." In a natural way, they were drawn into the role of pupils. Elisha noticed the woman's beauty, in the same way as he was aware of the full splendor of the mountains. In fact, he saw only Teresa. Her face was not smooth; around her eyes and mouth were small wrinkles and furrows. She did not wear a black dress today – the expected heat pushed her hand toward the yellow dress. Her body was relaxed, free of the need to stretch itself. Her hand held a small brown bag that radiated calming messages of tissues and aspirin and perhaps even a bottle of water. When his eyes rested upon her, he was suffused with a sense of home, like an eye detecting a family member in a photograph of unfamiliar people.

Elisha led them through the entire preserve, which was not big, enthusiastically explaining the scrolls of commentary and the sad denouement of the members of the sect: The prevalent hypothesis is that they joined the people of Masada, at the nearby tourist site, and found their death there. Were the people of Masada indeed heroes? A heated argument ensued. The Israeli man once heard that they did not really commit suicide and perhaps were not even Jews. The Japanese man defended their honor, in English.

He saved one scroll for Teresa. Before parting from the two couples (who looked a bit more satisfied now and a bit less deceived), they posed for photographs as a keepsake and took business cards from Elisha. Despite their good intentions, it was clear to everyone that the cards would be abandoned in the car and that they would never return here. Then Elisha told Teresa about the Copper Scroll. This scroll, unlike the others, was not written on parchment. Instead, it was engraved on a sheet of copper and contained precise instructions about the location of the Temple's treasures. There are scholars who do not believe this information. It was the favorite scroll of Nadav and Elisha. In both of their dreams, Nadav, the young and promising researcher, discovers a forgotten treasure and is chronicled forever in all of the right books.

It was a gift. In her wise and calm way, Teresa understood. She would not cause him the disappointment that heartless people sometimes accord to those who mistakenly share their assets with them; he could count on her. Their delicate relationship was based to a great extent on the mutual allocation of small security nets – if one of them said "this cake is excellent" or "I'd like to travel in Africa," he or she would never be insultingly challenged about the quality of the frosting or by noting that Africa has flies and diseases. At that very moment, her hand was placed on his arm in exactly the right balance. The treasury scrolls truly interested her. She asked several questions about them and then was silent, allowing him to shake the glass ball again until the snow fell upon the young Nadav, against the backdrop of the caves and the treasure, covering him.

*　*　*

On my third birthday, Mother called Father on the telephone and I discovered that he lived in Australia. Contrary to what one might expect, these were two minor events, almost insignificant and unrelated. In addition, I also discovered the wonders of the question "Why?" This already happened on the way to the hotel.

"SaltySea, SaltySea, I go SaltySea!" I sang excitedly. I wasn't actually the one who composed this ditty. At the age of three, it was still easy to instill happiness in my uncritical consciousness. All that was needed was to give the facts wrapped in happy smiles and spiced with "this is so much fun!" In the world of grownups, this type of marketing is considered predatory and unsophisticated; in my world, I was happy then. The exciting horizon, combined with the travel on the long and winding road, while sitting beside a sack full of birthday presents, produced a real sense of euphoria in me.

Darya was also traveling to the SaltySea. Her place in the song was omitted because it was so obvious. She took another toffee candy from the package on the seat next to her. (At this stage, I believed that the real purpose of the passenger seat was to serve as a table and had never thought to insist on sitting in front.) "Don't stick your hands out of the window," she admonished in fatigue.

"Why?"

"Because it's dangerous."

"Why?"

"Because a car could come and take your hand off."

"Why?"

As promised in all of the child development books lying by mother's bed and serving as a stand for tissues and a cup of water, I had reached the "why" period exactly on my third birthday. Mother discovered the new stage in my development only when we were already on the highway – if she had known in advance, she would probably have made sure to bring more cassettes. Instead, she turned on the radio. We sang loudly together "Give me planty, give me planty, it's fun to be a plant!" and my throat became parched.

At the end of the three-hour drive, I raced into the lobby of the Pomegranate Branches Hotel through the revolving door. It took Darya a little longer because the suitcase got caught in the door. She entered the lobby just in time: A moment later and I would have marched into an elevator by mistake and disappeared on one of the floors. She looked exhausted. The invisible thread connecting us was strained from being pulled here and there; her heart shrunk and expanded respectively. She could really beg Mika to take me with her for an hour or two, but then spend the free hours longing for me at home.

I gave her my hand and we approached the receptionist, who recognized me immediately. "Hi sweetie!" she bent toward me from the reception desk. "It's been so long since we've seen you. Look how big you've grown! Is it your birthday?"

"I go to SaltySea!" I updated her.

Shlomo the manager recognized Mother from afar. He crossed the lobby and came up to us. I really had grown. My hair, which was very blond, was starting to take on shades of brown. The shape of the person I would be someday was already visible in my maturing face. I made all of the other people in the lobby look very old. Shlomo also saw in me the three years that had passed since we first met. He mussed up my hair. "So, you've come back to us? How are you?" We conducted an insignificant conversation of an adult and a child.

And here, Teresa Holstein, my godmother and confidante, was sitting in the lobby! Our small and regular gang started to assemble. I might have assumed that she had remained sitting there since the previous year. Actually, I didn't remember her at all. Not only did I fail to remember her, it turned out that the past year had opened my eyes, like Eve after tasting the Garden of Eden's forbidden fruit: The world, which until then had consisted mainly of forms and crystals and sounds, suddenly appeared to me in its true form, and I felt embarrassed.

I hid my face in Mother's skirt as Teresa came up to her. (Her skirt still had the aroma of our morning visit to the Earth's Produce bakery that morning. I sudden had an urge for a croissant with butter.) Teresa tried to coax me with things and finally succeeded in drawing me out of Mother's skirt with the help of an orange candy. As she conversed with Mother, I rolled the sticky candy (it still had some of the plastic wrapping on it) around in my mouth and surveyed the expansive room. Now that I was discovering interest in children my age, the Morgenstern family was nowhere in sight. I vaguely did remember them. Every time Avi or Sarah appeared in the business section of the newspaper, Mother showed me the picture and said: "Look, here is Danieli's mother/father!" In my mind, Danieli had already become a blurred picture in a black-and-white newspaper.

I wandered back to the reception desk, where the receptionist was making funny faces for me. I liked her, without knowing of course that she held an important piece of information that directly pertained to life: With a wave of her finger, she could display the name, address and telephone number of my father on her computer screen. She herself did not guess that a particular piece of information that would shed light on a matter of concern to her was meaningless information for me. I knew what Teresa had done. A secret is a coin that rolls from your hand to the street – the more you look for it, the more it camouflages itself; however, the coin will shine happily in the sight of someone else. Sometimes the solution is simply to stop looking.

Mother finished checking in and conversing with Shlomo and Teresa. We went into the elevator ("Don't press all the buttons!" – "Why?") and we arrived – what a surprise! – on the first floor. Mother pushed the light switch. The first flash of the light bulb would signal, in a few minutes, the beginning of another chapter in my development, which included countless questions about the exact location of my father. (And this did not replace or shorten the "why?" period. Poor Darya.) In the meantime, I received birthday presents and was content.

Birthday presents: Spiderman. On one of the days when I was delivered to the care of Mika, she rented the cartoon version for me, assuming (correctly) that all children like Spiderman. Until then, Mother had thought (also correctly) that I was too young for Spiderman. Indeed, Mika had to simplify many parts of the story for me. And, indeed, Mother had to reassure me again and again that the bad guy from the movie was not hiding behind the bookcase. And still the result was unbridled adoration for the first masculine character in my life. I received a Spiderman shirt (that's from Father), a Spiderman backpack (that's from Mother), and a pile of coloring books (that's from Grandfather and Grandmother). I abandoned the coloring books quite quickly, while the shirt and backpack kept me busy long enough to allow Mother to change into vacation clothes, with a bathing suit underneath. When she emerged from the bathroom, all of the flashes of memories, the light bulb and the room, the beginning and the end, were processed in my mind into one short and not particularly original sentence: "Where's my father?"

It was not the first time I had asked the question, but there was still something new to it – until then, the question usually arose when seeing children and fathers together, and was later forgotten. Mother was not surprised. The scenery outside the window also stirred in her, involuntarily, the memory of my father, who was usually forgotten. Her answer was calm: "Father is gone. Just the two of us are here. You and Mother."

"Why?"

The question could sound very philosophical and heart-rending. But Mother did not fall into the trap. She remembered very well that I was just three years old. There was no blame in the protected and limited world she had created for me. She quickly came up with the one possible answer that would serve her during the coming weeks more than any cassette or radio: "Why not?"

Still, the question continued to echo after we left the room. On our way to the beach (I was in a Spiderman shirt, with a Spiderman backpack full of coloring books, and Mother wore a fluttering yellow dress), we passed through the lobby and met Teresa again, who was still sitting there. She waved hello to us. My mouth filled with a sweet orange taste mixed with plastic and I ran to her, but then stopped suddenly when I discovered that someone else was also sitting there. The man said, "Hello there, what's your name?" Teresa reminded him. When Mother arrived in my wake, he nodded and smiled a smile of an old acquaintance. Mother said, "Hello Elisha, how are you," without a question mark. For a moment, it seemed that the solidarity of the regular guests on my birthday at the Pomegranate Branches Hotel was impenetrable. In fact, years would pass before we all gathered again for a vacation at the same time. I stared at Elisha's short, well-made beard and reached the only logical conclusion. To make sure, I shot a glance at Teresa and asked, "Are you her father?"

My innocent question momentarily summoned in their eyes Teresa's deceased father and Elisha's lost son. The small, coincidental pains are the most painful, leaving bruises on the exposed skin.

At my young age and with my smooth and unscarred skin, I had no way of knowing this. And in any case, Teresa's eyes began dancing again a moment later: "No, of course not. You like Spiderman?"

I already noted that at age three it was very easy to distract me. I nodded enthusiastically. While I was showing her the bag and my coloring books, Elisha asked Mother whether everything was okay and how she was getting along. I noticed that people often asked her how she was getting along. The question seemed out of place to me. She's my mother, what other choice did she have? Only in retrospect did I realize how amazing and surprising it was that Mother thought like me, as well as the fact that she was telling the truth when responding that she was getting along wonderfully.

Still, as the days passed, she seemed to yearn more and more for the annual vacation as a real life saver. We said goodbye to Elisha and Teresa (not before Elisha whispered a promise to show me a surprise that evening) and went out toward the beach. As we approached the sea, the tranquil, standing water could be seen infusing a type of longing in my mother's eyes. We situated ourselves in plastic chairs. The moment one of the guests agreed to keep an eye on me, Mother shed her clothes as if they were a peel of cancer skin, with only the body underneath it alive. And within a moment, she was in the water, lying on her back and submitting herself to the sun. The ability to be weightless with eyes closed took on a meaning for her that I was not privy to, and I watched her from the beach. When she came out of the water, sparkles of salt crystallized on her skin. I ran a finger over them and told her in wonder: "You're beautiful, Mother." The woman who had kept an eye me smiled. Mother smiled too. This time she was willing to accept the sentence in all its depths and meanings, and ignore the fact that I was only three years old.

I did not go into the water, and the granular sand did not allow me to build castles and buildings in the sand. I was busy with my coloring books and colored intently while mother read a newspaper. My internal camera came out and captured the moment. I clearly remember how I meticulously colored the blue of the sky and the yellow of the sun, and Spiderman's shirt in read and blue. But Mother saved these coloring books for some reason and when I saw them again years later, all I could see were formless and colorless scribbles.

In the evening, I looked for Elisha in the dining room. When I found him, I hurried over to him: "You promised a surprise!" Elisha smiled in consent and asked my mother's permission to take me to the hotel courtyard. We went out through the revolving door and headed toward the back of the hedge.

The oleander hedge bloomed with pink flowers that gleamed from the remains of its last watering. I reached out a curious hand toward them and Elisha said: "No, no, never touch these plants. It's a very poisonous plant." I moved my hand away without giving it much thought, but the words were still not said in vain – a woman who was standing lost in thought at the entrance to the hotel would now take consolation in the possibility of a cup of tea from the oleander plant, to be on the safe side. I'm Darya's son and I was supposed to take consolation in memories of a different sort. Elisha went down on his knees and signaled to me to do the same and to keep quiet. To outsiders, we were surely a funny sight – a bearded man and a child kneeling in the twilight. If a guest noticed us, perhaps he mistakenly thought we were Muslims. But we did not laugh. We were very serious, even to the point of real awe and reverence.

Elisha said: "Look behind the bush, here," and a moment later I saw – a mother cat sat there, patiently licking a white and furry kitten. Three other newborn kittens were napping, cuddled up against their mother.

"Pussy cats!" I cried in excitement, my heart about to burst.

Elisha said: "Yes, this is their mother. She is taking care of them." "Why?"

As a father of three children of his own and as someone experienced with the "why" phase, Elisha did not respond. He stood up and I stood up after him, and I immediately bent down again.

"Pussy cats," I said to myself in wonder. The sight impressed me. It had many and mysterious meanings for me. They were absorbed inside me without words, perhaps in order to pop up someday.

When we returned to the dining room, Mother was already sitting. She chose a large table and invited Elisha to join us. After he agreed, his eyes surveyed the room with a perplexed look. Teresa was nowhere to be seen.

The cats quickly faded into the past as I ate pieces of fish without bones and gnawed on a roll. I received a surprise for dessert: a chocolate cake that Mother ordered for me arrived with a flaming sparkler. Mother, Elisha and the waiter sang "Happy Birthday" and some of the guests joined in with them, smiling. The story of my presence in the hotel circulated in whispers around the room. That's the child of the hotel. He was born here and therefore is eligible for a free vacation for life. There were no couples in the dining room who were young enough for their eyes to twinkle in mischievousness.

From the perspective of my three years on earth, my life was without particularly sensational developments. The long trip that day, the presents and the sea, the cats and the sparkler – made it one of the most exciting days I had ever known. It was also one of the most exhausting. When we went up to the room on the first floor, Mother turned on the light. I sprawled onto the double bed in my clothes and asked again, driven by a spark of memory: "Where is my father?"

"Father left," she said quietly, her voice adjusting itself to my eyes as they started to close.

"To where?"

I imagine that "to hell" and "to perdition" were only two of the answers that came to her mind. Aloud, she just said: "Shhh... go to sleep." She peeled the Spiderman shirt off of me. I submitted, already sleepy, to the maternal gesture. Within a few minutes, I was softly singing moon songs that took me onward, toward the world of sleep. I was about to miss the most important part of the day.

What actually impelled her to do the one thing she had sworn she would never do? Was it my questions that unintentionally hurt her maternal instinct? I tend to believe it was the moonlight. I assume that the dark and motionless sea visible from the window also contributed its part, and ultimately the location on the first floor was a decisive factor. On the first night of my third birthday vacation, Mother picked up the telephone, dialed to the switchboard and asked for the telephone number of a man whose name I didn't know, the stranger who became my father one night. She did not wait for her fears to pull back her hand, and she dialed right away.

For one short moment, we were a very banal picture: a child sleeping and a mother calling the father on the telephone. I missed the moment; I was fast asleep. In any case, there was no truth in that moment. The only information garnered from the telephone conversation was that the requested man – that is, my father – had received a job offer in Australia and set off without leaving a trace. His role in our lives was limited to an envelope of money every month. As it turned out, he had no desire to fill any additional role.

Did a tear run down the cheek that absorbed the information from the telephone? Did the body protest about everything that might have been? Did it shudder against the empty air? Or perhaps she simply put the phone down, yielded to the internal and innocent serenity that was inherent in her, a serenity that she had needlessly nurtured in meaningless workshops. Carpe diem, live the moment, the past is gone, the future is yet to be born. When I woke up, three years and a day, and full of energy, there were no foreign traces in her smile when she said: "Good morning, sweetheart. Let's get dressed and go to eat. Then we'll go down to the pool."

Except for two elderly women swimming back and forth with a grim expression on their faces, there was no one in the pool. Outside of the pool, several people were lying on towels, but most of the vacationers preferred to go down to the sea. After all, they came to the Dead Sea. Chlorine pools with no therapeutic value can be found anywhere.

Mother inflated a floating tube for me. I was Spiderman, spraying webs in all directions. It's hard for me to guess how much time had passed since we arrived, but Mother looked very happy when she saw Teresa entering the pool area. It was not surprising for us to run into her – all in all, we didn't have too many possibilities: sea, pool or hotel lobby. The guests at the Pomegranate Branches Hotel scurry around each during their vacations like a swarm of ants after someone has stepped in the middle of it. Nonetheless, we had not seen Teresa since our arrival. Her presence made the empty pool area appear less lonely.

I was a kitten who lived behind the floating tube bush, wailing and growling alternately and not listening to the conversation that Teresa and Mother were conducting. So I can only blame myself that an hour later they assigned me to Teresa's supervision in the lobby while Mother went down to get a massage. What did Teresa say to persuade her? Perhaps she offered the treatment as a birthday present. Perhaps she praised the wonders of the masseur. Or perhaps she preached to her that she should do something nice for herself and give herself a treat. Women do that sometimes.

Teresa bought a small puzzle for me at the souvenir shop in the lobby. There were three ducks and not a lot of pieces. I sprawled out on the floor and a moment later was entirely absorbed in the puzzle, accustomed to keeping myself busy. I hardly bothered to lift up my head when Elisha joined us. He and Teresa in my eyes were two sides of the same coin. They were the others and they were watching over me. The conversation they conducted above my head was no more or less understood than the rest of the conversations in the world.

Teresa said: "When I look at that, I simply admire her. It was a brave and correct decision."

Elisha responded: "Yes, though to be fair, there are still loose ends here. Still, a person should know his duty and fulfill it."

One could easily have assumed that they were talking about Darya and my father. When I finished the puzzle, I lifted my head from the carpet. Mimi the receptionist saw me from the reception desk and waved hello to me.

The next day, we went down to eat our last breakfast of the vacation. When we next returned, I would be four years old. Teresa Holstein would not be sitting in the lobby when we arrived – her annual vacation would be postponed due to family circumstances. (Who would think that she had other concerns besides spending time at the sea and the pool?) The newborn kittens would have newborn kittens. The white dress would no longer surround a salty bathing suit – it would have to wait in the closet. When the emotional connection between her and Mother wanes, the dress will become a Cinderella duster. I didn't know anything about all this, and still something of the cruelty in creating and then severing a routine seeped into my movements, slowing them down on that last vacation day.

When Mother returned to the table – it was a table for two that morning – with a selection of chocolate cakes and cheese and a croissant, I tried again to collect what was promised to me in this very hotel: "Where is my father?"

"He traveled."

"To where?"

"To Australia."

"Why?"

I imagine that if my father had been present for this conversation, with a third plate and another cup of fruit juice, he would have nodded in agreement with her offhand response: "Why not." Since I had yet to find a way to get around the obstacle of "why not," my face turned yellow and dropped, tugging on her threads of guilt.

Darya said: "But Mother is here. The two of us are together, forever. We're having so much fun together at the Dead Sea! Right?"

"Yes," I nodded enthusiastically, compelled for some reason to adjust the tone of my response to match hers.

"Want some chocolate cake?"

"Yes!"

The troubled conscience of parents who abandon their children would perhaps be hurt by the fact that, at least at some stages, it is very easy to replace them with something sweet to eat. The truth is that yes, it was fun for Mother and me at the Dead Sea. I didn't even ask when he would return. The question would only ripen later. I did ask whether Australia is far. The answer ("very") filled me with a sense of awe. My father was in Australia.

Teresa already said goodbye to us in the dining room. This time she gave me a green candy. I felt the pleasant, sour tingling and the internal camera gradually changed Teresa's color from orange to green. When we returned the key, Mimi hugged me and said: "See you next year!"

The sun was still in its afternoon location when we exited the revolving door. Mother led me to the seashore to say goodbye. There was something calming in observing the people still lying on the beach – elderly women in one-piece bathing suits, a couple kissing, and two men with a newspaper protecting their faces from the sun. Even when we entered the car, something of this would remain – though it left no impression on the silent sea or on me. While mother was inhaling the last sea air into her memory, I looked up. There was something there – my eyes were drawn to a grotesque Mickey Mouse figure, deflated and with sagging cheeks, hovering aimlessly and heavily there. It was definitely not my balloon, but still the sight made me feel the emptiness of a string in the hand and a familiar lump in the throat.

I was a child who had lost something and I wasn't at all sure whether it was in this incarnation. The internal camera, merciless as it is, of all the photogenic moments of that vacation, chose to perpetuate drooping ears of helium. We were very quiet on the way home. The radio played songs for regions of the country.

That day, as evening approached, a major power outage occurred – for two entire days an entire country was paralyzed, quite a marginal event in the life of three-year-olds. Fortunately, we made it home before the light disappeared. An emergency lamp was placed in my room to dispel dreams with a neon light. The hour was five o'clock in the evening, Israel Standard Time, and it was the middle of the night in far-off Australia. One could only guess that several expatriate fathers heard about the power outage on the news or on the Internet, looked out the window and wondered whether their children were afraid of the dark and whether those responsible for them were doing their job faithfully, in the meantime, until their return home.

*   *   *

That year, the earth was unforgiving. Soon after Yom Kippur, two sinkholes gaped open in the Dead Sea area. It was not the first time that the earth in the South had coveted its residents – once every few years, it becomes infuriated with the factories that are plundering its treasures in order to sell them in boxes and bottles with English names, and decides to suck in anything that crosses the lines, whose demarcation only it knows. The fact that the earth's surface becomes concave does not really bother anyone – people have no objection to valleys and gorges – but the unforeseeable timing, as usual, can turn simple events into tragedies. This time, the sinkholes were discovered so close to the hotel area that they merited a picture and front-page reference in the daily newspaper.

Usually, hotel managers are glad to be mentioned on the front page. The picture was also not bad at all – a hotel with an avenue of palm trees and the quiet, alluring sea in the background. But the caption declared: "False serenity?" and announced: "The Ministry of Environmental Protection will examine whether the sinkholes pose a threat to the Dead Sea hotels. See full article on Page 12." And this was already less to their liking. Many newspapers were tossed that day in anger, with their front page face down. In quite a few hotels the back page was prominently displayed, with the weather forecast and a picture of a sunrise with the caption: "Neta, marry me!"

Officials from the Ministry for Environmental Protection were quick to arrive and roamed between the hotels with an air of great importance. They had a reason to feel important – after all, at the moment they were the only ones in the area whose jobs were secure. The threat of closure orders for the hotels (and even worse – the danger of being sucked into the earth) hovered in the air and was whispered by the managers and the guests. The Pomegranate Branches Hotel stood in place like an island in a shark-infested sea. The first thing the sinkholes sucked in was the skin on the face of Shlomo the manager, which was now pulled down toward the area of his mouth. His face looked as if two arrows of accusation had been sketched in it, pointing toward the earth.

However, these lines of worry, even if impossible to erase, ultimately turned out to be unjustified. On the contrary, the only thing the sinkholes did in the end (actually the officials from the Ministry of Environmental Protection did this on their behalf) was to issued a temporary closure order for the neighboring hotel, the Royal Crown Hotel. There was poetic justice in this – a decade earlier, the two hotels had waged an all-out war over shared territory, and the court decided in favor of the Royal Crown Hotel. But now the ministry officials determined that the disputed area, which at the time included a parking lot that was very far from the two hotels, was likely to also include sinkholes that posed a threat to the safety of those in the area. The guests were asked to immediately evacuate, and the hotel was forbidden to take in new guests until the required steps were taken to confirm that no sinkholes were there. The manager of the Royal Crown Hotel did not want to disappoint the guests staying in the hotel (or even worse, to refund their money) and, therefore, he came at night to Shlomo, his old foe, and purchased alternative rooms from him in a relatively comfortable arrangement, considering the circumstances.

Among the guests who took refuge in the lobby of the Pomegranate Branches Hotel was a young journalist – alert, curious and diligent. While waiting with the other new guests, she glanced around with interest – who knows what stories the unanticipated move might generate. Undoubtedly, she would have been very happy to know that a former government minister had also packed his suitcases and moved to the Pomegranate Branches Hotel, where he had already stayed in the past. She would have been even happier to know exactly what had transpired as a result of that stay. What an article she could have written! And what a picture she could have presented to the editor – the minister standing on the hotel balcony looking sadly out toward the horizon. But how would the young journalist recognize the gray man? Her glance brushed over him for a moment and found no interest. She would have to suffice with the objective for which she came – a day in the life of the famous actress who was forming the entertainment troupe for children.

At the end of the lobby, behind the reception desk, Mimi immediately recognized the former minister – not so much from an interest in politics, but rather because of poor Kati. At the sight of the gray man, her initial instinct was to go up to him and explain to him in extreme precision and in a loud voice what she thought of him. (This would have made the journalist so happy!) But first she had to attend to the new stream of guests that continued to flow from the Royal Crown Hotel to the lobby. She had a responsibility and their lost look made her feel even more efficient than always. She passed out room keys, gave instructions and smiled encouraging smiles. For the time being, she sufficed with giving the minister an angry frown when she handed him the key to his room.

The minister situated himself in the room (was it the same room?) and sat down heavily on the bed. This was the last thing he needed, to return to this hotel. As if he had not made the long journey to the South in order to relax a bit from everything, in a place that was isolated and free of memories. But recently it seemed to him that his past was catching up to him and waiting around every corner. After years of speeches to the general public, he was accustomed to thinking in clichés. Now he was mulling over bitter thoughts about wheels turning and empires rising and falling. Yes, that's the way of the world. It was not a good period in the life of the minister, perhaps the worst one, though not necessarily due to the reasons his current setting demanded. That is, undoubtedly, his conscience should be tormenting him because of what he did to poor Kati. On the other hand, undoubtedly, people of conscience generally refrain from getting entangled in such situations in the first place, so it could be said with certainty that this was not the case. In fact, Kati held a very minute place in his life. It could not even claim the title of "the worst of his actions." She was just another thing that happened to him on one of those days whose memory has since become a colorful and muddy lump, like ice cream that starts with lots of alluring scoops and becomes an unappetizing concoction in the end. What a period it was! He had a government ministry, employed three secretaries and chaired two committees. Four months after the successful conference at the Dead Sea, they appointed him to serve as chairman of a third committee, this time for a project on collecting ground water. During the three years of his ministerial appointment, he had accumulated a handsome collection of brief love affairs, shady deals and some enemies too. Two of them conspired to eventually unseat him – one leaked to the media some pictures of him with a lover, actually not a very important one, and the other exposed a shell company funded from the state's coffers. The scoops of ice cream began to melt. His wife left the house and a month later the hypocritical and ungrateful party unanimously selected a new leader. What did all this have to do with poor Kati's baby? Perhaps cosmic justice had also ignored this. The minister's return to the Pomegranate Branches Hotel was the vengeance of the Dead Sea – not for Kati, but for the deal signed at that conference approving the continued mining of potash and salt from its treasures.

And Kati, nonetheless. Because from the time he moved to a rental apartment in Tel Aviv and lost the fight for his pension rights and started to work for a living as a lecturer in business administration in a college with a mediocre reputation and became a former minister in all of the crossword puzzles – he began to feel a need to think about everything in retrospect. This thinking started as somewhat utilitarian – perhaps it would have been better to give up a lover or two in exchange for the comfortable life he had. The deals that ended up costing him his job were also not essential in his previous economic situation. His sorrow was like drops of oil on water – little by little, they combined to form a large monster of sorrow.

After dinner, while all of the other guests gradually dispersed to tour the new space, some to their rooms and some to the promenade (it was, of course, the same promenade as that of the Royal Crown Hotel, but nonetheless the new angle mandated a renewed acquaintance), the minister went out to the balcony of the lobby. He knew that the Dead Sea had changed considerably since he was last here – the strip of beach was shorter and the entire sea was in danger of drying up. But the scenery visible from the balcony looked exactly as he remembered it, as if time had frozen. If only he could have also frozen the time! (He composed in his head a flowery speech, without an audience, imagining theatrical hand motions.) Despite, or perhaps because of, the backdrop of the polished Dead Sea, which cries out for precisely such sorrow, a surprising honesty crept into his sorrow. A brave tear emerged from the slope of his cheek on a hopeful voyage to unite with the great saltiness.

From her place by the reception desk, Mimi watched him and was also contemplative. Something in his limp posture and hunched back reflected the traces of that tear. She decided that it was an opportune time to approach him. "Will you manage here on your own for a few minutes?" she asked Alona, the new receptionist. Alona gave her a glassy-eyed stare.

On the dark balcony, next to the man with gray hair and gray clothes, Mimi's light-colored work clothes sparkled gaily. She leaned on the railing and asked: "Excuse me sir for interrupting, but I saw you've been standing here for quite a long time. Is everything okay?" The tone of her voice was very sincere; she was truly interested in knowing. The former minister remained silent.

After a few minutes of silence, when it already seemed to be the only state he was capable of, he suddenly replied: "Nothing is okay." He did not turn toward her, but continued to gaze out toward the sea with a veiled look, and Mimi realized that more words were coming. One after another the lights were lit outside, officially heralding the onset of night. The last bathers had already disappeared and a first boy with a guitar situated himself on the beach. It was an hour of kindness, a good hour for caressing and then delivering a blow. On the other hand, there was still some loss here, and Mimi did not have a vengeful nature, even though she sought justice. In the meantime, she remained silent.

"You know, I had everything," the minister told the dark beach. "Money, a wife, a family, a home. I had a position of power and I could have obtained anything I wanted. Anything." When he fell silent, Mimi said, identifying with him, "Power can also damage." It seemed to her that he was one of those people who like such sayings. Indeed, the sentence spurred him to continue. "Precisely! That's exactly what happened. So I had another young woman here, a bit more money on the side there. I didn't know when to stop."

Mimi wondered whether this was his only remorse. Nonetheless, she quickly formulated in her mind a very tough and educational response. The former minister unwittingly tempered her anger when he continued: "I look back and I'm simply ashamed. I had all of the opportunities and I wasted everything. I broke up a family, I lost a career, I hurt so many people along the way, and all this for what?" He turned his head and was now looking at her. "Do you understand? Everything was so unnecessary, worthless. For what?"

Mimi listened and, against her will, her heart softened. Unlike those who cleanse their conscience on Towel Day, whose remorse is driven by simple considerations of profit and loss (what is a towel, bathrobe or pillow in comparison to the Day of Judgment and the threat it entails?), the broken man looked to her like he was simply sad. It was also undeniable that she too held a piece of information pertaining to the minister that she wanted to get off her chest. She probably would not have gone to the trouble of searching him out, but now that he was here, it seemed to be the only possibility. She wondered how to make him confess to her about Kati, a mission that turned out to be easier than expected. All she needed to say was: "I'm sure you weren't so bad." Practiced in the burden of proof, the minister did all the rest by himself.

"You know, the funny thing is that my wife left me for all the wrong reasons. The affair with that woman, Varda was her name, was really nothing. That was when I was already getting sick and tired of all these flings. There were worse things – I formed a company, for example. I didn't steal, not really anyway, but the way it was managed was such that people did not really understand where the money was going. My best friend was hurt by this and we haven't spoken since. The problem was that he was also a member of the party and there was that committee then..." His stories and transgressions were gray like him, but the flow of his words indicated a sort of relief. He spoke without stopping. At first, Mimi looked at him with attentive interest and full of empathy, but as he continued she had to make an effort to keep her thoughts from wandering. Fortunately, the alert part of her brain made her refocus her attention when he got to the interesting part.

"...and there were other things. About four years ago, I got a young woman pregnant. You're too young, I'm sure you weren't here. (Mimi debated whether to feel frustrated or to take this as a compliment; she chose the latter). But she worked here, at this hotel. She apparently was impressed by my power, by my status. (He laughed a bitter laugh.) I was married, and when she told me... I was scared and I behaved like a schmuck. (Mimi made an effort not to giggle. The archaic word was crushed in his mouth and made him look older, or perhaps it was his true age.) She was very young. Look," he justified himself, "I had a wife and children."

Mimi shot a concerned glance at the reception desk. Her worries were confirmed – a line already stretched opposite the apathetic Alona, a line that was unreasonable for the evening hours. The line included a loud group of older and cheerful women speaking English, two couples and another man. Her eyes surveyed the small lobby. Under the yellow evening lights, she saw exactly what she was looking for. She said without too much thought: "I'm sure you also did good things. No one can know what tomorrow will bring. Nothing happens without a reason. Perhaps that's why you're back here, to come full circle." The minister nodded somberly. Mimi's eyes were not directed at him. She was looking mutely at Elisha. Her gaze made him turn his face from the eternal newspaper he read in the lobby. At the sight of the minister, his eyes squinted in surprise. "Excuse me for a moment, wait here a second," she said and crossed the lobby. The minister obeyed.

Good old Elisha! In her view, he was more suited to share the news with the minister. And besides, she preferred not to inform him by herself. Elisha, as usual, did not disappoint. What did Mimi whisper to him? It was only possible to whisper, though the looks on their faces, directed toward the minister, left little room for imagination. After no more than five minutes, they returned to the balcony. When he was a few steps away from him, Elisha already smiled at the melancholy minister. "Excuse me, you're not by chance..." he addressed the minister cheerfully. The minister was surprised by the flow of warmth he felt from the mere fact of being recognized and from the sound of his name being pronounced aloud. He examined Elisha and decided that this bearded man had good eyes. He also looked to him to be exceptionally athletic – perhaps a maharishi or Indian guru who sleeps on nails and eats berries.

"Yes," he said. "That's me."

"Nice to meet you." Elisha shook his hand. He allowed the minister to savor the moment of glory (a modest smile already emerged on his face) before continuing: "The truth is, I'm very glad you're here. I need to speak with you."

The minister looked at him hopefully. After years of political activity, he was no longer surprised to hear a stranger say he needed to speak with him. Besides, Elisha's beard gave him a very authoritative look. That is, there was a chance here to be rebuked by responsible people who would later work everything out. He was never a particularly spiritual type, but something in Elisha's prophetic eyes looked like a promise of redemption. He was ready to accept any solution that would make his life look different. His emotional state was the stuff on which devotional sects and cults are built.

"Come, let's sit," Elisha proposed. The strange trio turned toward a far corner of the lobby. Mimi sat facing the reception desk, shooting piercing glances at Alona, who pretended not to see her. The former minister sat opposite Elisha, with the wall behind him. In an unexplained way, he felt trapped.

Elisha spoke in a quiet and soft voice. "I understand that you've reached a certain point in your life, a low point." The minister did not resent the intrusive assertion. Mimi examined him closely. "You don't know me," Elisha continued pleasantly, "but I've been a regular guest here at the hotel for many years already. I'm very familiar with you and your story. From the media, but not only from there. There are several details you should know. They are part of your life and it's your right. Perhaps after you hear them, you'll see some of the things in a different light."

The minister looked at him in curiosity. Was he experiencing the long-awaited moment when a stranger out of nowhere brings him information that completely undermines the life he has led till now, information that transforms regular people to sudden heirs, to kidnapped princesses or owners of a plot of land on an African island?

"About four years ago, you visited the hotel here." Elisha spoke unhurriedly, like someone reading a bedtime story to children. "You met a young chambermaid here, her name was Kati. After this one-time encounter, Kati became pregnant. From you." Elisha continued, with increased emphasis: "When she told you about this, you said to her that she should abort the baby and you made it explicitly clear to her that you did not intend to acknowledge paternity and that if she told anyone you would personally make sure that she would be unable to find employment anywhere."

"It was not exactly like that." Like any guilty person, the minister had refined the arguments for his innocence over the years, with truth and falsehood forged into a single belief. "I didn't threaten her. I wanted her to have an abortion, that's true. How was I to know that the baby was even mine? It wasn't necessarily from me."

"It had to be," Mimi said. "I knew her. She didn't have anyone during that period. It had to be you."

"Kati did not want to abort the baby," Elisha continued as if he had not been interrupted. "Or more precisely, her traditional family did not want her to abort the baby. They pressured her and she was in awful distress. By the time she decided, it was already too late. She did not want any baby from a married minister. She was very young, you can understand her. So far, these details are known to you." After a brief pause, which all of the participants needed, the blow was delivered: "What you don't know is that Kati's baby died at his birth."

"Died?" A mixture of relief and shock appeared on the minister's face. "That is . . . so I don't have a child anymore?" Mimi studied his face apprehensively, searching for signs of loss in it. Was this the right way to tell a father about the death of his son, even an unwanted one? Naturally, she did not feel comfortable at this point. And as if the contradictory emotions flooding her were not enough, the line at the reception desk opposite Alona continued to grow longer.

"That's sad, certainly, but perhaps it's for the best," the former minister said, and hurried to qualify this. "For her, I mean."

Elisha stared intently at him. "Yes, what sort of life awaited this child, with two parents who didn't want him, with no family, with no financial support?"

"That's not precise," the former minister protested. "In the end, I did support . . ." Mimi and Elisha studied his face with interest, witnesses to the exact moment when information sinks in and then rises and emerges in a surprising form. Would it turn into anger?

"I sent her money, every month," the former minister said, and a threatening tone crept into his voice, a reminder from the old minister. "Just a minute, I opened a fund for this child and he receives an allowance every month. If she took money from me for no reason…"

"For no reason?" Now Mimi became angry. A guest in the lobby turned his head toward them on his way out. She spoke again in a quiet but malicious voice: "For no reason? Destroying someone's life is 'for no reason?' You got off easy, believe me. In court, they would have awarded much more than the pittance you send."

"How do you know how much I send?" Now the minister was the one raising his voice. The monster of amazement was already big enough to bare its teeth, and Elisha was there precisely for this. He hurried to restore calm: "Mimi is right. The young woman certainly deserves compensation. But that's not the situation. Kati did not take any money from you at all."

"She didn't?" the amazement shrank immediately. The minister was surely aware of the fact that he looked a bit foolish, but what he could do at this point?

"No."

"So… I don't understand. I deposited a sum with my lawyer and he sends a check every month. This was supposed to support them until the child reaches the age of eighteen. Where exactly did the money go?"

This was a critical moment that should be carefully sketched. Any half-tone or tiny twitch could derail the response they desired to elicit. It would take a split second to decide whether the raw emotion forming in the minister's face would ripen into anger.

Elisha did not seem worried. Of course, what did he care? Mimi thought resentfully. After all, he was just an onlooker. If shock and anger developed here, Mimi would be the one to bear the responsibility. Of course, this thought was not precise – Teresa's role in the story, if exposed, would be more significant for the minister than Mimi's role. But the complete story would mean betraying Teresa's trust, and it seemed that Elisha had decided to hold the story from the end that was easier to grasp. "Do you remember saying that you feel you haven't done anything good in your life?" he said. "I think you'll be happy to hear that the money went to a good place." The former minister listened intently. Mimi also listened, though all of the parts of the story were already known to her, at least as far as she understood. She remembered the moment when Kati went into labor pains as if it were yesterday. What a day that was, what a night! She also remembered the date – just after the second Towel Day.

* * *

Poor Kati. Lying exhausted in the white bed, her eyes fixed on a random spot on the ceiling. Her angry parents would only come the next day – she begged Mimi not to call them yet. She also refused to see the baby who had just been born. Contrary to her mother's predictions, no maternal feelings awakened within her when hearing the baby's first cry. The plans to travel and work and fall in love did not shrink to proportion as promised. Instead, they even expanded. And the only thing awakening in her was a need to powerfully weep. The baby was taken to the nursery. It was nighttime and the father of the unlucky child was surely deep in dreamless slumber next to his wife and the mother of his children, and did not even turn over. Thus, when Mimi left the room to finally buy something to eat, Kati remained completely alone. Mimi did not know much about children or births, and still she was sure that this was not how this particular moment was supposed to look. She's a woman who just gave birth, for heaven's sake, she thought gloomily. She had yet to imagine the tragedy of the next day, but a heaviness of bad tidings was already spreading through her limbs. Her lips were forever marred by a tiny wrinkle of dissatisfaction, which meanwhile was still invisible.

In a fair world, it should have been a night full of hope. A special night, one to remember. Three new babies spending the night in the little nursery in the South, which stands empty most days, despite having no fewer than five cribs and a shelf loaded with toys

for older children and a poster of African children and a cupboard
with soft sheets in white and light-blue sheets. It was once the main
delivery room for babies in the South, but since the construction
of the new hospital, a half hour away by ambulance, most women
prefer to give birth there. Of course, if possible – the birth of a baby
is an independent action that is not obliged to comply with plans
that preceded it. Those who come here are generally the babies
who insist on popping out prematurely or those who, for whatever
other reason, did not have time to get to the new hospital. This
happens once every few weeks, sometimes more, and usually just
one baby at a time. And today, in an amazing and exceptional way,
three babies gathered at once in the old delivery room! Another
nurse from the new hospital was summoned for backup. Three life
stories were about to begin.

The first baby to arrive did not come in an ambulance rushed
to the Pomegranate Branches Hotel. Instead, it arrived in a fancy
car, as befits the first-born child of Sarah and Avi Morgenstern.
Their identity is news in itself – the Morgensterns are well-known
business figures. A joint ranking in the list of Israel's 100 wealthi-
est people is reserved for them each year. Their nights out at the
theater and cinema are often covered in the gossip columns. With
the exception of a small number of friends, no one knew what they
went through in recent years – in the newspaper they always looked
so sure of themselves, backed by expensive suits and toothy smiles.
There are no photographs of weeping in the business sections, not
to mention the fact that at least sometimes the weeping was never
born, but was just left to fill the abdominal cavity. The hormones
thickened Sarah's face, which was usually lean, and in recent years
gave her the misleading appearance of a woman who had all the
comforts of life at her fingertips. In the living room conversations
of less wealthy people, they were sometimes cited, completely in
error, as an example of a couple who had forgotten basic desires
such as parenthood because of all of their money and businesses
and cocktail parties. Sarah had not forgotten.

And just now, after years of treatments and tears, and a moment before she was about to have her last period, a child was finally born to them. This was news that could have been very happy, were it not for the fact that the labor contractions, ironically, after years of waiting, were suddenly in a hurry to arrive. So, instead of arriving on the planned date at the private delivery room and using the doula they reserved in advance, Sarah Morgenstern was rushed in the middle of the night to the small delivery room in the South and gave birth there to a bluish and weak baby.

The Morgenstern couple, who stood opposite the crib with tearful and exhausted eyes, was not at all similar to the glowing and self-assured couple whom Mimi vaguely knew from the newspaper.

A day after the Morgenstern couple arrived, actually it was at night, the wailing ambulance brought two babies to the delivery room at the same time. Mimi was there, in the ambulance, holding the hand of Kati, who was shouting: "Get this out of me!" As if instead of a baby, a sort of dybbuk* had gotten into her.

Darya Cohen was accompanied by Teresa Holstein. The father, of course, was absent. Mimi knew exactly who he was – hadn't she seen him some months earlier carrying Darya in a white dress and with a look that left no room from doubt? The miniature romance between the two guests had touched her heart. When that strange group arrived again at the hotel some months later – that is, several days before Kati gave birth, she noticed that the young man did not arrive with them. Darya Cohen, on the other hand, was in an advanced stage of pregnancy. Mimi had indeed grown up in a small and outlying city, but she still knew a thing or two about this world. When she registered Darya, she casually asked about the young man who was with her in the group the previous time.

"He's gone, but he left me a souvenir," Darya smiled. There was

---

* In Jewish folklore, the wandering soul of a dead person that enters and takes control of a living person.

no bitterness in the movement of her hand over her round belly. The next day, she rode with them in the same wailing ambulance.

Every baby born in the hotel (there was only one so far) is also Mimi's baby to some extent. If not for worrying about poor Kati, she certainly would have been happier about the event. Now she thought angrily: One baby is ill, one is unwanted and one is without a father. The race of life is about to start, and three babies were dealt particularly lousy opening hands. After a well-aimed kick, the sandwich machine finally swallows the coin, but does not spit anything out in return.

"It's broken," said a voice behind her. Mimi turned around and recognized Teresa Holstein. "I have a snack. Do want it?" Mimi nodded appreciatively and took a bite of the chocolate caramel bar. The coating was too sweet and stretched between her teeth, refusing to be swallowed. "How is Kati?" Teresa asked.

"She's okay, I think. It wasn't easy for her. The minis... the one who got her pregnant didn't support her, the family is angry at her, she's young, she had other plans. She prefers not to see the baby. In any case, she can't raise him, so it's better not to become attached." This was a much softened expression of Kati's attitude toward the baby. Teresa nodded in empathy.

"And how's Darya?" Mimi asked. She felt that both of them were quite important – each of them was accompanying a distressed new mother, even though Teresa said: "She's feeling excellent. She looks very happy. The baby is adorable, healthy and that's the important thing."

"Right," Mimi concurred. Within a few hours, both of them would receive a chilling lesson on the veracity of clichés. In the meantime, they steered the conversation forward.

"Tell me, is Darya Cohen married?" Teresa asked. The question was a bit disingenuous, but led her surely to the answer.

"No, it's just her. The young man sort of panicked when he heard he was going to be a father, he picked up and fled. She's going to raise him on her own."

"That's not easy."

"No."

For a moment, both of them veiled their eyes in empathy, troubled by the plight of the world's single-parent mothers. Then Teresa said, "Why don't you go to sleep for a bit? It was a long night. We're in the next room and we have a mattress. If you want, come and take it. You look tired."

The word "tired" resonated like a command, sending waves of exhaustion through Mimi's body. She really was tired. He went into Darya's room and dragged the orphaned mattress (which was surely intended to serve excited relatives in more familial births). Before she left, she shot a glance at Darya, who was dozing, with a tired half-smile stretched across her face, clearing indicating that she was dreaming. Were they hopes or memories that caused her to smile? Mimi entered Kati's room with the mattress and went to sleep. Kati had also fallen asleep. Poor Kati.

The next day mistakenly started with what looked to be a good morning. A young and handsome doctor gently woke Mimi up – the doctor had to speak with Kati. Kati herself was already awake and looked more encouraged. Mimi also felt better. Daylight makes the world appear less cruel. As she left the room, she met the Morgenstern couple in the hallway. They looked a bit happier and a bit less famous this morning.

"Good morning, how are you?" she said. Avi Morgenstern smiled a slightly childish smile and said: "Tired but happy, thanks." (The nurses were anxiously anticipating his donation to the small maternity ward and trying to provide him devoted treatment, and the morning newspaper was full of congratulations wishes from business people and politicians.) Mimi smiled and went into the next room to visit Darya.

By nine o'clock, she had already conversed with a famous couple and visited the first baby ever born at the Pomegranate Branches Hotel, so the morning had been very pleasant so far. The news hit her by surprise. When she returned to Kati's room, the door was still closed, and the delicate voice of a very young woman invited her to come in. At first, she was surprised to find Kati sitting upright in her bed. A moment later, she was even more surprised to discover that the young woman with the delicate voice was a doctor and was holding Kati's hand.

"Do you want to be alone?" the doctor asked, and when Kati nodded she fled from the room in relief. There were only two doctors in this delivery room. She had a fifty-percent chance, and still she wondered how it was that the task of informing Kati fell upon her and not the older doctor. Later, she would wonder about the type of relationship between Mimi and Kati, and then forget.

"Kati?" Mimi sat next to her on the bed. "What happened?"

"He died." Kati's voice was mechanical. "He had an edema in his lungs. He's dead."

What was that look in her eyes? Guilt? Relief? Sadness? It was hard to say. A thin and foggy curtain covered them. It looked like a sketched map of a continent, perhaps it was the shape of America.

*

Details, details. That day is seared in her memory as a day with lots of tasks to perform. Mimi is good at tasks. Calling Kati's parents, ordering a taxi, updating Shlomo, signing and clarifying and organizing. Things that have a beginning and an end, things that provide something to do. The activity pushes thoughts aside, enabling them to strike roots. When the time comes to say goodbye to Kati, the news was already a known fact. In the meantime, she did not want to think of all the thoughts patiently waiting on the brink of her consciousness. It was for the best, what kind of life would he have had, it was God's will. She just wanted to take care of the necessary arrangements and leave. She did not enter Darya's room – it would be a shame to depress a new mother, she said to herself. (After all, this involved a hotel guest and the hotel's first child, and Mimi felt something like responsibility toward them.) Teresa was looking after Darya; it was best if Darya did not ask Mimi about Kati.

Two days later (Shlomo gave her a vacation day), Mimi was again sitting at the reception desk of the Pomegranate Branches Hotel. The familiar scenery visible from her usual place suddenly appeared warm. During the two days that passed, she tried to call Kati several times and received, again and again and without relief, her mother's response: "Kati is resting, she asked not to be disturbed." Two other chambermaids received the same response. In the end, they gave up trying. They would never meet Kati again. Did she set off for a big trip in America? They definitely hoped so.

Soon, the memories would start a natural process of evaporating and fading and relegation. In the meantime, they were still fresh in her mind. Though the conversation she had planned in her head so many times had lost its urgency (it should have taken place when the living baby was right in front of her eyes), she still thought it was worth a try. She waited for her break and then retrieved the environment minister's contact information from the computer and dialed. Conversations from hotels are usually related to a pleasant vacation. They are intended to confirm details like the size of the room, the Jacuzzi, questions that require a personal touch. This was apparently the reason why the number left on the registration form was a private number. The minister himself answered before she had a chance to think.

"Hello?"

"Shalom," she said in her official voice, "This is Mimi from the Pomegranate Branches Hotel at the Dead Sea. It's in regard to Katya Lovich. (What in heaven's name was Kati's full name? Perhaps it was actually Katrina?) She worked as a chambermaid here. I'm calling to inform you that Kati gave birth to a son two days ago." She had expected an uncomfortable silence to prevail, but a cheerful response was quick to come.

"Congratulations. I don't know her. But I wish her a hearty *mazal tov*."

"It's a bit late to wish her *mazal tov*, don't you think?" Her angry voice was an opposite reflection of the euphoria on the other side of the line. "And besides, as far as I know, you do indeed know each other. You met when you stayed here on behalf of the Environment Committee. You spoke on several other occasions when she told you she was pregnant."

"Ma'am, what do you want from me?" the minister growled, but did not hang up. That was a good sign.

"I think you know. It's your child and according to the law you are obligated to pay child support for him. You can deny it, but Kati could demand that you undergo a paternity test. And I can't promise you that this story would not leak – newspapers love things like this. In your position, this could be unpleasant." Could a paternity test be conducted on a dead baby? Mimi did not know.

"I don't have a child, I don't know her. You can't force me to take a test." The message was decisive, but the voice did not sound sure of itself. Unwittingly, the result sounded more like a question.

Encouraged, Mimi continued, "First of all, I actually can. Secondly, I certainly can approach the media. There would be a great splash, your wife would hear, your children would read about it, you get the picture. I suggest that you think about my proposal: a regular payment for the child or we'll take action. The money will be transferred through me. You won't have to identify yourself or be in contact with her. She doesn't want any connection with you."

"This is blackmail."

"No, it's justice. You got a young woman pregnant. She's not the only one who needs to pay."

Actually, despite Mimi's confident tone of voice, she was not completely sure that her proposal was what Kati would want. That is, what if the child decides that he does want to meet the father? And let's assume that Kati would decide to demand that the minister spend time with him, once a week let's say, to take him to the amusement park and to the doctor and to the park, like fathers are supposed to do? And let's say that he would refuse, would she suffice with money? The whole situation was very complicated in her view. Undoubtedly, at least from this perspective, the fact that the baby died made the situation easier.

"How much do you want?" the minister sighed.

"A mutual fund in the child's name, closed without any possibility of touching it, with a regular amount to be sent from it each month to a postal address we choose." Mimi cited a sum. (And she immediately regretted it – it seemed too low to her. She did not correct herself, of course.) Then she added: "Of course, Kati, Katya, promises to keep the entire matter secret. Take my phone number; I'll be waiting for your answer." She hoped this was the truth, it sounded logical to her.

What would she have done if he never called? To be honest with herself, Mimi was quite convinced that she would have dropped the whole thing. Her vague plan entirely sprang from momentary anger. Justice and courage are an elusive business. But the minister and fate complied, and already the next day a man called and introduced himself as the minister's attorney. The combination of words "Listen ma'am" led him easily to the bottom line: "The minister authorized me to transfer a fixed sum each month, in cash. Not because he admits that this is his child, but because this unpleasantness catches him at a critical juncture, prior to elections, and the hubbub it would create could hurt him. The minister regards this as a case of private charity, support for a woman who has a problem. The sum will be transferred on two conditions: The child will not know who is sending the money, and the young woman will promise not to contact the minister. Ever. The moment the minister discovers that one of these clauses is violated, the money will stop coming and we'll sue the woman for extortion."

This was a long speech that again raised many questions. The sum he cited was even a bit lower than the one she had cited, but it was better than nothing and he must pay for what he did to Kati! With relative ease, her righteous anger flamed again. "Okay," she said. "I'll give you the address." Quickly, with the telephone receiver still hanging on her shoulder, she went to the computer and pulled up the name of the guest Darya Cohen. So, one irresponsible father will pay instead of another irresponsible father, she said to herself. And, after all, he said himself that he wanted to support a woman who had a problem. A saint, she mumbled to herself, almost aloud. She read the address to the attorney.

Was it really justice? All in all, there was a falsehood here and money changed hands in way that was not intended to happen. He deserves it, she thought decisively. In retrospect, she realized that everything could actually have been more complicated – the minister could have demanded Kati's signature, releasing him from all of his obligations in return for the payment, the attorney could have demanded her bank account number. But bureaucracy is the domain of law-abiding citizens, and here guilt and fear ruled. The entire matter took just a few minutes. It ceased to be her business the moment she hung up the phone.

After this conversation, she had time to arrange another matter – there must be order. Mimi is the one responsible for order here. She makes sure the guests wake up on time and receive keys, towels and robes, and, if necessary, she makes sure that the guests do not shirk their obligations (especially if the obligation originated inside the walls of the hotel). Everything is included in the service.

She entered the saved record of guests and pulled out the number of a guest who had not been seen at the hotel for several months already and would probably not be seen in the near future. Then she picked up the phone and dialed.

The conversation produced no real results, at least not at that moment. Nonetheless, she felt more relaxed in the end. One guest was soon to receive an envelope that she undoubtedly deserved and a thread (admittedly, a very thin one) of a connection was stretched between one father and one child. Threads connecting parents and children are always a strange thing. It is not much compared to what other mothers and other children receive – flowers on Mother's Day, joint bank accounts, a picnic in the hills of the

Gilboa when the purple irises are blooming. But it is also not a little. When the child of the hotel and his mother come next year on their first vacation, Mimi will be happy to find that they look content with their lot in life.

*

"So, do you understand what you've done?" Elisha shot a penetrating look at the minister. "Though it wasn't intentional, you did something very special. You, personally (he accentuated the "you" and Mimi thought with a sort of pride that it was no wonder that his lectures were the most popular at the hotel; he was really an excellent lecturer), you, with your money, actually supported a single-parent mother, a young and needy woman whose boyfriend had abandoned her." This was a bit of an extreme description of another father and another mother, a truth with an objective. The minister was silent, digesting the thought. Mimi studied him anxiously – would the story of deceit become a story of a wonderful act of kindness, with all of the participants, including Mimi, benefiting in the end? There is more than one way to tell a story.

Elisha continued, "And this is the highest form of charity. Giving in secret. Mimi is right, Kati deserved compensation for what she went through. Since she didn't request this, you paid it to another child, a child who needed this assistance very much. And you said yourself that in any event you regard this as a private charity case. You prophesized and didn't know what you were prophesizing. Even if you don't do anything else significant in your life, you have already saved one soul. And you know, *whoever preserves a single soul, it is as though he has preserved an entire world*."*

In Mimi's opinion, Elisha got a little carried away in his story of saving a soul. All in all, Darya Cohen did not look like someone who needed help, though it could not hurt her, of course. But, it seemed to her, some brightness was starting to crawl onto the minister's face. This illumination grew stronger as Elisha continued.

---

* From the Talmud.

"You must think – but why shouldn't the father of the child look after him?" (The minister nodded. Yes, the thought had crossed his mind.) "The young man simply panicked. I believe you can understand him. He fled and left a pregnant woman behind him. But the young woman thought the whole time that the money was coming from him. Of course, God has not forsaken her (the biblical expressions flow through his words naturally, as if they had always been there) and someone would have taken care of her. After all, she works and there are also charitable organizations that mobilize to help if needed. But imagine if the young man decides one day to take responsibility and meet his son? She did not build up anger at him all these years. You helped her to get through them unharmed." (There was considerable injustice in this statement too – perhaps at that moment the tranquil and contented Darya ran her hand along the back of her neck in discomfort, without knowing why.)

"Just a moment," the minister narrowed his eyes. After all, he was somewhat experienced in financial matters. "And how do I know you're not lying? That is, if there's no child..."

"Do you think we would have simply taken the money from you?" Mimi asked in disbelief.

Elisha hurried to position his calming voice between the two voices that threatened to collide. "You're absolutely right," he said pleasantly. "You definitely are entitled to receive proof that what we're saying is true. Well then, all you need to do is to check whose address was given to you. I promise you that this is not fraud of any sort. You really truly supported a child who has no father. True, it was done without your knowledge, and if you'd like, you can argue that you were cheated, but you'll need, of course, to expose the whole story. In any case, the money went to a good place – that I can assure you."

The threat was diluted in Elisha's voice like an aspirin in a cup of Kool-Aid, sweet and disguising its effect. Nothing was said about unflattering articles or sensational news items. One could easily have believed that his decision was made strictly for reasons of conscience.

"Fine, I assume that the money really did go to a good place," the minister said, still contemplative.

"That's really very nice of you," Mimi smiled a sweet smile. "You see, don't say you've never done anything good in your life."

The minister smiled broadly. For a fraction of a second, he again resembled the minister he once was. Yes, he really did a good deed. Just a few years ago, this same story would have made him seethe with rage. Now it was a tentative ray of sunlight through the clouds. Who would believe it?

Elisha stood up. "I'm glad to have met you," he said and warmly shook the minister's hand. "You're a good man and you have a lot of merits, don't think otherwise for even a moment."

"Tell me, do you think I could meet them?" the minister asked. If she hadn't known him previously, Mimi would have sworn that he was almost embarrassed,

"I'm not sure it's a good idea," Elisha smiled.

"Yes, it's probably not a good idea. Still, I'm glad you told me." The minister also stood up, said goodbye to the two of them and walked toward the elevators, apparently heading to his room to mull over the new information, like a child going off to examine a toy.

Mimi watched the minister being swallowed into the elevator, unsure of how she should feel. A sense of relief would of course be expected (after all, Mimi was the one who initiated the deceit), but a buzz of unease still accompanied her.

*

The people who love surprises are precisely those who find it most difficult to enjoy them. The day after the three-way conversation with the former minister, Rabbi Elias entered the lobby. His entrance itself was surprising – he usually visited the hotel only on Shabbat. Undeniably, that same thought crossed Mimi's mind – after all, she called the minister before she knew about the amulet, right? That is, she performed an act of kindness without seeking to receive any reward. It is true that falsehood and theft were involved here, but the result was so successful! Even the minister was pleased.

So it is hard to say that she was surprised when Rabbi Elias approached her (though, still, she was about to discover a very surprising discovery). Her face was like that of a birthday girl when the rabbi asked whether she had seen Elisha. "I haven't seen him today, maybe he's at the pool," she said, brimming with innocence and the desire to help. To avoid disappointment, she did not put into words the thought that was drifting through her head. Instead, she told herself, don't be foolish. Nonetheless, her eyes wandered toward the back room where the safe was located, where all of the employees had become accustomed to the presence of a single towel, as if this were the way of the world. When her hand moved to her neck, as if on its own, she quickly pulled it back to its place.

But when Rabbi Elias returned to the lobby, with Elisha in his wake, she could no longer hide her excitement. She anticipated their footsteps: to the right, and then straight ahead toward the reception desk, and then toward her. When they stood in front of her, she turned a glowing face toward them. "So I see you found him."

"Yes, he was indeed by the pool. The man knows how to live," the rabbi said, and Elisha smiled. (In fact, the vacation unit caused him considerable aggravation – it was almost never rented out to people other than him. He and the other buyers were already organizing a class-action lawsuit.)

"Tell me Mimi," the rabbi said in an affected voice, "do you perhaps remember your trip to Tel Aviv?"

"I travel to Tel Aviv a lot." (She was lying, and to a rabbi! Shame on you, she scolded herself.) "You must be referring to my meeting with Rabbi Avram, right? Yes, I remember."

"I understand that he asked you to hold onto Rabbi Eybeschütz's amulet for safekeeping?"

"Yes, that's true," she said innocently, her heart about to burst. "He said that when the time comes to pass it onward, someone would take it from me."

"Are you perhaps keeping it here in the hotel?" the rabbi asked intently.

"Yes, I put it in the safe. Should I bring it?"

"Yes, if you don't mind." Now Elisha was doing the talking. "Bring it. We'll wait over there." He pointing to the tables in the lobby and Mimi nodded. Of course, this was Elisha's favorite spot, where he would always sit with the newspaper and observe the guests passing by, seeing and unseen. When Teresa Holstein is around, she usually joins him.

She did not wait for them to turn around and choose a table. Instead, she hurried to the small room where she opened the safe and took out the towel for the last time. So, this is it. When she pulled out the jewelry from the folds of the towel, she avoided looking at it, just to be on the safe side: Even more than she loves surprises, she hates disappointments. But the chances of being disappointed this time were slim – there was very little mystery in the whole situation.

When she returned to the lobby, she saw that Elisha and Rabbi Elias had already selected a table. She was happy to see that it faced the transparent wall. It was a partly cloudy day, but still very bright. Its colors conveyed a misleading feeling, as if it were the window that was covering the day in a thick coat of paint. Mimi had lived in the region for long enough to know this wasn't true.

She sat down in the empty chair and placed the necklace on the table. The knocking sound of the gold pendant touching the wooden table caught the attention of the three of them. For a moment, they looked like they were playing a game of Truth or Dare. To whom would the bottle point, bringing out demons and secrets? Then Elisha and Rabbi Elias exchanged a glance that left no room for doubt.

"So…" Mimi asked, trying to camouflage a stubborn grin hanging on the edges of her lips, "you've already found someone to give it to?"

"Actually, yes," Rabbi Elias smiled a meaningful smile, "we've found someone."

"Ah, that's great," Mimi said. "Can I ask who it is?"

She guessed that Elisha would be the one to respond this time, and indeed he was the one who said, "It's someone who did something very beautiful, a great *mitzvah*.* Someone who took care of a fatherless child."

Her body movements were already ready, waiting for years for any surprise that might come (Mimi winning an Oscar, a beauty contest, a Nobel Prize). She let her smile spread in slow motion.

"What, for me?"

Elisha and Rabbi Elias smiled.

"Yes, Mimi," Elisha said. "It's a beautiful deed, what you did. You took care of a child who has no father. You didn't look on from the side, you got up and took action."

"But I lied to the minister," Mimi said with uncertainty, "and it's forbidden to lie."

"That's true," Rabbi Elias nodded sadly. "It's forbidden to lie. But on the other hand, in this case you did something decent and correct. You helped a woman who needed assistance and made a person take responsibility for his actions, and all this without intending to receive a reward."

Elisha nodded in agreement.

"And therefore," Rabbi Elias continued festively, "I'm happy to award you with Rabbi Eybeschütz's amulet. May the good in both of you draw a little more divine goodness into our world."

"So … now good things will happen to me?" Mimi asked.

"You inflame fire with fire, you increase the might of water with water. Good attracts good, and therefore, I wish for you that the amulet will attract only good things to you."

Mimi was not sure she completely understood, but she felt almost saintly. She smiled another modest smile and then took the amulet from the table. When she put it on, it seemed to her that quiet prevailed, as if in a rare coincidence everyone in the lobby suddenly fell silent. The pendant was so beautiful that she was not sure whether she was breathless for the right and pure reasons. As

---

* A good deed, an act of kindness.

she wore it, it seemed to her that her body was relaxing with a warm sigh of relief. Finally.

But what should she say? She had to say something. She closed the clasp and then mobilized an ancient educational reflex and simply said, "Thank you."

"You're welcome, we're happy you'll be wearing it. It's yours for two years. If during this time you meet someone who is worthy of it, tell us. Perhaps you'll personally be able to pass it onward." Rabbi Elias stood up. "I'm glad to have met you Mimi. May you continue to do good deeds." He said goodbye to Elisha with a handshake and walked toward the door. Elisha remained seated.

Mimi relaxed in the chair. With the sparkling jewelry on her neck, she felt very elegant, as if she were one of the important guests at the hotel. She felt like having a conversation. She crossed her legs and said, "Just a moment, so you were the ones who sent that letter to me? About the necklace that was stolen from Teresa Holstein?"

And now, after all, there was a surprise for Mimi because Elisha said: "No, that necklace was indeed stolen from Teresa."

"But…" Mimi looked at him skeptically, "but she claimed that nothing was stolen from her. Why would she lie about something like that? She had nothing to be ashamed of, right?"

"Absolutely not." (Did he look amused?) "Teresa is a very special woman. She received the amulet of Rabbi Eybeschütz after she devotedly cared for the driver who was injured in the accident that killed her husband."

He peeked at her to gauge her reaction. Mimi was silent in awe, as expected. Teresa is apparently a really special woman.

"But what Teresa does not know," Elisha slowly dragged out the words, "is that if another amulet hadn't been stolen from her, she actually would have had two amulets, at least for a while."

"Two amulets!" It was a day full of surprises. The first question that came to her mind was not necessarily the first question that should be asked. It left her mouth before she had time to stop it: "But ... but what else did she do?"

*   *   *

The world is so big! That was my first thought. It is not particularly impressive, especially if we remember that at the time this thought occurred, the world from my perspective was the inside of a medium-sized ambulance. Still, the dim light, the human voices ("Get this out of me!") and the foreign air were impressive in their breadth. I did not think I could ever return to that position in the womb. I was a fish that was about to happily discover that he was a mammal.

Bundled in a soft blanket, I was placed in my mother's lap. A pair of eyes were studying me. They were not Darya's eyes. (I could not see them. It was only later that I became aware of the fact that I could move my head and see other things.) It was Teresa, the woman whose kind face welcomed me to the world. She smiled and placed a caressing hand on the blanket. The feeling was not foreign to me. I had apparently also been caressed with loving hands through the belly. The sound of a siren could be heard in the ambulance, an initial sound symbolizing new life. (About four years later, I would be profoundly excited by every ambulance or fire truck that sounded a siren in the street. I would want to be a fireman.) Through the window, fields of cotton glimmered. The cotton crop was left abandoned during the sabbatical year, which ended some time ago. The farmers had already started to polish their harvesting tools. Seven whole years would pass before the fields would again assume the form of a cloud.

When you are not the sole resident on the planet of the womb, sleep and wakefulness suddenly take on meaning. When I woke up, I discovered that the world of the ambulance had been replaced. I was situated in a small transparent bed in a warm room. Darya was nowhere in sight. I was supposed to cry, but I still didn't know that. (I developed late, from this perspective. I started to demand her constant presence only after she was convinced that I was a good-natured and independent baby.)

I was not the only baby in the room. Another small infant was lying next to me. It didn't look like he was thinking about anything, but two people stood at the entrance to the room and looked at him intently. The woman told the baby: "Be strong, hang in there my sweetheart." The man said more or less the same thing to the woman.

I don't think they were allowed to be so close to the baby. Approaching steps made them hurry outside the door. "Come, drink something," the man said to the woman. As far as I could tell, his voice was sad. The mention of a drink did not yet stir any bleating from me, nor did the sight of the couple rouse any sense of deprivation. No proud father stood and watched me through the glass window, but I did not think I was fatherless. My eyes were still blue, but they already bore a greenish tendency that would later constitute proof.

After a few minutes or hours of staring at the ceiling, a surprise came: I had guests! The steps approached and became a nurse in a white uniform, carrying another baby in her arm. She gently placed him alongside the baby next to me. "Come sweetie, don't they want to feed you?" she said to him compassionately, and then went to a small table on the side of the room and pulled a bottle out of one of the shelves. The milk from the unwilling mother was replaced with a substitute. Would he feel the difference? I expected a flow of nurses to continue to come and fill the nursery, but no, it turned out that only the three of us would share that night.

And still, I wasn't referring to the nurse or the baby when I said that I had guests. Through the window, I recognized Teresa's kind eyes. She smiled and waved hello to me.

A strange smell drifted through the room. The nurse cradled the new baby in her arms and pushed the nipple of a bottle containing a whitish liquid. The baby rejected the bottle angrily. I suddenly remembered Darya and started to cry.

Things naturally have their own order. As always, the beginning is a bit unclear in a new place. I was taken back to Darya and placed at her breast. Her familiar skin had the smell of home. "Hi, my sweetheart," she said. I'm a sweetheart, just like the baby of the sad couple in the nursery. The confusion of identities would soon intensify. But the internal camera, still inexperienced in taking pictures, captured a cuddle. Me and Mother.

Darya moved her hand over my hand. We were one body with limbs intertwined. Both of us were surprised that I could suddenly move independently. I cautiously bent two fingers. After a few moments, the joy of the renewed meeting waned. I remember that I cried and received compensation in the form of a nipple pushed into my mouth. The warm liquid was manna from the Sinai desert – it had no flavor or smell, it was all of the flavors and smells together. Serene and satiated, I fell asleep.

When I woke up, I discovered that I was again in the room with the two other babies. The first nurse was replaced by the nurse who had accompanied us in the ambulance. She was sprawled in a chair with her eyes closed and her mouth drooping to the side. The baby who drank the milk substitute also closed his eyes. I had no way of knowing, but the hour was late. The world around me was sleeping. I could only gaze at the ceiling, and wait.

But no, a surprise! Teresa came to visit me again. At first, she stood next to the window. Then she entered the room. She shot a glance at the sleeping nurse (maybe she too was bored?) and then came inside.

To my great disappointment, she did not come straight to me. Instead, she stood above the bed of the unfamiliar baby. Something happened. Her heavy breathing, the breaths of a mother, high-lighted his lifelessness. For one moment, perhaps inspired by the natural inclination of most of the residents of the room, there was a tangible possibility in the air of an outbreak of screams.

What was she doing? Teresa was probably asking herself the same question. When she placed the newest baby in the crib next to me, I wondered – maybe she wanted all of us to sleep in the same bed? But no, she removed the baby who was next to me from his crib and moved him to the far crib.

A secret was born, he was gently situated in his new place. The action appeared completely natural to me – so far, all of the people I had met were engaged, in one way or another, in moving babies from place to place. Then she stood by my bed and, finally, her eyes glowed with the light that appears in the eyes of those who observe babies. (I would only learn to identify this light when I grew up a bit and felt its absence.) When the nurse shifted in her sleep, Teresa smiled a small smile at me and left. She shot a last glance at us from the window of the room.

When did I fall asleep again? When I awoke, the sun's first light was already rising. One of us cried, and then we cried together. A new nurse took the baby from the crib next to me, apparently to the room of the couple I met the previous day. Two people in white gowns arrived and stood above the crib of the baby in the far crib; that is the last thing I remember of him. During those first days of consciousness, we were, if you will, like a school of minnows at the bottom of the ocean. If one of us grew weak or ill or died, the information existed and fell off on its own. Nothing stopped the quiet flow forward.

In retrospect, I assume that the situation was probably confusing – if the baby from the far crib was taken to the couple who belonged to the middle crib, when would I be taken? But already in those initial days of my existence, I was very sure about where I belong. Me, they take to Darya. The new name she whispered in my ear had a familiar and consoling tone. Her smooth skin, her warm milk, the movement of her hand on my head through the belly. All these were wonderful signs of certainty for me.

*   *   *

Even though she had barely slept a wink during the past twenty-four hours, Teresa Holstein did not close her eyes on the way back from the maternity ward to the Pomegranate Branches Hotel. Instead, she pressed her forehead against the window of the taxi in the back seat and stared at the neglected fields out the window. The exhausted trees, laden with fruit and waiting in vain – none of the trees had been cared for, no fruit had been picked or eaten for an entire year. The sabbatical year was over, but it seemed that the farmers had yet to awaken from their hibernation. No one was harvesting or planting or hybridizing the avocado trees. There was apparently some logic in this. It was not evident to Teresa and she was not willing to accept it. The sight of the overburdened trees filled her with anger – something had to be done. When they drove quickly past a cotton field, she could not get the milky sight out of her mind – a field of mother's milk was flowing and no one wanted it.

What a night it was, and what a day. And what a night afterwards. At ten o'clock in the morning, the taxi finally arrived at its destination and Teresa paid and entered the hotel lobby. The weariness of the past day began to creep into her eyes in the form of blue-gray depressions. Teresa had already personally experienced orphanhood and love and parenthood and loss, but all these were forced upon her or at least seemed to be compulsory. The events of the night and the morning stunned her with their incomprehensible pace. Perhaps for the first time in her life she was truly in turmoil. For the first time in the life of the wise, level-headed and good Teresa, she encountered the small chill that freezes the heart: What have I done?

It could be said that three participants took part in the act – Teresa and Kati and even the place itself. (In the new and orderly hospital, this type of act would be unimaginable.) One could also blame the heat of the moment, the rare convergence of circumstances that consolidated into a decision. But Teresa was the one who placed the dead son of the Morgenstern couple in the crib of Kati's baby. So she alone carried the weight of this memory. It's not too late, she told herself. One anonymous call to the hospital, a small mess and within a few days everything would be forgotten and back in place. But what place was this? Her mother's heart cried out. To whom was this compassion addressed, this compassion that had welled up in her and lacked an address till now? To the dead infant? To the living infant? To the childless parents? She was probably touched by all of them that night, but her heart actually went out to poor Kati in the end. She was no more than a young girl herself, Teresa thought. Too young to bear the Cain's mark of regret and guilt. While in Darya's maternal eyes she saw profound and complete happiness, with no remorse, the main thing she saw in Kati's girlish eyes was distrust. This could not happen. And Teresa longed to liberate those eyes, to create a world for them in which, in some cosmic way, everything falls into place. Yes, she also wanted to dry the tears of the anguished Sarah Morgenstern and to place the unlucky baby to rock in her arms. But it was Kati's look of desperation that made Teresa feel like the representative of some entity that had betrayed its responsibility in the most miserable and despicable way. There was a sort of promise in Kati's eyes that had never been made and Teresa longed to fulfill it.

What happened to the Morgenstern couple's baby? Only the God of babies in the cradle has the answers. Perhaps his heart did not withstand the expectations attached to every sole heir, and perhaps the doctors had a more logical explanation. Teresa did not remain in the small ward in order to find out. Here was the simply, illogical plan that she concocted in her mind while her hands carried it out: The live baby belongs to the Morgenstern couple and Kati would receive the dead baby. While Kati's wounds from the unplanned birth were healing under the warm hand of time, Sarah and Avi would give the baby everything that till now was only a vision they stored in the back of their minds and which sometimes trickled from Sarah's eyes in the form of tears. After all of the attempts, they did not deserve to lose a child. And the child did not deserve for them to lose him. So, everyone was pleased. It was not too late, she reminded herself again, and in the same breath she knew – what was, will be.

She was planning to head straight to her room and go to sleep, but she saw Elisha near the reception desk. His familiar appearance almost moved her to tears for some reason. And perhaps it was the fatigue overcoming her. The good Elisha, was she entitled to look to him for justification or consolation? Elisha, who found such kindness and generosity in her that he believed she was worthy of good and could draw goodness to the world. What nonsense. People award themselves prizes and amulets while the world continues to mete out destinies in its random way. What would he say if he knew?

As she was passing by him, she slowed her steps, hoping he would notice her on his own. Her hope was fulfilled, though not as she expected: Shlomo, the hotel manager, was just coming up from the bottom floor. She he saw Teresa, he walked straight toward her.

"Teresa! Good morning. How are you? And how is our new mother?"

For a moment she wondered which of the mothers he was referring to. But it was clear that he was referring to Darya. After all, Darya was the one who gave birth to the hotel's first child and she was the one Teresa had followed into the ambulance. Was he even aware of Kati's situation?

"She's feeling great," she said. "The baby is healthy and she looks very happy."

"Wonderful, excellent! This is the first child born here." Shlomo looked as excited as a birthday boy. "I intend to adopt him. Like a good luck charm. The birth of a baby is a good sign. He will be the baby of Pomegranate Branches. You know, just like someone who's born on an airplane receives free flights for life."

Teresa nodded and smiled tiredly. Elisha, of course, had already noticed her. He watched them.

Shlomi added: "It was really good of you to go with her. I understand there's no husband or family in the picture. It was truly a *mitzvah*. Do you know what? I'll add another vacation day for you, at our expense. After all, you didn't have time to enjoy yourself the past day." In order to illustrate the seriousness of his intentions, he immediately turned to the unfamiliar young woman staring at them from behind the reception desk and said, "Abigail, write down another day and night for Ms. Holstein. Everything included and no charge." Abigail nodded.

Elisha joined the conversation. His eyes were serious when he turned to Shlomo: "I heard that one of the chambermaids also gave birth yesterday."

"Yes, yes," Shlomo's face darkened and he looked worriedly at Teresa. "Were you there when they told her? Do you know what happened?"

His concern for her feelings touched her heart, which was exposed from lack of sleep. She nodded. "Yes, I heard."

"Poor girl," Shlomo said. "Young women these days drive me crazy, they don't have a bit of good sense, they simply don't know how to be careful and they ruin their lives for themselves. She probably doesn't even know who the father was. Well, it's terrible to say, but in this case I get the impression that it's the best for all concerned. What kind of a life would such a child have? God apparently knows what he's doing."

Now Shlomo looked a bit lost. Elisha, as usual, saved the situation: "Yes, it's really sad, but everything is for the best. That's how it is in life, mourning and joy combined. Teresa, you look tired. I'll walk you to your room?"

"Yes, you really should go to sleep," Shlomo quickly concurred and stepped back to make way for the unified body Elisha-Teresa. "Great, then Teresa, you'll stay with us another night as we agreed? Excellent, excellent. Again, thank you. And again, you really did a *mitzvah*."

When he turned around and left, Teresa and Elisha walked together toward the elevator. An old intimacy settled in Elisha's eyes. His concern was sincere when he asked: "You look exhausted, is everything okay?"

"Yes, it's just that I was there all night and..." and she was definitely ready to stick with this lie, but the tears decided on their own volition to appear. The fatigue, the fear, the endless guilt. Elisha looked at her in a strange way. The elevator door opened in front of them. "Come, let's go up. I'm sure you want to sleep finally," he said in a soft voice. The voice echoed toward her from a distance and struck a familiar chord. They entered the elevator.

"Tell me, can I ask you something?" She pressed the button and stared at him. The large white yarmulke gave him the appearance of a cleric. Was she waiting for forgiveness?

"Of course."

"Could it be that a child is born by mistake at the wrong place? That is to say, is it possible that God would send an orphan child into the world?"

"Many times I've thought that my Nadav could have been much happier with another father," Elisha said quietly.

"That's not what I meant."

"I know."

They were silent for a moment, she in her exhaustion and he in his sorrow. The elevator door opened again and they spilled out. A slight twinge of surprise ran up each of their backs when he walked into the room behind her. She sat down on the bed.

"You're asking a tough question. You're asking whether it's possible that God makes mistakes and waits for us to fix them. The truth is, I don't know."

His look was too distant to read the disappointment on her face, and in any case she softened a bit when he continued: "There's no doubt that some people feel that they were mistakenly born into the wrong reality. I assume that in most cases, the parents and child simply must make an effort to do their utmost. I didn't try enough. I imagine there are people who hang on to this as an excuse, and there are situations in which human compassion should simply intervene."

The missing night weighed down upon Teresa's eyes for a moment and they closed. At the same moment, she clearly saw Avi and Sarah Morgenstern waiting for a taxi outside of the hospital building, guarding with their bodies the precious package held close to Sarah's milk-laden breasts. It's not too late, the small chorus of night demons chanted softly. The Morgensterns looked very happy and serene. She opened her eyes and said: "I have to tell you something." A sort of intimacy gave way to closeness of a different type, a sort of relief at confessing a sin. From now on, another person would carry part of the guilt with her. Elisha listened to her in silence.

When they parted for the night, she felt more at peace for some reason. The tranquility derived from the decision she made: She decided not to do anything. As far as she was concerned, the matter was closed. If the living baby was destined to live with the unwilling mother, God or fate could intervene. She had done her part. If there are thoughts and misgivings, she would bear them, while the baby naps in his cradle and poor Kati in her childhood bed in her parents' home.

And sleep actually came very quickly. Already as she undressed, she felt how it was spinning a pleasant web of slumber. She did not hear the quiet steps of the chambermaid when she entered and immediately went out. (Teresa forgot to hang the "Do Not Disturb" sign.) She also did not hear the quiet steps of Elisha, who came again to the door. What did he place there? The customary legend places smiling infants on the doorsteps, but the object in his hands was inanimate and sparkling. It was undeniable that the way in which Teresa's good intentions touched his heart was also related to the previous summer, when they spent time together at this very same hotel. Good actions can stir the heart. His heart went out to the wise, good-hearted and brave Teresa. He wanted to give her a second amulet.

One could say that the amulet itself poetically objected to being given as compensation for such an action. People of the realistic sort immediately realize that someone who leaves an expensive piece of jewelry on the floor should not be surprised. A junior waiter bent down at the threshold of Teresa's door and his eyes glowed. It was his first theft. A few months later, his conscience would bother him before Yom Kippur and he would seek to return it to its owner. An ancient and universal nightmare stole its way into Teresa's dream: She was trying to scream, but no sound came out. She woke up just in time for dinner.

*   *   *

The ride to the SaltySea for my fourth birthday was going to be very crowded. Four people stuffed into a small and rickety car, and maybe even a fifth – it depends who you ask.

I was sitting in the car, with a seat belt, and Furry sat next to me, also in a seat belt, after Mother acceded to my pleas. Furry complained. "It's not comfortable for him," I told Mother.

"So tell him that he just better get used to it."

Like her voice, her movements were also quick and rigid. I don't think she was happy to have Furry back with us. You couldn't blame her – it had been almost a year since he left us to play with the boy in that other country. The truth is, we had already gotten used to being without him. Just before my fourth birthday, he apparently felt with his all-knowing sense that I would need a friend.

One of the probable reasons for his return was also crowded into the car and sat next to me. "Isn't he a bit old to have an imaginary friend?"

"He's here, and he hears you. Besides, he's only four," Mother answered her.

"You didn't have imaginary friends when you were four."

"How do you know?"

In my previous incarnation, I didn't have a grandfather and grandmother. When I met with these ones in my current incarnation, I had no memory in my body of this instinctive grandchildish longing. I had a mother and also a father. The fact is that my body remembered my father with boundless affection even though we had never met. I studied Grandpa and Grandma warily.

Darya also did not exactly long for them. When she decided to give up the better future her parents wanted to provide her and to return to Israel from America, they did not bid her farewell with a hug, and the string was severed. Every subsequent hug seemed out of place. This specific relationship, with all its bitterness and blame and longing, was conducted till now mainly in nocturnal telephone conversations above my head.

When one door slammed shut, another door opened. Would Flurry agree to sit next to the man who is Grandfather? Both of us understood that it would not be good to upset Mother. We made do with turning up our noses together. Furry looked very funny with a wrinkled nose. We laughed. The woman who is Grandmother shot a skeptical glance at me.

We were driving to the SaltySea to celebrate my birthday with Grandfather and Grandmother, who came especially from America to see me. These pieces of information had been drilled into to me countless times during the previous week, but they still had quite a weak connection to reality. If you were not in America, you could not be Grandfather or Grandmother. I relaxed in my seat.

From the place where I was sitting (on a raised child's seat between Grandfather and Grandmother) the scenery was spread out before me – blue skies and a winding road. Grandfather could only see Mother's back. Grandmother's scenery was the back of the empty seat. In fact, one of them could have sat in the front seat, but I was unaware of that and Darya did not say anything. (Unless you consider that slamming of the door to be a statement.) And so, they crowded together in their secure and familiar closeness, only with me planted between them.

And in any case, the purpose of the visit, as Darya explained in one of those telephone conversations when she decided to invite them, was for them to finally get to know their grandson (and not, heaven forbid, a reunion with estranged parents). If you don't come, you'll regret it when it will already be too late," she said severely to the telephone. "You have a smart, charming and successful grandson. You can be proud." But the people in the back seat did not look proud. The main impression they made was of worried people. The internal camera caught a sweet perfume, and a future chemistry with perfumed girlfriends was determined. The smell of Grandmother.

When Grandmother grew tired of staring at the back of the empty seat (the wise Darya did not turn on the radio), she turned to me: "So, do you already know what you want to be when you grow up?"

The familiar question dispelled a bit of the foreignness and I answered enthusiastically: "A fireman! And Furry too! And we'll have a helmet and a red fire truck!"

"That's great," Grandfather's voice said. "Which one of you will drive and which one will hold the fire hose?"

"I'll drive!" Furry and I said together. "Do you know how a fire truck goes?" Without waiting for an answer, we burst into a loud imitation of a fire siren. We saw the future firemen very clearly. At the same time, we were imbued with the reassuring awareness that this future, in which we would be grownups and firemen and policemen and doctors, was not really about to happen. The fire truck joyfully sounded its siren.

Grandmother gave Grandfather a look that I didn't recognize. The internal camera also caught this. I grew up a bit, unknowingly. A slight crack was made in the repertoire of innocent expressions of my childhood. She tried another question: "Do you know where Grandfather and Grandmother came from?"

"From America!"

"And do you know what language they speak in America?"

"Hebrew!"

"No," Grandmother celebrated a small victory for some reason. "In America, people speak English. Do you want to learn a song in English?"

"Yes!"

The excitement from the trip and from the rare event of additional people in the car inflamed a supersensory exuberance in me.

If she had asked me whether I wanted to jump out of the moving car, I probably would have been enthusiastic to the same extent. Grandmother was pleased. She said, "Repeat after me," and immediately started to sing: "Jack and Jill went up the hill…" She left the verse hanging and said to me in an encouraging voice: "Okay, now you!"

"Jacknbillventpadeh eel," I sang cautiously and Grandfather interrupted: "First, he has to learn the words. Here, repeat after me – 'Jack and Jill.'"

"Jack and Jill"

"Went up the hill."

During the next hour, Jack and Jill traversed a long and bumpy road and ultimately managed to coalesce into a more or less reasonable song. Furry sat on the side, insulted, but Grandfather, Grandmother and I sang together enthusiastically. "Mother, look, I'm singing in English!" I said. Through the rear-view mirror, she shot a glance at me. We sang and sang until the singing gradually petered out, and we all drifted into our own worlds. Grandfather looked out the window. He seemed to be deep in thought and perhaps those thoughts were memories. He had always loved the Dead Sea, especially at the end of summer when the skies were already beginning to turn gray in central Israel. Grandmother stared stubbornly in front of her, at the back of the empty seat, as if it would constitute some sort of confession if she allowed herself to look out the window at scenery she might like.

Many years had passed since the last time Grandfather and Grandmother visited the Dead Sea, and exactly one year had passed since Mother and I celebrated my third birthday there. On my fourth birthday, Grandfather, Grandmother and Mother were reminded, and I suddenly discovered, that the drive there was actually very long.

After many hours of travel, almost without stops, emerging from the car were four faded versions of the people who had entered it. I was half asleep and Darya lifted me out of the car. Grandmother stretched and looked exhausted in an accusing way. Only Grandfa-

ther obediently drew a deep breath into his lungs and said: "Ahhh ...
what air!"

When we passed through the door of the hotel it was already
possible to say: The comfortable routine Darya and I had shared
was broken. Instead of one grownup watching over me, there were
now three. While they were arguing over who would carry the
suitcases (Darya is younger, Grandfather is a man, Grandmother
could take care of herself), still woozy from sleeping, I entered
the revolving door and got my finger stuck in it. My shriek of pain
added to the general tumult. For a moment, it seemed that the pain
was unbearable and would never go away. When the doorman gave
me a candy I forgot about the pain and continued on my way into
the lobby.

I stopped at the reception desk and thrust my nose at the eye
level of the receptionist. In order to accomplish this, I had to stand
on the tips of my toes, but the effort paid off. When she saw my
eyes peeking at her, the receptionist exclaimed: "Look who's here!
It's our birthday boy! You're so big, how old are you?"

"Four!" I said proudly.

"Really? Do you remember me?"

"No."

"Do you know my name?"

"No."

"Very nice to meet you," she said, offering me an official handshake. "I'm Mimi. I was here when you were born."

I shook her hand and compensated her for this gesture with
information: "It's also Furry's birthday!"

"Is that right?" Mimi enthused. "He's your friend?" At this point,
the three grownups in my life managed to finally get through the
revolving door. Mother stood above me.

"Ms. Cohen, great to see you again!" Mimi said.

Mother smiled at her with relief. "Yes, it's nice to be back. Would
you believe that he's already four?"

"It's amazing how time flies," Mimi concurred. For a moment, both of them looked at me and saw a decade slipping by and a first wrinkle and one apartment in Tel Aviv. Afterwards, Mother said: "This time we're four. His grandfather and grandmother came especially from America to celebrate his birthday with him!" She spoke mainly to me. Mimi also was addressing me when she said: "Yes, I saw that you're four. That's wonderful!" Her voice sounded decisive. The glance she shot at Grandfather and Grandmother looked a bit more skeptical. We received two keys to two rooms on the third floor.

Birthday presents: A real knight's sword (from Mother) and a suit of armor (from Father). I ran around the room, brandishing the sword and shouting "Yeahhh!!! I'll kill you now, you fire-breathing dragon!" When Grandfather and Grandmother walked into the battlefield, I ran toward them. "Grandfather and Grandmother, look what I got!" (I still saw them as a single unit, Grandfatherand-Grandmother.)

"Wow! Who bought that for you?" Grandfather said excitedly.

"Mother the sword and Father the armor!" I said.

Grandmother gave Grandfather a piercing look. "Why are you telling him this?"

"Not now, Mother."

"Do you want to give him a complex?"

"Not now, I asked. Besides, he really did buy it. I told you, he sends money every month. He bought him lots of other things too."

"Oh right, father of the year."

"Mother!"

At the beginning of the short dialogue, Grandmother looked to me like the fire-breathing dragon. At the end, she looked more like Mother. Which of them should I fight against? Confused, I stood for a few moments with the sword drooping at my side. When Mother said: "Sweetie, do you want to try on your armor and show us?" the fire-breathing dragon was immediately forgotten. Father volunteered to help me, and we spent a few pleasant minutes while he used the sword to check the strength of my armor. I was four and I had a suit of armor and I was very happy. How easy it was to be invincible.

"Do you want to see what Grandfather and Grandmother bought for you?" Grandmother asked me. I nodded and a large package appeared in her hand, as if out of nowhere. It was wrapped with promising and sparkling silver paper. I ripped the paper with excitement that immediately gave way to a confused expression. What is it?

"It's a game to learn English," Grandmother explained. "There are all of the letters here, and also a cassette with songs!" Her beaming face stood in complete contrast to the gift itself. I stared at the box and tried to understand from which side to look at it. Mother recognized the disappointed expression on my face and hurried to intervene. "Say 'thank you' nicely to Grandfather and Grandmother!"

"Thank you," I saw and immediately gave each of them, in order, a hug. That's how we say thank you. Apparently Darya started to hug as a sign of appreciation only after she had left them. They seemed very surprised.

"And now," Mother said, "who wants to come to the sea?"

"Me! Me!" Grandfather, Furry and I shouted together. Our loud voices almost completely drowned out Mother's scolding question: "Don't you think he should first of all learn to read Hebrew?"

We went down to the SaltySea. It was still early in the afternoon when we set up on the beach. The sun had yet to complete its daily, Sisyphean climb to the highest point, exactly in the center.

It was hot, very hot. The beachgoers wore looks of revulsion on their faces, as if in another decade they wouldn't give much of their wealth to return precisely to this day. While Mother spread sunscreen on me, I looked around. Mud people were scattered here and there on the beach. One face was covered with a newspaper. There was no love-struck weather forecaster on the back page, no messages for Neta under the tidings: "Weather – more of the same." The man whose nose was under the barren forecast did not even sense their absence; it seemed like the sun alone had been here forever.

A fairly large family sat next to us: a father, a mother, and three children. The father and mother were very light-skinned, and the two older children also had transparent-white skin. Through their straight blonde hair, you could see their scalp turning red. The baby was dark, with curly hair. He crawled on the ground joyfully and brought a fistful of sand toward his mouth. The woman called out: "No, Jimmy, don't!" and the clump of sand froze in his hands. The familiar sound caught Grandmother's attention. She smiled at the baby. The baby smiled back at her and also made Mother smile, a chain reaction that created an opening for a conversation. Grandmother definitely intended to take advantage of it.

"You're also English speakers?" (An unexplained twinge of tension runs through me, probably coming from Darya. In her view, "you're also" was intended to place her and me in the other camp.)

"Sort of," the woman smiled. "We worked overseas and just returned now. It's hard to go back to Hebrew."

"Jimmy only speaks English still," the father interjected and proudly declared: "All of our children will have two languages."

As far as I could see, Jimmy did not speak at all. Nonetheless, Grandmother was impressed. "Where were you?"

"In South Africa."

"We're from America. We came for our grandson's birthday. It's been a long time since we were here. It's difficult, very difficult to come back."

"Mother, you just came for a week," Darya said, spreading sunscreen on the back of her neck. Grandmother said, "Yes, but after you become accustomed to a certain mentality, it's not simple to deal with this. Even for a short time. With us, the education is different." (She shot a side glance at Mother.) "The people are different. The whole atmosphere is different."

"Yes, I hear you," the blonde woman said. "It was also really hard for me to come back. Everything was so perfect during this period abroad, we felt really at home. I wanted to stay another few years." Her eyes filled with longing when she added, "at least."

"I actually didn't mind returning," the blonde father said. "There's no place like Israel." He lifted the dark-skinned boy in the air. The baby started giggling.

"Do you work in the Foreign Ministry?" Grandfather joined the conversation for the first time. The man nodded, and the conversation slowly was pulled out of the hands of female camaraderie. Grandmother returned for one more sally when she asked: "Tell me, do you have some nice unmarried men in the Foreign Ministry?" The man did not have a chance to answer, but both Grandmother and Darya had a chance to feel ten years younger for a moment when Darya rolled her eyes and said, "Really, Motherrrrr!"

I was a white spot jumping between three black spots. Grandfather, Grandmother and Darya spread dark mud on their faces and arms, and Grandfather said with delight: "There are some things you can only find in Israel. Look at this, natural minerals. People from all over the world pay a fortune to buy these products."

Darya said: "Yes, they're ruining the sea, these factories. People will do anything for money. If they don't stop them, they'll pump all of the minerals from it and it will dry up. Only the desert will remain."

"I thought you're not going out with that awful fellow from the desert anymore," Grandmother said. "What was his name, Crip?"

A long sentence shrunk into a single facial expression, saying: "I was never going out with him, his name is Trip and he was just the facilitator at the workshop and I regret telling you about him." Grandfather winked at me, "Want to see something nice?"

As we got closer to the water line, the voices of the two black faces we left behind faded away. Grandfather said, "Bring me a big stone." I bent down and immediately found a smooth rock with a reddish color, which I placed in Grandfather's open palm. Furry and I were very curious.

Grandfather took the stone, cocked his arm and threw the stone toward the water. The stone hopped three times and that was just the beginning. When it finally was swallowed into the water, I stood spellbound: It seemed as if the entire sea was full of rays of light and small waves, circular and glimmering. The sun broke in them, with glittering colors; circles of salt flooded the sea far beyond the horizon visible to me.

"Do it again, do it again!" I yelled when the sea calmed down, and Grandfather complied. My grandfather is a magician, a master of the water and a champion of the stones. I looked at him with admiration.

"Do you want to learn how to do this?" he asked.

We spent the next hour pleasantly. When we went back to our spot, it turned out that it was just in time because Darya said, "That's the end of that. I don't want to hear anything more about it." And she went to the shower at the end of the beach to wash off the black mask. I ran to catch up with her and stood next to her, closing my eyes under the stream of water.

"Did you have a good time with Grandfather?" she asked.

"Yes, I learned how to skip stones!"

"Good for you! And you were able to?"

"Yes, I made waves! Grandfather knows how to make waves in the water."

"Wonderful, I'm happy that you had a good time." She seemed contemplative. Something from the mud mask and her melancholy thoughts dripped onto me with the water flowing from her chin, or perhaps I felt a need to dispel the trace of the thought that passed through her – how good it is for a child to grow up surrounded by family. I suddenly hugged her. "Mother, I love you." Darya was the one who taught me to hug and kiss and to declare my love, yet for a fraction of a second she looked very surprised. A moment later, she was already my mother again without a mask. She said, "I love you too. Want to race to the towels?"

*

The next morning, we went down to the pool. Mother wore a white, one-piece bathing suit, with a robe over it, also white. She was very beautiful, her face beaming. Grandfather and Grandmother each wore blue bathing suits under their robes.

When we arrived, Mother chose a yellow beach chair, took off her robe and spread the daily newspaper across her knees. For the first time in four years, she had the chance to spend an hour in the sun on vacation by herself. She did not intend to miss this opportunity. "Do you want to go into the water with Grandmother?" she asked. Her voice was childlike and enthusiastic, but it still seemed to me that it was not directed toward me.

Grandmother, for reasons that would later become clear, did not raise any objection. "Here, Grandfather will inflate the float and we'll go in," she said. While Grandfather was blowing air into the float, Darya closed her eyes facing the sun, yielding and indulging herself, looking gorgeous. The lifeguard adjusted the angle of his chair. Grandmother glared at him.

I showed Grandfather how I swim. It was very easy to swim (I was a captive inside the inflatable tube), but Grandfather was still impressed. Then he showed me how he swims himself – his arms struck the water, making it white and stormy. He was a big and splashing whale.

When Grandfather reached the other end of the pool, Grandmother, who was holding my float, said: "Do you know where Grandfather and Grandmother live?"

"In America."

"Right. And do you know what there is in America?"

"No, what?"

"In America, there are lots of cute children like yourself, and they have lots of games."

"We also have games in preschool."

"Right, and in America there's a beautiful lake by the house. In the winter, you could skate on the ice. Do like to ice skate?"

"Yes!"

"Do you know," Grandmother said, as if sharing a secret, "maybe you'll come to us once, to America."

"With Mother?"

"Of course. Maybe you'll come to visit and, if you like it, maybe you'll even come to live near us. Would you like to live in America?"

I took a moment to think about this. I wouldn't mind living in America, I thought, but the thing is, I was already living in my house. Grandfather the whale surfaced next to us with an enormous spray of water and said, "Come on Bracha, leave the kid alone."

"I'm just suggesting an idea. Wouldn't you like for them to live near us, for Dorit to advance a bit, for the boy to receive a proper education? Chris could arrange a job for her at his office."

"She's okay here, it's their home, they seem happy," Grandfather said and his voice was soft. That was the end of the little conversation for now; its fruits, planted now, would only sprout the next day.

When I came out of the pool, a surprise was waiting for me. "Look who's here! Danieli, your friend! You remember Danieli?" Mother sounded so convinced that I had no choice but to believe that this boy was my friend. I assume Mother would have been happy in any case to meet the Morgenstern family, but her happiness was undoubtedly doubled and tripled by the impressed look on Grandmother's face. When Mother introduced them – "Father, Mother, these are our friends, Sarah and Avi Morgenstern and their son, Danieli" – Grandmother said "pleased to meet you" and her voice left no room for doubt: She knew very well who Sarah and Avi Morgenstern were.

Danieli also had an inflatable tube. While Mother and Grandmother were talking with Sarah and Avi, Grandfather put both of us in the water. We had swimming competitions in the tubes, going both forward and backwards. "Where are your Grandfather and Grandmother?" I asked Danieli.

"At home. Where are your Grandfather and Grandmother?"

"In America."

"We live in America, but now we're here because we came to visit you," Grandfather intervened. I wasn't convinced, but still I said, "Ah."

Danieli said, "My father is the strongest."

"No way," I objected. "My father is the strongest!"

"My father can pick up a desk!"

"My father can pick up two desks!"

"My father is as strong as an elephant!"

"My father is as strong as a tiger."

"An elephant is stronger than a tiger!"

"No way!"

"Of course!"

This conversation made both of us laugh. We continued to laugh after Grandfather interrupted it and asked us to count out loud how many seconds he could stay under water. We counted till ten and then applauded, and then swam some more in the tubes. The hotel photographer took pictures of us on the edge of the pool, click, in order to hang the picture on the board in the children's club – fun at the Dead Sea. When I was an Indian woman, I believed that each picture takes a small piece of the soul with it.

The children's conversation seemed to have been forgotten and Grandfather breathed a sigh of relief – Darya's heart was spared. However, when we finally got out of the water, I ran to Mother, who was waiting for me with an outstretched towel. I wrapped myself in it and asked: "Isn't it true that my father is the strongest?"

In retrospect, it seems that even the water stood still for a moment. Grandfather looked down and Grandmother gave Mother a hard stare. But even if my innocent question or Grandmother's eyes stabbed her, it was only for a second. The next moment she quietly said, "That's very true," and continued to dry me off. The answer satisfied me and the question was forgotten; the water in the pool resumed its frolic. Father owed this fleeting moment of glory to Mother – the strongest woman in the world.

*

Our warped, restless vacation apparently left an impact on the other guests in the hotel; no one left it completely intact. At lunch, a child's scream was suddenly heard, followed immediately by a woman's shriek.

Several guests, including Grandfather, abandoned their forks and knives and ran to the hallway. Grandmother continued to eat, her face clearly indicating that in her view it was not polite to scream, and certainly not to abandon the lunch table. But when Grandfather returned and said to Darya, "The son of your friends, the Morgensterns, fell," everyone got up and went after him.

When we arrived, we found Danieli Morgenstern lying on the floor, with blood and tears streaming from his chin. His location did not leave any doubt about the circumstances of his injury – he was lying directly underneath a square pedestal on which the statue of a man stood in a transparent box. He had apparently climbed onto it earlier. Sarah Morgenstern (her shriek was the one that shook the dining room) knelt at his side and made soft comforting sounds. Avi Morgenstern stood by her side, discomfited to find himself with no role to play.

"Everything's okay," Sarah smiled – not at Danieli, but at the small crowd that had gathered around them. "We just had a little scare, that's all."

But the crowd was unwilling to downplay the event it had witnessed. "We need to call a doctor, he's bleeding" one of the guests declared and demonstratively whipped out a cell phone.

"You don't need to be alarmed, it's only a superficial cut," Sarah insisted. "Here, it's nothing, right Danieli?"

"Ma'am, do whatever you think is best, but if I were you, I wouldn't play around with this," the stranger said. He sounded a bit ominous, though his intentions were undoubtedly pure. If he didn't follow his impulse to call an ambulance upon seeing the bleeding child, maybe he would at least rescue the boy from the hands of the neglectful mother. It was clear that he did not recognize Sarah and Avi Morgenstern.

And here, who came to save the day? It was none other than Elisha! I recognized him immediately as broke through the small circle of onlookers and knelt down beside Danieli. "Let me through, I did a first-aid course." The course accorded him the momentary status of a wonder healer.

The small crowd awaited his pronouncement and sighed with relief when he announced: "Oh, it doesn't look serious. He got a bit of a fright, there was a bit of bleeding, and that's all." He ignored Avi and looked at Sarah when he asked: "Do you want to call for an ambulance?"

What silent understanding flashed between them at that moment? Or perhaps it was just a spark of solidarity between concerned parents. The crowd was disappointed to hear Sarah say in a decisive voice: "There's no need."

"We prefer keeping our hospital visits to a minimum," Avi explained. "It can be very traumatic." The "we" was a noble expression of collaboration on his part – in fact, it was Sarah who had developed a strong aversion to doctors and medical instruments and examinations and records since the birth. This could be attributed to the long period in which she spent between doctors and injections when she was trying to get pregnant, though this was only a very small part of it. Meanwhile, Danieli had stopped crying and was lying on the floor with his eyes surveying the ceiling with great interest. Elisha bandaged his chin (where did the first aid kit suddenly come from?) and examined his eyes. He asked him a few questions and then helped him to his feet. "He looks okay to me," he said.

Danieli came over to us, feeling his bandaged chin. Mother patted his head. "Did you get a boo-boo?"

He nodded, and suddenly put on a miserable face. I observed him with admiration. A bandage on the chin, how wonderful!

"Come, do you want to join us for lunch?"

Now it was Sarah's turn to nod. A few moments later, Danieli was already sitting next to me, at a bigger table. Grandmother conducted a lively conversation with Avi. The bandage on Danieli's chin was the only trace of the small drama that had already vanished from the hallway. Later that afternoon, Furry fell from the window in the room and hurt his chin. I knelt over him like Elisha and treated him with the medication bag and my magic sword. No trip to the hospital was needed.

*

The last day of the vacation was completely ruined with the active help of a four-year-old traitor. We were planning to go down to the sea again ("you don't breathe air like this every day" my good grandfather said, his words covering up the limited range of activities), but the argument already started in the room. Grandmother knocked on our door, dressed in a bathing suit. Mother had just woken up. While she was in the bathroom, Grandmother asked me: "Do you know where we return to at the end of the week?"

"Where?" (I was used to answering a question with a question, even if I knew the answer.)

"To America! We live in America."

"Me too?"

I didn't attach great importance to the question, but when Grandmother replied, "Sweetie, you want to come too?" her voice was so tender and full of empathy that I became overwhelmed with sadness.

"I want to go to America too."

'Sweetie, I also would like you to come to be near us. I would like for you and Mother to live with us and I would like you to have a new father. But you have to ask Mother whether she is willing for me to help her."

And the timing was perfect, just as Darya stormed out of the bathroom. She wore a red bathing suit with a robe over it, but the serenity from the previous day was absent from her eyes. She glared at Grandmother and I hurried over to her: "Mother, can I go to America?"

"No."

"Why?"

"Because we live in Israel."

"Why?"

"Because our home is here and we have fun, and because you love your room."

"I want a new father from America."

"You have a father. He sent you a sword. Besides, you need to go to preschool."

The explanation was sufficient for me, but not for Grandmother. She said: "Dorit, I really think that you need to give it some thought. Forget about us, but think about the child."

Mother said in an ominous voice: "What exactly do I need to think about?"

"Here, he'll never receive half of what children his age receive where we live. And I'm not only speaking about him." Grandmother's voice was gentle. "About you too. You're young and talented. In America you'd have so many opportunities. Isn't a shame to waste your life this way?"

"I'm not wasting my life, I'm living it. I have a job and a child and friends and a home and I'm happy."

"Oh really, Dorit. You expect me to believe you? A dull job at a bank without any opportunities for advancement, a child without a father, you don't go out, you don't even try. I realize that you came back to Israel because you were angry at us, but now you have to show responsibility. I already asked Chris and he might have a job for you. To receive a little help from your parents is nothing to be ashamed of. After all, you don't really think that his father will suddenly appear and assume responsibility, do you? You have a child to take care of. I didn't raise an irresponsible daughter."

The gloves were off, and merciless truths were about to be set free. I brought my sword. Mother seethed, "You asked Chris? You suddenly care so much about me and your grandson? Four years he didn't see you, and now he's supposed to run and move in with you? I don't need any help anymore, I'm managing. The only thing I need is for you not to try to change me and criticize me."

Poor Grandfather chose to enter the room precisely at this

miserable moment. When he innocently asked, "What is this, no one is hungry here?" two sets of eyes directed their anger at him.

"I thought you came to visit me and to finally see your grandchild," Darya said. "If I had known you were coming in order to fill his head with nonsense about America, I wouldn't have suggested it."

"It's not nonsense," Grandmother insisted. "Tell her that she must think about her child." She turned to Darya again. "What do have here? In America, you have a family, we'll find you a better job, and maybe you'll meet someone. A boy doesn't have to grow up without a father. Look at him!"

"I'm looking at him," Darya said, but didn't look at me. "And do you know what I see? I see a happy boy whose mother loves him as he is."

"Love is wonderful, but it's not enough. What about a spouse, a family, what about a male role model for him?"

"He has a father. Everything in due time."

"In due time, I will hasten it,"* Grandfather quoted, no longer able to restrain himself, and both of them turned their glances to him again. Tell her, their eyes glared. He sighed. "We'll wait for you in the dining room," he announced.

When Mother and Grandmother arrived, we were already sitting with a plate full of pastries and cheeses. Furry pecked at blueberry jam on my napkin. We ate the meal in silence.

The dispute might have subsided or at least been relegated to trans-Atlantic conversations far away from my ears if I hadn't decided to stir it again. I was not the only one to blame for the incident – on the shore of the Dead Sea, even before we skipped rocks or entered the water, Grandfather fell asleep.

I'm used to keeping myself occupied, but now when I had become accustomed to his company, I became bored. I lay next to Mother's towel and said again: "I want to go with Grandfather and Grandmother to America."

* Isaiah 60:22

Grandmother turned a page in the newspaper, all of her senses focused on us. Mother said: "You live here, with me, in our home."

"So you come too."

"I can't. I need to go to work."

"You'll have work in America. I'll take care of that. Just say." It was Grandmother's voice from behind the newspaper.

Mother said: "Yes, you always take care of me so nicely." Her voice was mixed with bitter sea salt.

"I want America."

"I said no!"

Oh, the weeping. The uninhibited and unrestrained weeping of a child. I would later miss this. But at the time it burst forth from me, accompanied by a ridiculous look of insult, and it continued until Grandfather woke up and whisked me off to the water with skillful quickness and without saying a word. He gently placed me on the ground. We skipped stones and then went into the water and floated on our backs; the sun dried my tears. Grandfather understood the drying of tears. Once, when Darya was still only Dorit and they lived together in Israel, he took her to the sea in Tel Aviv. It was a very wintry day and the waves crashed. "Look, the sea is happy," he told her and at once dispelled future stale and depressing thoughts of adolescence.

It was quiet and pleasant with Grandfather. Unfortunately, I was already too old to fully enjoy the moment itself. In the middle of the last day of vacation, there was already an element of longing. When we got out of the water, I lay down on a towel next to my silent mother, and without checking the expression on her face, I fell asleep. While sleeping, I felt how someone was caressing my clenched hand. Beyond my closed eyelids, it seemed to me that it was Grandmother's face. She put something in my hand, perhaps it was a clue. When I woke up, it was time to go home.

Did Darya expect a different visit? Different parents? Did she mistakenly think that time blurs and erases, with its pain and anger washed away like a name on wet beach sand? On the way to the hotel, she had been full of tense hope and I was hesitant, but now we were traveling in the opposite direction. I like playing with Grandfather and Grandmother. I'll travel to America when I'm big. The gate that opened before me was the gate that Darya had carefully locked. We were taking them to the airport. What conversations took place while I slept in the car? They were probably similar to the ones I had heard. When the time came, we parted easily. I waved to Grandfather and Grandmother and shouted: "Come back soon to take me to America!" Grandmother waved back to me.

Furry flew to America just at the right time. He made room for Thomas the cat. The day after that vacation, I came home from preschool and a surprise was waiting for me.

"Here, this is instead of the game in English. You always wanted a kitten," Mother said.

This instantly became the truth. I had always wanted a cat! And now I finally had one. A sweet cat with thick gray fur was napping in her lap. She ran her fingers through his fur with a maternal touch.

"He's ours?" I asked. She smiled and nodded. I looked at the curled up bundle of fur, my Thomas, the pussy cat, my compensation.

It would later break my heart, thinking of how she walked restlessly in the street after that day when we had all turned our backs on her. She must have let her legs lead her aimlessly – she does this sometimes. Outside the pet shop she stopped, signaled "hello" with her finger on the transparent glass and adopted the kitten, who yielded to her heart unconditionally.

* * *

The few guests requiring services from the reception desk at the Pomegranate Branches Hotel did not notice anything unusual about the receptionist. Her movements (she gave them what they requested: paper and pen, a telephone book) looked a bit decisive against the backdrop of the serene and indolent mountains, but they did not reveal the tempest raging in her head. Arguments for and against drifted from one side to another, though she had actually come to a decision already: Mimi received a promotion. Mimi would not go to Tel Aviv.

What's so special about this Tel Aviv, she scolded herself as she arranged the "Lectures – The Fig Room" folders on the shelf behind her in alphabetical order. (What if someone wanted to find details about a lecturer from five years ago, let's say? And who besides Mimi could take care of such things?) It not the seventies here, today the center of the country is close and available, there's convenient transportation and besides, it's not like the ice cream is sweeter there. (That's a saying Mimi once heard. Absurdly, when pulled from the depths of her memory, she could really taste the ice cream she ate during her last trip to Tel Aviv.) Today there are computers and telephones, and location has become irrelevant. Besides, she could enjoy the new position a little, save a bit, and then go.

But time was more pressing now. The colorful stores and tiny apartments and the young men and women who could teach her to be different would not wait forever. In her mind's eye, she saw an adolescent girl in jeans and a T-shirt, the same teenager she had imagined until recently when thinking of herself. "Mother, you've really lived in these boondocks your entire life? You never left the South at all? Not even once?" she asked in amazement. Her eyes, Mimi's eyes, were a bit disappointed.

A young woman approached the reception desk and asked what time dinner is served. She was young and vivacious and smiling and her hair was a bit wild. A few hairs stuck out; one of them was white. If she had noticed it, she undoubtedly would have plucked it out. Now it was hanging over her like Damocles' sword and there was something intrusive in this. Mimi tried to ignore it, but she still had to contemplate for a moment the passage of time. Who needs this Tel Aviv anyway? It's not every day that one receives such a promotion.

The official reason for the promotion was unimportant, even silly: On a day that was not particularly busy, one of the chambermaids decided to enter one of the rooms and take a bath instead of spending the time cleaning. To her credit, it should be noted that she remembered to lock the door. On the other hand, she found the radio button, which was set to a classical music station and was broadcasting The Magic Flute opera. She did not hear the temporary but lawful owners of the room trying unsuccessfully to enter, so she did not get up, get dressed and ask them to wait while she finished cleaning. Instead, she continued to weigh clouds of bubbles in her hands and sing to her delight. When she finally heard voices, she quickly jumped out of the tub and thus the couple and their small son, the locksmith and a shocked Mimi encountered a naked chambermaid covering her body with a handful of suds to the sounds of the aria of the queen of the night. The guests, of course, raised a big fuss – not so much over the use of the bathroom, but more about the shameful disruption of the natural order. The chambermaid was fired that same day and compensation in the form of free dinners for the rest of their stay ultimately resolved the matter.

The one who handled all this was Mimi, of course. Temporary guests mistakenly think that they are the main event at the hotel. But, in fact, the hotel's hidden layer – invisible chambermaids, cleaners, cooks and waiters – constitutes the real heart of the place. Mimi orchestrated them with skill that derived from her experience and character. The place, she told herself with satisfaction on more than one occasion, operates like clockwork. In recent years, since his divorce, Shlomo's presence had receded and Mimi's authorities had gradually expanded. They say that during the first days of the hotel, he himself chose every carpet, every tablecloth, and every decorative candle that illuminated the faces of the dinner guests. Now he simply let the place operate.

The chambermaid in the bathtub was just an excuse, of course. The real reason for the promotion was a nearly imperceptible lack of concentration that snuck into Mimi's eyes, a grayish shroud that emerged from time to time and then disappeared. Shlomo feared that she was about to leave. In light of her age, her terms of employment and the new grayish shroud, he had to take action. At the Pomegranate Branches Hotel she had Michael and enjoyed an undisputed status, but Shlomo's senses told him that this was no longer enough. Two days after the saga of the chambermaid, he called Mimi into his office. "I don't know what I would do without you Mimi," he told her candidly. "I think you deserve more. What do you think about being the administrative manager of the hotel?"

Manager. Administrative. During the following days, Mimi rolled the words on her tongue. They sat there with a natural ease that quite surprised her. Her salary improved, of course. And she had a lot of plans. For example, to redecorate some of the rooms. For there to be a red room and a blue room and a white room, and the guests could choose rooms according to the color that matched their mood and find peace of mind in them. At night, they would curl up in bed in precisely the color that suited them. The hotel's breakfast experience would be a colorful feast for the senses. But in order to achieve this, she would have to be a real manager. That is, she would need to continue to acquire experience, perhaps at other hotels – in Tel Aviv, for example. And maybe not? She consulted with Michael that night.

"The way it sounds to me, it would be a shame to miss an opportunity like this," he said. "So you won't be going to Tel Aviv, is that so terrible? Believe me, Tel Aviv is not as glamorous as it sounds. The apartments are expensive and rundown, and the people are searching for themselves. They would die to find peace and quiet like there is here. You had the good fortune to be born into this, you belong here, and you're flourishing. Why should you give this up?"

She noticed that he didn't say "Why should you give me up?" The little girl with Mimi's eyes asked: "Really, you and Father met in the hotel where you're still working? Wow, you're in the same place for so long? It's strange that you never felt like trying other things." Is it possible that Michael also saw her?

"Look, if you want to go to Tel Aviv, I won't stop you," and thus Michael also noted the sentence that went unspoken. "I'm happy being with you, but I think that people should not stop their dreams. I don't think you need to stay because of me. I just think that it's a shame to miss the opportunity for such a promotion. You're real Mimi, and you have something real here. You don't need the pretense of Tel Aviv."

This sentence itself sounded a bit pretentious to Mimi. And the fact that Michael did not think that she needed to stay because of him moved uneasily inside of her until situating itself in the right place. The facts were still soft. Soon the process of consolidating them into an irreversible story would begin.

"It's not that I'm looking for other people," she hurried to establish a fact in their hearts. "I just think there are more opportunities to advance in Tel Aviv." And nonetheless, in the end she convinced herself to stay.

On a Thursday during the afternoon break, Shlomo convened the staff in the conference room. This was the usual place for making a toast on holidays and for lectures on personal empowerment and taking initiative at work. But this time no one (except for Shlomo and Mimi) knew what it was about. The pessimists spoke about layoffs, and the optimists guessed that Shlomo would announce a recreation day for all of the hotel's employees. No one was surprised when Shlomo festively announced: "You all know about the wonderful work Mimi does in our hotel. We all know that we wouldn't get by without her. We, in the Pomegranate Branches family, appreciate effort and are pleased by the successes of each and every one of us. I would like to make a toast in honor of the hotel's new administrative manager." As he turned toward the table, where little cups and a bottle of wine had been prepared in advance, the small group of employees applauded. Mimi let the warm feeling spread through her (What was this feeling? Pride? Joy? Love?) and she smiled at them with a broad grin. If one day her life flashes in front of her eyes, at least for now she had no doubt in her heart that this moment would appear as one of the highlights.

Still, a twist of almost indiscernible uneasiness crept into her limbs, preventing them from completely relaxing. This feeling of home, a warm and tangled webbing. And what if this is all there is? And what if Mimi, like the towels on Yom Kippur, always returns to the little (and homey, according to those who love it) hotel in the end, pulled by invisible ropes, and is unable to fit in anywhere else? Good is attracted to good, fire to fire, water to water. It is possible that Mimi is attracted to the Pomegranate Branches Hotel? If it once had been clear to her that her current life was a waiting period for the real thing that was yet to occur, she now started to come to the frightening realization – it could be that this was actually her life, that this was all there would ever be. There would be no shiny uniforms of the Sheraton Hotel and hikes on the soft sand of the Mediterranean Sea. The girl with Mimi's eyes gave her a look of "I'll never be like you." Mimi searched for Michael's eyes to see whether he understood. Michael exclaimed with everyone "Lehayim!" and looked at her proudly.

*

Shortly before the beginning of Mimi's seventh Towel Day, she informed Michael that she was leaving. That is, she did not even have to tell him. The winds of the South are experienced in announcements about leaving. But even though she postponed the conversation with him until she could smooth all its edges, she was obliged to tell Shlomo. She forget to ask him not to say anything to Michael or hoped he would understand this on his own, a hope that turned out to be unfounded. "So, I'm sure it'll be tough for you without Mimi," he patted Michael on the shoulder two days later. When she found out, she felt the tangible unraveling that began to erode her trust and permitted her for the first time to think that Shlomo, with all due respect, was not a particularly smart man.

She had planned to take a walk with Michael to the abandoned train station, which was once active and now served mainly as an inspiration for frustrated local artists, and to tell him there. It seemed appropriate to her. Those who leave sometimes do this, hoping that the right backdrop will leave a softer impression in the memory of the person left behind. But, as indicated, the walk to the station never took place. The question tossed and turned on Michael's nervous fingers, reached his distant glance and finally landed on his lips. One afternoon, at the end of Mimi's morning shift, he walked her to the parking lot and then stopped next to the car and instead of parting from her with the usual "see you tomorrow," he look straight into her eyes and said: "So, I hear you're leaving in the end to Tel Aviv."

There was no anger in his voice, though anger was clearly to be expected. And since there was undoubtedly supposed to be anger there, it actually found its way to Mimi. Excessive understanding was just another way to make her feel guilty. And who told him? And who said she was really leaving?

But then she recalled that she was indeed leaving. She had already given notice to Shlomo. It was now or never, and she chose now. An attempt that turns out to be a mistake could still be included in the list of erroneous and reversible choices of a young woman. But there was no justification for mistakenly staying in one place. Michael could not understand this. He had not grown up under the chalky air of the South that threatens to cover everyone with a layer of dust.

She looked down and said the short, required and useless sentence: "I'm sorry."

She shut the door of the car without getting in, and leaned against the fence of the parking area. Michael leaned against the wall next to her. A stranger passing by could have thought that they were supporting the wall and not the opposite.

"I don't understand," Michael said. "I mean, I know you've always wanted to leave, but why now of all times? You have an excellent job here and they just promoted you." He looked at her, but his eyes focused on the lower part of her face. "And besides, I thought we had something between us."

"You're right, and I feel good with you, and the work is really okay." Mimi turned and looked toward the sea, which actually appeared very beautiful and blameless, smooth and blue, with that island squatting in it, circled by salt. "But I just need to go, and to do it now. I'm afraid that if I don't go, this place will close in on me forever. There is so little here, it's as if… as if there's nothing to wait for. Do you understand?"

"No." Michael did not understand. "You have work here, you have a home that doesn't cost much, and scenery that people fly from all over the world to come and see. You have clean air. What else do you want?" Nonetheless, a small bit of revenge waited patiently – he didn't say "you have me."

Michael brushed a hand by his ear, and then tucked his shirt into his pants for no reason. Mimi took a close look at him: brown hair, green eyes, a perplexed look. How could she explain to him what every local kid understands without words, simply from the air? Everyone knows that they should leave. And perhaps it's just that she, Mimi, unlike him, did not know how to find serenity in the hills. Perhaps just as there are people who are attracted to a particular place, there are also those who are always pushed away by an invisible gravitational force, as if someone had attached the wrong side of the magnet to their back.

"Look," she said, "it's not that I'm unhappy. But what do I have to look forward to here? Another promotion from Shlomo to the rank of … of what actually? I won't get another promotion in the next ten years. There's nothing here except for hotels, there are hardly any young people our age, and the big city is a half-hour drive away. I feel like I've come to the final station too early."

The last sentence she had planned, of course, when she thought they would walk to the train station, but it still seemed to make an impact.

Michael was silent for a moment and looked contemplative. Was he convinced that she was actually right? The relief had yet to set in when he said, "You lack options, that's what you're really saying. You want a lot of everything so that you can choose. Lots of jobs, lots of young men, lots of places to go at night. Right?"

She lowered her glance. "Maybe."

And she realized too late that she actually had meant exactly the opposite. Once, long ago, she heard a common and evil sentence: In the desert, every thorn is a flower. The sentence stuck with her against her will and drifted in her mind as Michael gazed at her with that tender look of his and she was unable to wipe the moment clear of the thought: What would have happened if they had met, for example, in Tel Aviv?

And all of those guests, **she remembered them**. Of course she remembered the regulars like Elisha and Teresa, but sometimes she also recognized guests who had stayed at the hotel two years earlier and more. They, of course, didn't remember Mimi, which put her in an inferior position to them, because it was clear that much more had occurred in their lives in the meantime. After all, what had occurred in Mimi's life? Work and Michael and that standing sea, which does not go anywhere.

She realized that she had been digging into the wall with her finger for several minutes already. She would have to do something with her fingernails.

"I think you need to consider this very carefully," Michael said. "This promotion is a very good opportunity for you. Listen, I grew up in Tel Aviv and it's not really as glamorous as it seems from here. It's true, there are more parties and more people. But between us, how many parties will you go to? Things are going well for you here, and you're still young and everyone here loves and appreciates you. Believe me, you're not the type who'll enjoy it there. The fact that you were born in a particular place doesn't mean that you have to leave it. People like me have to search for themselves, but you're different. You simply . . . belong. Save up a bit, enjoy the promotion. You have things to do here, perhaps you'll even manage the hotel yourself. If you still want, you could always leave later."

That is, what he was saying is that he, Michael, actually belonged to the big city, while she, Mimi, clearly belonged to the hotel area at the Dead Sea. The big city was not for her in his view, and in the end she would discover this herself. Mimi was well aware that there was a small chance that he was right, but still the insinuation angered her. Besides, it seemed to her that the fact that she was curious and vivacious did not make him want her more, and perhaps the opposite was true. Her passion made him uncomfortable. It was not the first time she felt that Michael did not see and appreciate and was not impressed with what she defined as her best qualities. Complete parts of her remained unloved. Left with no alternative, she did what she knew how to do: She became very practical.

"I already spoke with Shlomo. He wrote me quite an impressive letter of recommendation, you know him. I hope that it will help me find work as quickly as possible. And I need to find an apartment."

For a moment, they both thought of the same thing – they could look for an apartment together. But where? The idea drifted above them and landed on the ground, useless.

"What about us?" Michael asked. Really, what?

"I really wanted for this to work. But you have to understand, I'm simply suffocating here. I have to try. I think we just met at the wrong stage of life. You understand? I don't want to feel that life decided for me, that I simply let it happen."

Mimi did not look at him. In fact, she looked exactly in the opposite direction. The sea suffered the insults without raising a tempest or blushing. It remained standing there, blue and powerful in its quiet way. This was hardly surprising. The sea needs no proof. It can, merely by its very presence, make people from all over the world fall at its feet and spread mud over themselves.

"I'm sorry," she said again. She would have preferred for him to get angry. But he did not.

"You're a talented and strong and funny young woman and I'll miss you," he simply stated. "But I can't keep you here against your will. Maybe we really did meet at the wrong time. If we're meant for one another, perhaps we'll meet again when we're more ready." The concepts of "meant for" and "to be ready" Michael discovered in the South with the serenity and the calm. These are treasures the hills do not reveal to the locals, but save in order to impress the new-comers. He looked too radiant and that annoyed her. A moment later he brushed his hand on her cheek, and for a short minute their silence really blended in with the silence of the mountains and the sea. It was very much his moment. Possible hope padded the sadness. Perhaps the backdrop of the hills was, nonetheless, more appropriate than the train station. And perhaps now, when they understood that she was really leaving, they decided to share something of this with her too.

"See you tomorrow," he suddenly broke away from the fence and went back into the hotel. She was still looking at the sea as he walked away. That is the problem with ill-timed farewells – during the entire next week they would have to meet and converse and carry this awareness between them and then bid farewell again. When she approached the car and this time opened the door and got in, the thing happened that should give pause to all of the world's parting couples: With the sadness and regret and fear, a light and irrevers-ible breeze of relief snuck in. Emotions flamed inside her that were not necessarily connected to love, but more to the time that was fleeting and the possibilities that were peeling off and vanishing, like dead cells from the body. And as if to clarify this point, already the next day she received a reminder of the passage of time in the form of a square brown envelope, without a return address. Folded inside the envelope was a white towel – Mimi's seventh Towel Day was approaching. It was now or never.

What was left for her to do? Last memories would be seared on their own, the separation would also creep away, pretending to be forced in order to stir sympathy. For the last time, she would receive the regular guests who were a part of her life, the Morgenstern couple and Elisha Natan and Teresa Holstein. Unfortunately, her favorite guest would not come to the hotel this year to celebrate his fifth birthday, an absence that would take on the semblance of a small tragedy. She had no way of knowing this, of course, when she went into the computer records, typed a very old date and dialed the number of the man with the green eyes.

*   *   *

Who is the man with the green eyes? It is easy to describe his outward appearance (average height, relatively broad shoulders, short-cut and curly brown hair). His life's center of gravity depends on how you look at it. Is he a young man who fell victim to the caprices of a young woman with a greedy womb, a conscienceless man who was neglecting his duties, a man who fell in love once, or perhaps the successful owner of an Australian company that sells fish? All these are only ostensibly contradictory, different sides of the same Rubik's Cube. The cube is an extremely complex game. It is often placed on a shelf and serves as nothing more than a colorful decoration. Older people say that it is more beautiful like this anyway, and who said that the correct order is the conservative separation of colors? Self-deception, like wisdom teeth, is one of the growing pains that reflect maturity – a child who receives a Rubik's Cube knows that there is only one possible solution.

The events of this man's life are easier to describe, even if they raise some questions. For example: How did a person like him happen to come to a moondancing workshop at the shores of the Dead Sea? By profession, he is an engineer. By character, he is calculated by content – that is, not exactly the type of person who is likely to dance on beaches on full-moon nights or to follow the directions of an instructor named Trip. One might suggest that he was drawn to the Dead Sea region and to the Pomegranate Branches Hotel at this particular juncture in the same way that people and objects sometimes tend to be drawn to him. The more precise answer is a birthday present. While having lunch a few days prior to his birthday, he felt the pangs of existential emptiness, the province of the young and satiated. As a result, he registered for the moonlight workshop, a gift from a colleague at work. "It's a different experience, just give it a chance, it will bring things out of you that you never knew were there," she promised him. And, we will not deny it, lots of young women participated in it.

Young women with twinkling eyes and beautiful legs, their bodies submitting to the generous, soft moonlight. The beckoning possibility, a gleaming negative of the dull routine, led him to ultimately agree to join the group that assembled one evening on a chartered bus to the Dead Sea. So, love was already there, waiting to materialize. All Darya had to do was simply to be, and this, after all, has always been her expertise. And she indeed was there, young and happy, two qualities that unperceptive people call beauty. Most of the members of the group knew one another and divided into pairs. The seat next to Darya was usually reserved for Trip, but he had to take the microphone at the start of the trip and say a few words to the group. That is, the seat was empty. She smiled at the man with the green eyes and he sat down next to her – the two magnets were placed close enough, and on the right side of gravitational pull. The conversation was not at all similar to the theoretical falling in love she had imagined when she registered for the workshop, but it was still a very long trip to the Dead Sea. When they arrived at the hotel, Trip's enthusiastic words already seemed like an affected and superfluous backdrop, like background noises that were about to hinder them from pursuing the new intimacy that had developed and from celebrating it in all the known ways. Within two days, Darya would draw from the green-eyed man things he did not know he had in him. At least from this perspective, the gift justified itself.

A baby, for example. Who would have believed that he had a baby in him? He was no more aware of this than he was aware of the unrealized potential of tomato and pepper seeds. (Darya, of course, was the type of person who nurtures avocado pits.) It could be said for both of them that there was some misunderstanding there.

That is, the conversation and the looks and the new feeling that here, something here is happening, were definitely understood, as was the decision to ultimately leave the group. When he said things to her like "I've never felt this way," he definitely meant it. He even was not lying when he said, "I love you." Darya, a moon child, danced as if there were no emptiness in the world or anything lacking. How could he have not fallen in love with her? How could he have known?

The days were short, but very full and heaped with possibilities. He planned dinner and other meals and conversations and perhaps a trip to the North, a slow and sweet march to a foreseeable but distant and abstract end. To his regret and surprise, all this was taken from him before he had a chance. To her credit, it should be noted that this was not a real case of theft here – she actually was on the pill. It was one of those instances when the chemical compound is defeated by human willpower. Though he felt with a hidden sense that he had been defeated by forces greater than him, he had no logical reason to be angry at her. When she informed him that she was pregnant she bore no remorse, and he realized that he was being pushed out prematurely and without having chosen this. In his eyes, this was already nothing less than deceit: He had not chosen to come into the world, so it seemed only fair that at least the decision to bring offspring into the world would be something under his control. From Darya's point of view, it was inconceivable to give up the child. In the same breath, she promised not to demand anything from him. Now he could not get the woman he wanted without all of the other things. He swung between various dosages of sadness and anger and a sense of missed opportunity. When he left, it felt like leaving a room after thinking that the door handle was stuck – the world you left outside just a moment ago suddenly appears full of an air of relief.

Darya kept her word. She did not come to him with any demand to forgive her or love her or support her, and at his explicit and angry request she did not even inform him about the birth of his son. "Come when you're ready," she told him without anger in their last conversation. "Come if you want." So, from all perspectives, he was free of responsibility.

But it was impossible not to know, simply to forget this. It was the same stubborn picture that sometimes forced its way into daydreams; the awareness of it made it impossible to discard. And, nonetheless, he knew the date in the end. Not immediately, but several months later came a businesslike and focused telephone conversation.

"Hello sir, I'm calling from the Pomegranate Branches Hotel. You stayed with us when you participated in the moonlight workshop. I'm calling to inform you that Darya Cohen gave birth to a son and the hotel manager decided to give her a free annual vacation with us. As the father, you're also entitled to enjoy a free vacation, so here's the date for you to write down…"

This conversation was very official, seemingly free of accusation (if you ignore the fact that he never registered or identified himself as Darya's partner or as the father of her child. The hotel clerk's official-sounding voice was a disturbing hint of the existence of a parallel universe in which one-dimensional people behind reception desks and telephones also continue to exist after providing the service, and they see and hear and know).

What did the receptionist want to tell him? The free vacation, of course, was not the subject. Your Darya is here, the voice from the desert was telling him, your child is here. Get up, go to the woman you loved, to the child who is yours even if you did not choose him, to a different possibility of life. Like Jonah the prophet, he fled from his obligations to rest under the shade of his protected life, but in the end, the knowledge that a child was born did not intend to wane. At least once a year, it brought to mind Darya in her white dress walking to the beach with this child – one year old, two, three – enjoying the free vacation and remembering. After all, there was no doubt that she remembered him. He could, of course, travel there, take a peek at them and flee. But this would be unfair toward them, he tells himself piously, perhaps inspired by the approaching Yom Kippur. And what would happen if the child catches his glance?

This was only one layer of life. On the other layer, he continued to keep his job for awhile, and yes, there were also other loves. No one was like Darya, and the truth is, he tells himself, it is better that way: One unplanned child is more than enough. When a friend offered him to leave everything behind and go to Australia to take advantage of a one-time business opportunity, he was young and unfettered enough to agree. The eternal office, with its regular lunches and meetings that stretched on and on, became a fading memory. Within two years, they were the wealthy owners of a flourishing business for importing and marketing fresh-water fish. There was a sense of relief in the relatively independent work, in the open air, in the foreign language. It turned out that he was a free soul after all, and life outside of the office painted his skin with a more correct color. They opened another branch, and then another. Every year as the known date approached, he wondered and also felt a bit guilty for some reason (as if an historical conversation with the hotel receptionist and the offer of a free vacation were obligations he could not betray, of all things). What kind of eyes does the boy have? At this stage, it is impossible to know. His were blue at first, and then gradually turned green later. If the child is similar to him, it is reasonable to assume that they now have the same eyes, because his own eyes were returning to their original blue color the more he immersed himself in the long days of fishing in the open sea.

The business continued to prosper. After the third branch, they sold the business and returned to Israel. It was hard to be banished again to dry land after all those days, the disparity was very large and the chance that he would become an engineer again was very small. The two of them joined a company that was developing an innovative method of raising fish in fresh water. At this stage, he was quite sure that Darya had already married and that the child he didn't want was calling someone else "Daddy." So, every-thing worked out. The detachment he felt since returning to Israel, together with the belief that Darya was no longer possible, led him to think about her less and less. He would have called her long ago if not for the child. He did not choose this child; could he suddenly change his mind after all these years? In any case, calling her would be acknowledging responsibility. Was he ready for this? He had no moral obligation, of this he was sure. His disappearance was very justified. Darya was very Darya. And he has a boy.

There was no seminal moment that made him want to turn back the hands of time. It was impossible to talk about a sudden reve-lation, but since his return to Israel, he suddenly noticed couples sitting in cafés for breakfast with strollers next to them. Sometimes he considered uniting with one of his many female friends for a pressing and shared matter in the guise of a good ending, which is falling in love. In such moments, which were gradually growing more frequent, his thoughts usually wandered to Darya.

A surprising conversation joined this emerging backdrop: "Sha-lom, this is Mimi from the Pomegranate Branches Hotel." The official-sounding voice was mixed with a sort of hesitant frankness. "I called to remind you that this year too you are entitled to a free vacation with us. In honor of your son's birthday."

He waited a moment, as if he needed to jog his memory and then said, "I understand, thank you."

"It's just that I'm leaving the hotel" Mimi said, "I'm going to Tel Aviv and I wanted to remind you before I leave."

"She comes every year?" he asked.

"Every year." Mimi, charitable enough not to wait for him to ask, added: "And the child too, of course. What an adorable boy, he's really our good luck charm here. The child of our hotel. He has green eyes."

He was silent. And as it sometimes happens, despite all the efforts to say or do the right thing, she likes him now precisely because of his weakness.

"She comes alone?"

"Usually," was her cautious reply. "This year she reserved the usual room."

Five years and eight months after the workshop drew from him what he didn't know he had inside, the man with the green eyes again embarked on the windy road to the Dead Sea. The hills stared at him in boredom.

Who is the man with the green eyes? A father-in-the-making who was almost, almost ready, a lover who fled but now changed his mind, or perhaps a person who was still quite young, who was rescued again at the last moment? It would be overly optimistic to assume that he planned to immediately reunite with his obligation-right. It would be optimistic to assume that he had any plans at all of any sort. He just wanted to peek for a moment at the woman that he loved for the shortest period of time with the mightiest intensity and with a five-year-old outcome of this magnetic pull, to see whether something remained in her from the memory and to look into the green eyes of the boy. It was not an acknowledgment of consent to what he regarded as an act of deceit. Nonetheless, he bought a large remote-control car wrapped in tin foil, and on the designated day he sat in the lobby at a safe viewing distance and waited.

Would he recognize her? He did not recognize her. Because Darya did not come.

He did not think to go up to the reception desk to look for that receptionist, Mimi. How would he recognize her? He simply sat there. After several hours, Mimi approached him herself. "Nice to meet you," she extended her hand officially, "I'm Mimi." The wrapped package looked pitiful when she said, "I'm sorry. I didn't have time to inform you, she canceled this morning, really at the last minute. But look, I saved something for you. It's from last year."

The birthday boy's disappointment was transmuted, with only a modicum of success, into a picture taken by the hotel photographer exactly a year ago. Two children gleamed from it and there was no need to point out the hotel's child to him. Now he knew how the boy looked; he absorbed the picture in an irreversible way. Light brown hair, green eyes, looks like a happy child. The twinge in his heart could be interpreted in more than one way.

It was a very small tragedy – there was nothing in the world to prevent him from taking Darya's number now and shifting his life to that track. Get up and go to Darya, whom you love. But who knows what layers have piled onto that night – dust and anger and tears and debts. The mountain landscape made him uneasy. He did not stay to take advantage of the vacation (which he did not really deserve in any case, as both he and receptionist knew full well). He could, at least, send a present. The remote control is not sufficiently remote. He took the address from Mimi. In the end, the car wrapped in aluminum foil was sent by mail.

* * *

Elisha drove to visit Teresa. The hills knew where he was heading and were not abandoned.

Like the northern city of her childhood, Teresa's current city of residence is also situated on the coastline. Apparently, it makes a difference. It seems that the residents of Israel are divided into two – those who have a beach and those who are distant from it. The mayor of Tel Aviv once gave a beach to the capital city as a gift and named it Jerusalem Beach, and thus forever established the supposed supremacy of the beach dwellers. The residents of the South cannot say that they have a sea. On the other hand, it is impossible to say that they don't have one. Thus, they were gradually pushed out of the argument.

Elisha had a few things to do in the city – a visit with Aya and the children, a meeting at the synagogue about the charitable organization, and he would deliver a lecture at the university the next day. Nonetheless, he was traveling to Teresa, the visit's center of gravity was drawn entirely to her house on the outskirts of the city.

Teresa's house was not big. She had always preferred a small house, as if she could guess that she would live alone in the end. Still, the house was very familial: a living room that was worn-out to the right extent, oil paintings on the wall and also things of a more personal nature – a Polaroid photograph of a relative inserted in the frame of a large drawing, notes on the refrigerator, and a specific and regular type of breakfast cereal – intimate items that are always a bit strange to encounter in the homes of others. While Nati's room no longer corresponded to his age, it was clean and aired. The kitchen was small and had cabinets in a woody brown color. (It recently became very fashionable again.) The kitchen window was her favorite window – you could see a quiet street and a small garden from it; in the mornings, it let in the chirping of birds. Teresa always loved them, until she discovered one day that their songs did not rise up to her from the open air, but rather from a cage on the window of the neighbors from the first floor.

There were days when time stood still in this house, for example, the days after Nati left and after Ephraim died. Teresa then conducted herself on an internal level, undefined yet very active, and mostly waited impatiently for nighttime so she could retire to bed with her belongings and go through them again and again. The house suffered no damage from the periodical stoppage of time. On the contrary – it looked younger and fresher than it was liable to appear.

When did she become present again? She had not always been the wise, calm, impressive Teresa she is today. Her skin had always been pale-shining, her hair black, and her eyes large and dark. Externally, no change had occurred in her. Nonetheless, these, yes these, were actually her beautiful years. With the obligatory retreat of the body over the years, a sort of blur was lifted from her. For too long, the young woman Teresa had succumbed to the temptation to please the audience in her life story. After all, if she hadn't married Ephraim after a two-year friendship with him, what sort of ending would this have been? And indeed, they were a handsome couple and so suited for each other. Of course, this was not the reason she married him, and they did indeed build a home and a child was born to them. And, at least according to the precise definitions of those watching from the side, it was a very successful ending. In those insecure days, this was no small consolation. Teresa believed then that she had no tangible assets. After all, her fields of interest were the humanities – that is, of the type that demands self-justification. However, Teresa gradually realized that her main asset was actually herself. People listen to Teresa. There was considerable irony in this – the moment she decided to stop being a story, she became a much more compelling story.

The march of time resumed, signaled by an Italian actress whose name she didn't recall. A magazine featuring the actress on its cover had been lying by Teresa's bed for a long time. "Mia bella!" the caption declared. She put it there at one point with the intention of reading it, but the right time for reading it refused to come. Every Thursday, the housekeeper would demonstratively change its location and Teresa would encounter the date that grew older from week to week and remember that she read in other publications that the actress had already gone and returned and traveled, but still Teresa kept it. The fact that she remembered the exact day on which she placed it there turned the passing time into a horrifying fact. It was before the accident. She kept it for a long time it. One morning, she simply tossed it and the date stopped disturbing. When she met Elisha, the turnabout was completed in its calm and creeping way – she started to see, to hear and to remember small everyday experiences in a way that she could share them with him later. That is, she became the story teller herself.

Teresa was sitting in the living room, wearing her eyeglasses, with her notebooks spread out on the table. She was preparing a lecture for an introductory course for undergraduates. The radio in the kitchen was playing softly. The song that once precisely recounted the story of her life emerged from it in a cover version by a young singer. She hummed it while working, without paying special attention, yet she suddenly wondered: Was the original singer also sitting now on the sofa in his home and humming? She never sits in Ephraim's study, though it is reasonable to assume that he would have no objection. And still, the trapped girl Teresa had to be secretly impressed by the sudden absence of other people from the home. Something in the air became free. Now she was waiting for Elisha.

He would spend the night with her and deliver a guest lecture to her students the next day. The course is entitled "The Messianic Element in Agnon's Writings." (No one bothered to ask how the messianic element is connected to political poetry, and Teresa on her part did not bother to explain.) So far, the course had won only partial success. She gave them a poem to read that the boy Agnon wrote about mission and revelation and waging war against Satan. The students took notes diligently, but it did not seem to her that they were impressed. She hoped that Elisha's lecture about Shabbetai Tzvi and his followers and about Rabbi Jonathan Eybeschütz would manage to stir their interest.

It was not the first time that Elisha came to visit Teresa. Since that Southern vacation when they met for the first time, their relationship had gradually developed. He visited her whenever he came to Aya and the children, or to meet with his fellow members of the charitable organization or any other echo of his previous life. Their first meeting in her Tel Aviv apartment was a bit strange – like the first time an unfamiliar person addresses you by your first name. Gradually, they both also became accustomed to these meetings, a relaxed conversation and coffee in the living room. Sometimes they would go to a play or a movie or eat at one of the places that open and close and change their names and leave monuments for the culinary dreams of others. The bustling restaurant area was familiar to them – both Teresa and Elisha had visited it in their previous lives quite a few times and, who knows, they might have even met there. It is easy to imagine Ephraim and Teresa waiting patiently in line behind Aya and Elisha, with Nati glancing at the trio of children at the neighboring table. A meeting of this sort, if it indeed occurred, would have been meaningless. In the isolated South, their shared process of collecting memories began, only there did they truly meet. For both of them, the annual vacation there, once a year, was something to look forward to.

Before Elisha arrived, he visited Aya and Rabbi Avram and Darya Cohen and her son. In the meantime, Teresa finished organizing her papers and sent e-mail to the department's secretary.

Elisha's visit with the child of the hotel deviously seared a shared memory that was mistakenly stolen from them, Elisha and Teresa and a visit with the child. When she thinks of him, her heart swells. This, despite the fact that the boy's height is also the distance growing between her and the day she became guilty. At any moment, there could be a knock at the door and someone asking her to explain her interference in the workings of fate. She did not regret it. If asked, she would not object to paying the price. There was so little that could be taken from her, compared to everything that was given. When she heard the doorbell, she knew it was Elisha. As usual, it would take the molecules of the home several minutes to reorganize around his presence. Then the present would again appear as if it had always been like this.

*   *   *

Over five years had passed since Nadav left home. It is essential, therefore, to look back and try to understand what exactly happened. How did this sequence of events come to be? Why this particular string of events and not another? The attempt to place the memories in order is like trying to line up a litter of kittens – they wriggle and cuddle and scratch and mainly move from place to place.

The freshest relevant memories were, of course, more available. Elisha did not like to recall them. For example, the day that he and Aya went to the police station to report Nadav as missing. That was two days after he left the house, when they thought he was on his way to his mother and brothers in Tel Aviv. When he did not arrive at either the house or at any of the acquaintances they could think of, Aya boarded a bus and joined Elisha at the Southern police station. The long trip was understandable, of course, but it did not indicate a new closeness that grew between them as is customary, so they say, in such cases. They entered the station together, Elisha placed his hand on her shoulder and poured her some water from a dispenser standing in the corner of the room. Still, even the policemen understood from the first moment: These are two parents who came separately. Nadav was no longer a child then and not yet exactly an adult – a grayish age in which it is very easy to disappear. Since he declared in advance that he intended to leave and not return, the policemen did not seem to be particularly concerned. "We'll do our best, of course. But that's how kids are sometimes," they told them empathetically. Their eyes showed relief – that's how other people's kids are.

The hidden accusation stung even more in light of the fact that if Elisha had been asked to point to one ray of light in his previous life, before he accepted the research position at the Qumran Caves Research Institute, he would have undoubtedly circled with a fluorescent marker the fact that he has three children. Boys actually, not girls. He would see girls in the garden, characters with highly developed consciousness whom you needed to compliment on their clothing, fold the sleeves of their dress, and braid their hair. With boys, he thought, he knew exactly what to do. And in fact, the children (this unfair bundling, as if they were a single body with multiple limbs) usually looked relaxed and simple and happy. Nadav was perhaps the happiest of all of them, and during the last year it seemed that he was flourishing, despite everything. Etched in his memory was the time they allowed Nadav to lead a tour of the caves for a class of fourth graders. They joined him, of course. He did this fluently and passionately, and the two other researchers said, "You're a little Elisha, you." From a distance of time, this sounded like an accusation.

Thus, the year in which an additional layer of life pulsated, conducted in parallel, entered their lives. Elisha and Aya called the police, at first every day, then every week. No one happened to see Nadav traveling on a bus, purchasing a roll at the grocery store, playing in a band. He disappeared as if swallowed up by the earth. Elisha, in any case, was one of those people who harbored in the back of his mind the awareness that every regular day is a windfall – someone lets his guard down and here, the telephone is about to ring, the alarm will sound, an earthquake will occur that will change everything. The day Nadav left signaled the beginning of the realization of all this. There was something familiar to it.

These are the known facts: If Elisha had not accepted the job offer at the Qumran Caves Research Institute and left the Department of Biblical Archeology at the university, they would not have left Tel Aviv, he and Aya would not have separated and that particular day when Nadav left that particular home at that particular hour would not have taken place. That is, there is no alternative to determining that Elisha is guilty. He does not deny guilt, but who shares the other part – Teresa? Aya? Amnon Wolfer? And perhaps he is guilty from a different perspective of primordial DNA that refuses to put down roots? When he thinks of Wolfer, he recalls his last months at the Department of Biblical Archeology, and this memory clearly points to the fact that the decision to leave the department, the city and the home appeared like the only correct course of action.

It's not that Elisha did not like the department – the sterile surroundings, the lawns and the libraries and the temperature that was always under control, gave him a feeling of home. He liked the walls covered with gray wallpaper with the feel of cloth, the bulletin board and the schedule of class hours and all of the things that truly spoke to him. He knew how to use them and so they were his. When did the feeling of revulsion start to trickle into him? Apparently, the moment it was decided that he would share a room with Amnon Wolfer, the department's new acquisition. Amnon Wolfer was a very nice man and very wise too (that is, he was able to combine a basic interest in the field with common sense in the right places), and at first it seemed that except for some initial apprehension, it was a successful partnership. But it was not exactly a partnership – something elusive happened between them. The first time Elisha noticed this was several days after he told Amnon about the meteor shower. Every year on August 12th, Elisha and Aya would pack a blanket and the three children and drive to Mitzpe Ramon, which was then just a distant and once-a-year point on the map, in order to watch the start of the regular meteor shower on that date. It was a tradition. **Their** tradition. In truth, most times they did not see more than two or three shooting stars and the children would usually fall asleep on the blanket spread out under the open sky, but they would still set out each year with the same excitement. When the date approached that year, he shared this with Amnon, who appeared interested and excited. "I have to take my son," he said, and this actually sounded okay, and was even to be expected. A few days later, Elisha was making coffee in the office and heard Amnon casually tell his secretary and one of the professors that he was going with his son to see the meteor shower. "Every year, there's a regular meteor shower on the same date, on August 12th," he said offhandedly. He was not really lying, but still he made it sound as if he had always been going with his son to the observatory on a regular basis. Elisha already had seniority of several years in the department, but he was too honest and calm to boast about his actions, which in his view would drain them of content. No one knew that these were his meteors.

It was the opening shot of a campaign to steal Elisha's persona. It was a quiet and undefined crime that was impossible to complain about. It was expressed in loud and charming reflections. For example, Elisha would put on a disc of the Israel Philharmonic Orchestra playing Tchaikovsky as background music when he was alone in the room. Sure enough, several days after allowing himself to listen to music when Amnon was around, the latter brought several discs of Mozart operas. He happened to run into the department head, just as he was climbing the stairs with the discs in his hands. Of course, he invited him and the secretary too to come listen to them. One time, he turned on the stereo at full volume by mistake and the entire department knew that Amnon Wolfer listens to Mozart. After that, listening to Tchaikovsky was pointless. The music that had pleased Elisha till now was suddenly tainted with a bitter taste of mimicry.

And the walks around the campus, and the preference for pens of a certain type, small and delicate signs of Elisha's character were duplicated at high volume by Amnon. In addition, Amnon was the type of person who nods when he hears the name of a book or article familiar to them and thus appropriates them as their own. Gradually, Elisha started to feel that the room had become crowded. It was the desecration of small pieces of personal property, a cynical use that could easily be labeled inspiration. This also had a practical impact – Elisha's work was not done in a vacuum. He saw himself as a type of funnel. When he read inspirational articles, inspired ideas flowed from him. When he read fluent texts, he wrote fluent texts. Amnon Wolfer, by his very presence, diluted crystals in his funnel and Elisha started to fear that the bulk of his work here was behind him. Of course, he could have simply requested to move to another room. But in addition to feeling uncomfortable, there was also a real concern that this new and likable researcher who listens to Mozart and takes his son to watch falling stars was quite certainly slated for rapid and vocal promotion. So, from a great many perspectives, the offer to move to the Qumran Caves Research Institute came exactly in time. Aya, of course, was not enthusiastic, but the children were excited, and it seemed that their calm family conduct would overcome this too.

That is, it seemed that the departure was the most important thing in the story. But from the distance of time, the picture becomes skewed. Nadav becomes big and prominent and Amnon Wolfer small and flat.

What did the move give him? For a long time, he considered

it the boldest and wisest decision he ever made in his life. The previous life seemed impossible to him now. He has the job, of course, and the salary, and primarily the quiet. What he likes is not necessarily the heat – in fact, it seems to him that in his new lifestyle he is mainly similar to residents of Finland, Sweden, Norway, who live in wide-open spaces and enjoy a peaceful existence and the ability to live the things themselves, without the need to display a colorful personality. The Community Rule group was also peaceful. He shared it with a few very important scholars – he did not share it with Amnon Wolfer. He had time and conditions and emotional quiet for working. All this made the move worthwhile, even before taking into account the fact that the Southern region introduced him to Rabbi Elias and, of course, of course to Teresa.

There is indeed the possibility that if he had not met Teresa, Nadav would not have been forced to seek refuge and he and Elisha would still be spending beautiful days together investigating the Qumran Caves. Even if the source of the earthquake was in Tel Aviv, it cannot be denied that Teresa was there precisely when the cracks started to widen. But Elisha remembers the sight of the teenage boy turning his back to him and does not really believe it. In the weekly telephone call with Aya, they assure each other that he will come back when he is ready; it is impossible to shorten the path leading home. Elisha does not blame Teresa. He loves her. That year brought them even closer and turned them into mirror images of separation and loss. (After all, she also lost a husband and her only son is roaming the world. They imagined possible meetings between Nadav and Nati in India, in Thailand, in Nepal.) Their togetherness was built very slowly; like expectation and longing, it gradually settled in. No, Teresa bears no blame. On the contrary, he finds consolation in her.

* * *

My fifth birthday party was organized indirectly by an unfamiliar woman named Rivka, with the assistance of the department for employee compensation. This Rivka worked on the second floor of the same bank branch where my mother worked. They had never met, and Mother did not even know her last name. She only knew her by the nickname that everyone knew – "Outstanding Rivka." She rightly earned her nickname because she made a habit of being the person with the greatest output at the bank. Monthly, yearly, daily, from whatever direction you could measure, she always came out on top and won free breakfasts and certificates and desk clocks and dreams of early retirement. About a month before my fifth birthday, Outstanding Rivka outdid herself and won first prize for the entire branch in a national competition for recruiting customers. In honor of the event, all of the employees of the branch (including those from the first floor) and their families were invited for a fun day at the Sea of Galilee. And what a day it was.

For me, the excitement already began in the morning when I discovered that it was a group excursion and that it would be by bus. Until then, I had lived my life in quite narrow confines that included our neighborhood, short trips in the car and a vacation at the Dead Sea once a year. The confines had indeed broadened a little during the past year, but Mother still had a clear policy on riding in a bus – no babysitter, not even Mika, was allowed to travel with me on public transportation. In addition to the regular fear of bombings, she worried that I wouldn't get off on time and the door would close, and the invisible thread would be stretched and crack and become full of soot.

So, we headed for the Sea of Galilee. The merry group that settled into the bus was unlike anything I had known – people of all ages and sizes, families with their children mingling with each other in a buzzing tumult. Unaccustomed to family gatherings, I was entranced to be part of all this. I also liked the attention that was showered upon me. (Darya, it turns out, is a very well-liked employee.)

On the way to Tiberias, we passed a field of sunflowers; they all turned their heads as if to signal the way for us in an amazingly uniform dance. The decision to hold my breath until the last sunflower proved to be not simple at all – we drove and drove and the route remained green-yellow. The end of the field came at the very last moment. I released the trapped air with a sigh of relief.

On a global scale, the Sea of Galilee is no bigger than a lake. On a local scale, it is a source of national pride, nearly the only source of water for an entire country and the only fresh-water lake. As such, it spawns a fair number of tourist traps, boat renters and other water attractions, and ice cream vendors. All these are likely to be considered a nuisance when you are a grownup on a tight budget and an acquired revulsion to noise. When you are nearly five, these are excellent tidings.

Someone planted grass on the ground bordering the lake water, and the beach we arrived at was completely green. The grass nearly reached the blue waters of the Sea of Galilee, and the yellow beach umbrellas planted around were the final touch of a perfect picture with strong colors. Sea of Galilee, my wonderful first love! My heart went out to it, quivering in amazement.

We were shot from the bus as from a cannon. When I say "we were shot," I am not referring to me and Darya, but to myself swallowed into a gang of boys and girls my age, laughing and shouting, intoxicated from freedom. Mother conversed cheerfully with two of her friends from work, a woman and a husband, and occasionally shot a not-too-worried glance at the bloc of children moving further away. The bus passengers were divided into Group A, which included adults and very small children, and Group B, ages five and six and seven, old enough to roam around in a group and young enough to stick with each other without prior preparation. An invisible shared thread encircled all of us. The parents' camp shot an inquiring and lazy glance at us from time to time.

After a quick survey of the territory and a quick rub of sunscreen, we raced as a single body toward the water. My body felt that the water was freezing, but my legs were not mine alone to stop them. We jumped. What a wonderful splash! Clear and pure water, quiet as a pool, but from time to time serving up small waves of heat and cold from the foreign land of the border.

Nearly five years old, in a new and different group of children, I discovered the magic of atoms, which arrange themselves in each body in a coincidental and completely different way. Among us, for example was a very beautiful girl. In her first-grade class in Herzliya she might have just been a regular girl, located somewhere in the middle to lower chain of the kingdom. We swam for her. We were not permitted to go beyond an imaginary line on the water, and a responsible adult was assigned to guard the borders. This did not bother us, the cold water and the children's voices created new dimensions of endless space. When I say "we swam" I am referring to the slapping of water, the splashing of arms by children who are not allowed to let their legs leave the ground. Nonetheless, the internal camera captured a group of children swimming, diving, and flapping fearlessly in the depths of the sea.

I was the one who discovered the water slides. In a moment of absentmindedness, I looked toward a random horizon, and there they were. Three winding and inviting slides. "Look, water slides!" I called excitedly. Within a moment, we charged out of the water and galloped toward them as a single, shapeless body. I was in front, the children behind, and behind us trailed the responsible adult sent by the mothers in the group to check that everything was okay.

To our relief, the grown-up forbid us from going near the really scary slide. So we lined up for the two other slides, the blue one and the red one. They twisted gracefully and sprayed water, promising us long moments of pleasure.

When my turn came, I stood there for a moment, freezing in my mind the picture of the water and the hills behind it and the voices of the children screaming beside and in back of me. Why do I need a mucousy and salty sea, with old people plagued with psoriasis and seborrhea, when only a few hours away, at the northern end of the same country, the sea is blue and the grass is green and there is one girl who is worth swimming for? I will think about all this later, now I will swallow the air of this moment, which will echo in my belly – I am happy, I am happy.

I was swept away by the water with a scream. What fright, what happiness, what uncertainty.

Therefore, it was no wonder that a month later, when Mother donned that particular smile and began with "Do you know where we're going for your birthday?" I refused to jump up and down on the bed with excitement as I had done just a year ago. Instead, I covered my child's face with the adolescent facial expression that was starting to develop within me and declared: "Don't want the SaltySea."

When I think today about that conversation, my heart twinges. Poor Darya. Her entire being was maternal and responsible, and she, who would tend to her small joys? There was no adult there to recognize the deprived girl whose sole possession was now taken from her, "But why?"

"It's no fun at the SaltySea. The sea is disgusting and there are only old people there."

"What are you talking about? There are also children there. I can check with the Morgenstern family, maybe they'll come with us. Do you remember Danieli? He's your friend. You were born on the same day."

"I don't want. I don't know him at all. And there's nothing to do at the Dead Sea. I want to go to the Sea of Galilee."

"But they give you the vacation as a present because you were born there. We go every year."

"Don't want."

"So we'll stay home."

"That'd be better."

"We were at the Sea of Galilee not long ago."

"So what. We've been at the SaltySea loads of times."

I was once an old Indian woman who read tea leaves. I remember that they showed us a movie at school about an Indian reservation and I was filled with a strong and wonderful feeling of déjà vu. But nothing remained in me of that wonderful ability to predict future events. How could I have known that my insistence on a vacation at the Sea of Galilee was liable to bring about not one, but two disasters? I won. On the morning of my birthday, we got into the old car and headed north, to the green road, in the opposite direction from the Pomegranate Branches Hotel.

The trip took three hours, during which we heard the same disc over and over. Mother happily and softly sang her favorite song:

That what there is
shall go to those
who are good for it.
Children to the motherly,
that they prosper;
carts to good drivers,
that they be driven well;
the valley to the waterers,
*that it yield fruit**

The words, a Hebrew translation of Brecht's song, sound to her like a real prayer. In fact, for quite some time she has already been adding them to the blessing she makes every Friday evening on the Shabbat candles. As the All-Powerful One, the assumption that God is familiar with Brecht sounds logical.

In the end, the Sea of Galilee in all its blue splendor came into view through our window. From afar, the yellow hills, the blue sea and the green grass created the flag stripes of a new and wonderful country. The air was very hot when we got out of the car. On the sidewalks stretching along the beaches, children in bathing suits were running to and fro, and families with infants and a dog created a moving picture of freedom and proved, in my opinion, that I was right.

The beach at our hotel, the same beach where we played on the

* From *The Caucasian Chalk Circle*, translated by Eric Bentley.

fun day, courtesy of Outstanding Rivka, looked quite empty. The revelry of the children from that day was missing, and their absence painted a gloomy picture. I knew very well that they had simply returned home, the beautiful girl returned to the first grade at the school in Herzliya. But those children, in that wonderful group of atoms, no longer existed, not in the same way. I experienced a light sense of loss.

Still, I was determined in my decision to enjoy the vacation that I had arranged for us. I erased the lost children from my mind (after all, I did not really expect for them to be there) and pulled Mother toward the entrance of the new hotel. "Come on already, so we'll have time to go to the pool!" A moment later, we were walking through the gates of the unfamiliar lobby, tourists in a still unfamiliar land.

The receptionist did not recognize us, of course. The hotel manager also did not emerge from the back office to see how much I had grown. He did not know that I was the child of a hotel and that Darya was the barefoot moon dancer in a white dress. In their eyes, we were just a mother and a child, guests. The receptionist handed us a key with a tired look. She did not ask my name.

Our room was on the third floor. It was my vacation. Mother walked behind me as I marched determinedly toward the elevator. She wore white pants and a red sleeveless shirt and looked very beautiful. If she was harboring sadness about the abandoned crystals of salt, she hid it well. When we emerged from the elevator, I observed the family that came out of the adjacent elevator, and a simple truth that was always there suddenly sprang up. I reached out my hand in an initial masculine motion, which became routine from that moment, and took the small suitcase from Mother.

Birthday presents: A "Young Scientist" kit with a real telescope (from Mother), a "Folk Tales" series (from Father) and a world map for children for hanging on the wall (from Grandfather and Grandmother). All of the gifts were very exciting – amazingly, all of the Santa Clauses in my life choose my presents as if they really know me. After spending a few pleasurable moments checking the new treasures, I lay on my back on the double bed and asked, "How is it that the presents from Father and Grandfather and Grandmother always come in the same wrapping?" The answer was clear to me, of course. The question was no more than an exercise of my still-limited powers of cynicism. The sting was completely removed when I stared at the ceiling miserably. Mother was not moved. "Sweetie, you know that Grandfather and Grandmother love you very much. They can't fly here because Grandfather is working very hard, so they send me money and ask me to buy you things here in their place. And your father also sent me money from Australia in honor of your birthday. That's all."

And that was really everything. One mother and envelopes of money. (What would she have said to him if she had known the true location of Father at that hour?) The other things came and went. Indeed, I spoke with Grandfather and Grandmother on the phone from time to time (Grandmother never gave up on the idea of bringing Mother and me to America) and I was full of anticipation of a promised father who would arrive when the time comes, a father cake rising in the oven. Still, in the end we were only two, a small unit that fully provided for the two of us (so I thought until that vacation at the Sea of Galilee).

I debated whether to nevertheless start one of the "Why isn't Father coming to meet me" conversations, which yield varying responses and loving declarations from Mother. There was something consoling in this. But when I turned my head, I discovered that she had disappeared into the bathroom. A moment later, she emerged wearing a one-piece bathing suit on a body that was adapting to the passing years, with a sleeveless dress on top. "Sea or pool?" she asked. I jumped from the bed. "Pool! No, actually sea!" I announce. "If you don't put on a bathing suit, we won't go to either of them." There was no threatening tone in her voice. We laughed. That is the way it always is. For every sad moment, she makes sure there are two happy ones, so that in sum total we can say that we are doubly happy.

It was early afternoon when we dragged chairs for us onto the beach. Around us, there were no gray mud monsters lying on towels. Instead, families were bunched together on the strip of beach, a group of young people with a guitar sang unfamiliar songs in English. After she attached inflatable floats on my arms, Mother took from her straw bag a book in English and a bag of sour candies. I ran straight into the water, abandoning my body at once to the invigorating cold blast that was not long in coming.

I was sure I knew how to swim. At the Dead Sea, there was no chance to demonstrate your swimming abilities – the salt will turn you onto your back if you only try. The Dead Sea likes its guests floating. But the Sea of Galilee is cool and calm, the fresh water minimizing any disaster of a mouth or eyes remaining open by mistake. I splashed at the waterfront, Mother glancing at me from time to time or waving. Was I ever a fish? I wondered.

When I grew tired of swimming, I came out to rest on the water line connecting the beach and the sea, and sifted sand and small seashells with two hands. A few yards away from me, a girl was doing exactly the same thing. A man came up to me and asked, "Is it your first time at the Sea of Galilee?"

"No," I answered, almost insulted. At this stage, I already loved the Sea of Galilee in a sort of declaration of ownership, it has always been mine.

"You look like an intelligent boy, I'm sure you know to be careful," he said. The man was tanned and very muscular. I listened to him. "The Sea of Galilee is treacherous. It only appears calm, but it has subterranean currents. You need to be careful and not swim without supervision."

"Yes, I know," I lied, refusing to grant him the pleasure of revealing new information. He apparently wanted to shower me with metaphorical clichés of men for men-in-the-making, to compare the sea to a woman or a country or something else, but Mother noticed the conversation, got up from her chair and approached us, staring suspiciously at the stranger. The stranger smiled at her. When she asked, "I'm going in, want to come with me?" I nodded. We ignored him together until he felt superfluous and disappeared.

While in the water, I watched her slowly acclimating her body to the cold streams. She laughed and shivered and tried in vain to get her arms used to the water by dripping gently on them, until I ran out of patience. She noticed me too late. Her shout "don't you dare" met the wave of water I showered on her, her words freezing from the cold and the shock. She immediately retaliated. We laughed and sprayed water, and then we held short swimming competitions. I was amazed to discover that Darya, the woman of the desert, is herself not a bad swimmer at all. So how could she prefer all these years the strange sea and the barren landscape? In my eyes, this vacation was a thousand times better than all of the other vacations. It remained so when we came out of the water and lounged on the beach and went up to the room to change clothes. My first disaster was waiting patiently in the dining room all this time, smiling and joking with the waiter.

The dining room of the hotel at the Sea of Galilee was more magnificent than that of the Pomegranate Branches Hotel, or maybe it just seemed so to me because of the piano. In place of one of the walls, there was a large mirror that created a festive sense of a grand ballroom. I looked around, furtively examining Mother's reaction, and was pleased as a gentleman bringing his sweetheart to a fancy restaurant.

A masculine voice surprised me from behind, and even though I did not see who it was, I could tell he was smiling.

"You really are an excellent swimmer."

I turned around and returned a smile to the man of the metaphors from the beach. Now he was wearing a white shirt and pants, and for some reason seemed very happy to meet me.

"I'm Roni. What's your name?" The name Roni fit him like the shirt. Mother put a hand on my shoulder, Roni now turned to her. "You've raised a fine swimmer."

"Yes, he's okay," she pressed my shoulder.

"Are you alone here?"

"No, we're together." As I already mentioned, I had yet to master the fine line between the bitter and the cynical. It was a very innocent question and, in any case, Roni was not offended. "I'm here with my brother and his daughter (glances at me), she's about your age. (Back to mother) would you like to join us?"

When he made a sweeping gesture with his arm toward the table, my eyes involuntarily were drawn to the place he was pointing to. There sat an unfamiliar man and the shell collector from the beach. I looked at our distorted and frightening reflection in the mirror, and then at Mother. When she said, "With pleasure, why not," all of the candles on all of the tables glowed at me from the mirror in a thousand red lights.

The older I get, the range of my vision broadens. At that moment, I understood a simple truth: Mother was also once a mother kangaroo. Her pouch is empty now, and the air fills it with bubbles that send small quivers to her chest. Her eyes sparkled with a strange light, as if she had emerged from the darkness and was getting used to the sun again. She shook hands with Benny, Roni's brother, smiled at the tanned girl, and sat down.

I sat down beside her with my mouth clamped shut and stared down at the plate. I could hate the girl Dafna or love her, either way I fit in well with the optimistic, amusing scenarios that Benny and Darya were wordlessly sharing above our heads. In fact, I had no influence. Was it any wonder that I was embittered?

The waiter served us an unidentified first course, drowning in sauce. After hours of swimming, I was very tired. The candlelight, the rattling of the silverware and the well-orchestrated laughter of the diners made me feel hallucinatory. Maybe all this was not really happening? Perhaps if I concentrated, the treacherous Sea of Galilee would disappear and outside the transparent window the silent, unsurprising image of the Dead Sea would appear. Suddenly, after my stubborn and successful campaign of persuasion, there was nothing in the world I wanted more than to be again at the Pomegranate Branches Hotel, to move on the slow, regular path from the sea to the pool to the room, to rock gently with arms spread out on calm waters, to meet Elisha and Teresa Holstein in the lobby, to hear from the manager and the receptionist how another year has gone by.

I have no power to turn imaginings into reality or vice versa. When Mother interrupted my thoughts with "You don't like the food?" I was distraught to discover that Benny and Roni and Dafna were still there. In response to her question, Benny started to devotedly cut Dafna's fish and pick the bones from it. They were conducting an unconscious contest for the good parent title. Dafna and I, on the other hand, made no effort to demonstrate that we were the more successful or satisfied child. Dafna was also very focused on her plate.

So, this was the situation: After five years of a more or less satisfying mother-son partnership, Darya felt ready for another partner and another child too, perhaps even a marriage proposal. All of this was well and good, and even logical. After all, I was already too big to be her kangaroo baby and too small to be the man. Still, there was a problem – I have a father and he will come to meet me when he is ready. And what will he say when he returns?

The waiter served soup. I wondered whether Dafna would ask for soup almonds. She did not ask, but Roni did. As he asked, he winked at me. For some reason, he thought there was some sort of pact between us. I did not smile, but still thought it was a shame I have no uncles like Dafna does.

While everyone was trying to imbibe soup without slurping, I said to Mother: "But you didn't even try, you and Father. You didn't even try. It takes him time. Father is coming slowly, but he's thinking about us and until he comes we have to wait patiently."

All of these things I said in my heart, of course, but it just so happened that exactly as I finished, Mother suddenly choked on the soup and started to cough. Roni got up to pat her on the back and we all watched. After a few seconds, she signaled, embarrassed, that everything was okay, but the perfect picture was still a bit ruined.

We spent the next morning on the beach – Roni invited all of us for a ride on a motor boat. Mother and Benny refused and waved to us from the beach as Roni, Dafna and I sailed off. I shot a worried glance at them. Until then, I had not known the infinite sense of responsibility for the actions of someone else, what he was saying now, what he was thinking about. It is very tiring feeling. It is usually the domain of lovers, and then a sweet taste of longing was added to it. I was aware of every movement of the couple receding in the distance. Were they talking about us, or about themselves? Was he touching her in a demonstration of ownership, or perhaps she was the one who was putting her hand on his shoulder? "My father also has a lot of money," I sent her a message over the waves. "He'll come and take us sailing, you'll see." The water remembers, it was moving slowly toward the shore. I become mesmerized by the sound of the boat as it picked up speed.

After a nighttime stroll in the teeming pedestrian mall, another sail in a tourist boat, and another day on the beach of the Sea of Galilee, what chance was there for the vacation to reach its end without a gloomy feeling portending the ensuing emptiness? When it was time to part, Roni said, "It was an excellent vacation, I'm glad we met. Maybe we'll have the chance to do it again." He shot meaningful glances at Benny and Darya. Dafna said, "Come on Dad, let's get going so we won't arrive in the dark." She perhaps felt a small victory when telephone numbers were not exchanged, but I already knew that they had been exchanged the night before. "So we don't lose each other in the pedestrian mall," Benny said, and the cell phones received a new memory. The internal camera forced on the album of memories a picture I would prefer to forget: Mother and I standing next to Benny's car, Mother leaning toward him and laughing and waving goodbye to Dafna.

The car was quiet and empty on the way home. Mother asked whether I had a good time and if I liked Dafna. She had a different, distant look in her eyes that filled me with foreignness. I soon pretended to fall asleep. As she softly sang quiet songs with the radio, I contemplated my disaster. What would happen if Mother and Benny become a couple and even decide to get married? Where would we live? And what would happen when Father comes? Everything seemed so disastrous and overwhelming to me, and all this without having the faintest idea of my other tragedy.

After all, how could I have known that a man came to the lobby of the Pomegranate Branches Hotel that very morning? For at least three hours he sat, read the newspaper from right to left and from left to right, with his foot tapping nervously on the rug and a bag with a package wrapped in aluminum foil at his side. What was the expression on his face when finally Mimi the receptionist approached and informed him that this time Darya had actually chosen not to make use of our regular vacation gift? Upon looking at the picture of the child with the green eyes, a stolen piece of Indian soul stared back at him in disappointment.

*

Many maxims are so obvious that they become worthless. Money is not everything in life, for example. Home is where the heart is. And still, most people would be happy to win an astronomical sum of money in the lottery or change houses. They tell themselves that it would be different in their case. Therefore, the moment they personally experience the cliché in reality, it is always a bit embarrassing. There is a predictable sobering in front an imaginary audience that guessed the ending and is now smiling.

The regular guests of the Pomegranate Branches Hotel scattered that year like an aging dandelion, disseminating seeds of the South throughout the entire country. Mimi did not go as far north as the Sea of Galilee, but she did go to Tel Aviv. Not just to Tel Aviv, but to the Sheraton. She fulfilled a dream and moved to the center of Israel, found an apartment and a job as a hotel receptionist, no less ("with a possibility of advancement, sure," the bored manager told her).

It took a lot of courage to admit the simple, banal truth: She had already been there several long months, and she was not satisfied. That is, and it is important to be precise: It could not be said that Mimi did not enjoy Tel Aviv. The city did not lie in its colors and voices. It was truly colorful and full of possibilities. The small apartment she rented (with a roommate with dreamy eyes who almost never slept there) was really ideally located, close to the sea and the road and the street. Her legs already seemed to walk the short distance between the hotel and the apartment on their own, a well-known sign of acclimation. She learned to recognize the landmarks by heart: a tree, a bench and an old bulletin board. The board did not contribute much to the dynamic image of the city – it was old and peeling and most of the notices on it were no longer relevant. No one bothered to remove them or post new notices on top of them. Mimi knew most of them by heart: "For Rent – a three-room apartment on Ibn Gvirol Street at a bargain price," "The Angry Blue band will appear at The Street pub," and an irate handwritten note – "I recited a chapter of poetry for 40 days and wasn't saved."

But further down the street, the trees looked very ancient and were well cared for, the stream of cars never completely stopped, not even at night, and the bus stops were always filled with people who seemed to have a clear objective. There, the bulletin board was actually very active – on more than one occasion, she has seen a young man or woman post a piece of paper with detachable stubs. The way in which the notice takes leave of them and becomes part of the board makes them stare at it in surprise at first. No, it could honestly be said that she did not regret coming to Tel Aviv. Everything really happens in the center of the country.

The Sheraton Hotel also glittered exactly as she had imagined it. During the first month of her work even Madonna stayed there. Journalists and fans filled the lobby; a report featuring the most elegant suite in the hotel was broadcast on television. No one spoke to Mimi, of course. She was not, at least yet, even the head receptionist, but she still enjoyed all of the action. And her salary was higher than at the Pomegranate Branches Hotel. She wondered whether Shlomo had seen the reports on television and remembered that she was there, and she corrected guessed that he had. Shlomo was not really surprised when she left. In fact, he would have been disappointed if she had not left. This is the tragedy of those with clipped wings – they are held tightly, but still expected to fly. Those who surrender cannot give their captors anything that is not blended with disappointment.

However, for the price of a spacious apartment in the South, she was renting a room here. A small and old room, with all of the street noises barging in when the window is open. Mimi was used to sleeping in quiet. Indeed, there is something consoling in knowing that life continues to make noise after you go to sleep, a sort of sedation of senses that is not unpleasant. However, this is also accompanied by a feeling of lack of control that Mimi found difficult to get used to. In addition, she had to admit that her expectations about saving money and rapidly advancing never seemed more distant. At least as distant as the Dead Sea, a small place where a chambermaid could become a head receptionist and even an administrative manager. A place where people like Michael could realize a dream and build their own private spa. Here it seemed that there was too much of everything, so that each person takes a smaller part of the sum of occurrences.

"Tell me, do you get used to it in the end?" she asked him soon after she arrived. (After all, Michael is a former Tel Avivian, and the fact that Mimi left does not mean that they cannot talk on the phone. In fact, she called him almost every evening. It took only two unplanned conversations to establish a routine.)

"Why, the noise?"

"Among other things."

"There are people who have a hard time acclimating to quiet. It depends on one's nature, apparently. I think you get used to it in the end."

However, several months had already passed since that conversation and Mimi was still not used to it. That is, she had definitely settled in. Small signs indicated that she was already a Tel Avivian long enough to impress the girl with the Mimi eyes, for example. Her toothbrushes were already worn out. When she arrived in the city, she bought a sale package of toothpaste and two brushes, one blue and one red, as if to indicate that here in this city it was also necessary to pair up in order to be saved from this big flood. She alternated between this one and that one, and both were already tired. It was time to buy new ones.

Her social life was also satisfying, if not electrifying. Mimi's greatest fear – to be swallowed up and become invisible – was already dispelled. There were so many young men and women that it seemed statistically improbable that no one would take an interest in her. And in fact, already during the first week, the dreamy roommate invested her to join her for coffee. A few acquaintances joined them and since then Mimi was invited to movies, to housewarmings, to parties. But to her surprise, she discovered that it was hard for her to accustom her body to relax when sitting around without purpose. She did not like staying up late and conducting meaningless conversations and arriving at work tired. And, in general, the whole scene was like a pajama party that lasts too long. If in the Dead Sea region time stood still and was placed in the open air for anyone desiring it, and people could calmly engage in their activities, here it seemed to her that the stagnation of the people is what forces the air to move impatiently.

If you were born in the right place, you do not need to leave it. But it is very worthwhile for you to choose it anew. Michael said this to her and was referring to the South, to the Dead Sea. Now she was thinking that this was also true in regard to relationships. Because there is no other way to express this – as time went by, Mimi discovered that she longed for Michael.

It could be, of course, that it was not really longing, but instead the consoling power of habit and perhaps the same fear one experiences before skydiving – it might very well be that if she had only dared to let go of his hand and jump, she would have lost her breath for a moment and then would have landed in a different place. But Mimi was not interested in skydiving – there were so many possibilities and none of them seemed true. What difference does it make why she finds consolation in his familiar voice? When she calls him in the evenings, he sounds calm to her, and also very distant. He was working very hard, Michael, saving money to start his own spa. It usually seemed to her that he was happy to hear her, but who knows when a new receptionist or chambermaid or just a caretaker would arrive at the Pomegranate Branches Hotel? Mimi knew how easy it was to stand out against the backdrop of the barren hills. A calm realization started to germinate within her. She did not touch it for the time being. Her experience taught her that unripe realizations are always accompanied by a stomach ache. Once ripe, they are sweet and easier to digest. This awareness sort of tied an invisible thread to her previous life, and this calmed her. And indeed, the awaited signal was soon to come. The guest Lily informed her, unknowingly of course, at the end of one night when Mimi was waiting for an important call.

The nights at the Sheraton tired her. Men and their lovers and the businesspeople who just landed visit the lobby at nearly all hours. In fact, it seemed to her that the hotel was more active during the nighttime than during the day. Not that she was complaining. After all, she was very lucky to find work like this. But still, the nighttime guests, with their haughty smiles and the open secrets made her uncomfortable quite often.

The work, all in all, was quite similar to her work at the Dead Sea: take reservations, do wake-up calls, handle the requests of the regular guests. Here there were no towels each year on Yom Kippur or children of the hotel with a free vacation. If a piece of jewelry is stolen, someone will almost certainly file a police complaint. Nonetheless, there are regular guests with regular caprices, Lily for example, the elderly woman from the seventh floor, who was now approaching the reception desk. Mimi looked at her tiredly. Before World War II, Lily was the oldest and most beautiful of three sisters. Since she was very beautiful, she was also very choosy. Courters came and went, and her two younger sisters, who were not allowed to marry before their stubborn sister, watched her longingly.

When she finally married, her two sisters also hurried to get married, but the world war, widowhood and loss did not make them forget their stolen youth. In old age, the three widows moved in together and Lily was required to pay her debt on a daily basis. Now she was approaching the reception desk with bleary eyes, "Do you have some aspirin perhaps? Daisy doesn't feel very well."

"Why doesn't she come down herself?" Mimi asked. (Of course she knew the reason. The two younger sisters, Daisy and Rosy, shared their story with the hotel staff at nearly every opportunity. "Lily will wait for the key," Rosy explained immediately upon their arrival and turned toward the lobby with Daisy. "It's not a big deal, we also waited.")

"She has a headache," Lily said. While Mimi rummaged through the drawers looking for aspirin, Lily observed her. "You're new here, right? Before you, there was Bella. Where is she?"

"I don't know," Mimi shrugged her shoulders. What difference does it make who worked here previously? The thought made her twinge.

"Where did you come from?"

"From the South."

"Far," Lily nodded her head, and as if it were possible to compare, added: "We came from Romania. In Romania, I met my beloved. I waited a long time until I was sure. I was ready to do a lot for love. You, do you have love in your life?"

Mimi nodded. "I think so."

"So now listen to Lily: Everything is nonsense. If you love him, go with him. Everything else will work out. Memories of love are something no one can ever take from you."

Mimi finally found aspirins and handed them to her. "I'm just not sure that he's the one."

"Listen to Lily: Everything is nonsense. Don't be like the women of today, chasing after a career. If you have love in your heart, you glow from inside, you're rich, you're beautiful. Follow your heart. It will already tell you where you need to go."

The advice was, of course, the regular clichés. But Lily's face was so illuminated from the memory of her few years of grace, and Mimi believed her.

When Lily disappeared in the elevator, Mimi thought: But how do you know? The question was much more ancient that Lily. It seemed that Lily had found an answer for her, but she still needed to ask and be asked. Does she really truly love Michael? Does she really love Tel Aviv? The night was very long. By 2:00 AM, Mimi had checked in two couples and received a telephone reservation. There was no doubt about it, the work at the Sheraton was more difficult. But, she reminded herself, it was the Sheraton. The girl whose eyes were Mimi's eyes looked at her with admiration. The promenade visible through the quiet window was teeming with life even now. The receptionist who was supposed to replace Mimi also arrived a quarter of an hour late, but Mimi was too tired to scold her. She said goodbye to her and hurried to her small apartment. Sometimes the events of the night release stubborn adrenaline and do not allow her to sleep. This time she barely was able to take off her uniform and immediately fell asleep. She slept until 9 AM and woke up when her telephone rang. On the other side of the line was a familiar voice and it took her a moment to match it to its owner.

"Mimi?"

"Shlomo," Mimi sat up in bed. "How are you?" Her voice was warm and her body was warm too. Shlomo, who would have believed.

"I didn't wake you up?" he asked, embarrassed as usual, and

Mimi smiled. "No, it's okay," she reassured him. They spoke like old acquaintances.

Like acquaintances, not like an employer and a worker. She noticed this right at the beginning of the conversation. At the end, the feeling was officially affirmed in the form of an offer that was difficult to resist. Shlomo had married the new spa girl and now they were planning to take a year off and travel on a long honeymoon. Michael would continue to manage the spa, of course, and would hire another worker or two, and perhaps she, Mimi, would be willing to take upon herself the management of the Pomegranate Branches Hotel for a year? It is true that she has no official experience in management and he realizes that this was coming out of the blue, as a surprise, but she knows the staff well and with a little guidance he believes she could do a great job. She does not have to give an answer now, but if she thinks it is a possibility, then she should call and they will set up a meeting. He is happy that she is enjoying Tel Aviv and is sure that she is doing excellent work.

When she answered the phone, she was just Mimi, a receptionist at the Sheraton and not even a head receptionist. When she hung up, still a bit astounded, it was the beginning of Mimi, the manager of the Pomegranate Branches Hotel. And with Michael too. That is, to leave Tel Aviv and the Sheraton. What an offer! How could she turn it down? On the other hand, what will happen after the year is over? Arguments for and against bounced around inside her in excitement.

Method of decision making: toss a coin. If you are disappointed with the result, you will know what you prefer. If the result stirs a feeling like the "click" of a coin falling into its place in a machine – it is apparently the answer. Here, this is how great loves and critical questions are decided, on simple nights and in unmistakable signs. While imagining herself and Michael working together again, she suddenly noticed that she was smiling. That's the way it is, she thought as she brushed her teeth, you need to back away in order for the compass to show the way home with certainty.

* * *

In the end, no hotel had to close as a result of the studies conducted by the officials from the Ministry of Environmental Protection. The report they planned to submit did include an assessment that the pumping at the Dead Sea would definitely encourage additional sinkholes to open, but months would pass before the final version of the report was formulated. In any case, it was safe to assume that nothing would happen until after the opening of the Lowest Place in the World Center. The center was designed to be a global tourist site and it would be a great shame, the minister of tourism hinted to the minister of environmental protection if someone spoiled the celebration. Still, the sinkholes produced at least one significant result. The fissure, a many-legged creature with a life of its own, twisted under unseen layers of earth and finally shook the ground under the feet of a local real estate broker. As a result, Elisha and Teresa purchased a small home in the Southern city at a bargain price.

A handsome couple, Elisha and Teresa. When they stroll down the street in Tel Aviv or on the dilapidated promenade in the hotel area – Teresa with her graying hair and usually in her dark dress, and Elisha with his increasingly white beard and skin that remains unaffected by the tanning rays of the Dead Sea sun – they look like a pair of opposites. The faces of the people who look at them usually break into a self-righteous, satisfied grin. They automatically assume that here is a couple who has survived everything and reached this point, a victory of love over the hardships of life and time. Their interpretation, of course, is mistaken and, still, they are right.

Elisha gave this picture to Teresa, as well as the right to finally enjoy simple things like a sale at the supermarket or a recipe for a casserole, things that tend to be blended with loneliness, but the presence of serenity in life makes room for them. There is no urgency in this love, it is very relaxed. It is without the haste that burns the hearts of younger lovers with the need to establish a household and give birth to children.

And so, the home – Elisha and Teresa do not share a home. In fact, they do not even share the same part of the country outside their windows. Teresa still resides in her home in Tel Aviv; she is now a senior lecturer specializing in political poetry. In the center of Israel there is more poetry and more politics, so the choice to remain was natural. One could assume that she would want to cling to the memories of Ephraim and keep Nati's childhood room for him in order to make his return, if he indeed returns someday, one continuous line. All this indeed rested unformulated in the back of her mind, but it is hard to say that she decided to remain. She simply remained there. The addition of Elisha to her life turned the place into a home.

Elisha, of course, would not think of leaving the institute and moving back to the center – just like her, the knowledge that some-one belongs to him somewhere has become part of his general disposition and enables him to love his current location even more. They speak often, but their meetings are relatively rare – twice a month he comes to see his children in central Israel and sometimes she travels to visit him. The months of the year revolve around her annual vacation, which is now extended, when she spends a week at Elisha's vacation unit at the Pomegranate Branches Hotel. A hasty heart would not agree to this. It would insist on sharing reality in the customary ways. Elisha and Teresa share other things.

The house stands at the far edge of the city. It is not really a house. That is, it is not a place where you could live before a long period of renovations by a loving hand; it demands patience and a generous purse. The garden was ruined, of course – pampered plants that demand frequent watering do not survive desert heat waves. Only the bougainvilleas, real survivors, have bothered to leave a flower and a leaf here and there, like a monument: Once there was a hedge here. In the house itself, a wooden door indicates naïve construc-tion whose time has passed, the walls need paint of course, that's the easy part. Small spots of mold indicate more severe problems.

They came across it by chance when they lost their way heading back from the city's small shopping center to the hotel area. They were staying at the Pomegranate Branches during their annual vacation. The need for aspirin, newspapers and pantyhose does not disappear upon setting out on vacation and sent them to the shopping center. On the way back, Elisha missed a turn and they continued to the less familiar edge of the city. It seemed to end with a clear border – a last house and then mountains and earth. Before he turned around, Teresa asked: "What house is that?" and he stopped the car. They had free time and the acquired right to be curious about ostensibly mundane things. They got out of the car and looked around. The house was neglected and it was obvious that no one lived there. This fact shouted from the peeling walls, but also from the "For Sale" sign.

They called the telephone number posted on the sign. At this stage, their intentions were nothing more than a moment's caprice.

"We're calling in regard to the house," Teresa said, as if one could order a house for oneself at a distance of a telephone call.

"Ah, yes," the man answered on the other end of the line. "Do you want to look at it from the inside?" It turned out that he himself lived a few streets away from there. They waited.

The whole thing seemed a bit like a practical joke that was out of place. They smiled at each other and for some reason felt excited. The owner, named Akiva, arrived within minutes. He proved to be not an especially shrewd salesman. "We inherited this house from my wife's mother," he disclosed. "We thought we'd renovate it for the children, but will all these sinkholes, we decided not to take the chance. In any case, it's not very likely that they'll remain here. It's better for us to save for their studies."

"How old are they?" Teresa inquired.

"Fourteen, ten and seven," Akiva said, opening his wallet. "So, it needs a little renovation work, it's been quite some time since someone lived here. But all in all, it's a nice house."

"How much are you asking?" Elisha inquired. The price led them to again exchange glances.

A few days later, Elisha and Teresa were already on their way to becoming the owners of a shared property on the outskirts of the Southern city. Since Elisha had his own opinion about the danger of sinkholes and he expected home prices to actually appreciate, one could regard them as an older couple who became partners in a joint real estate investment.

But, in fact, they were building a home. Not now, not at the moment, there was no urgency for a place to unpack boxes and build a nest and send children to kindergarten and school. It was a future home that they would enter one day. This knowledge gave them both a sense of tranquility. Elisha would not leave the Qumran Caves, not as long as the scrolls continued to stir the excitement that makes the mornings more alive for him. Teresa would not leave her work in central Israel as a lecturer in political poetry, though she started to look into a job at the university in Beersheba – after all, the South also has politics of its own. They hired a home renovator, chose bookcases – in any case, their libraries were gradually becoming a joint asset, with borrowing and gifts and memories. When would they move in? They did not have a defined date. Elisha has to sell the vacation unit, Teresa must find a job. The home in progress is an island of certainty. Together with it, an unfounded but inevitable hope sprung that it was the right home for hosting children. After all, Nati would eventually grow tired of traveling, Teresa was convinced. And perhaps the twisting crack would continue to search for a place to erupt and would also send messages of home under Nadav's feet.

*   *   *

It would have been nice to maintain symmetry. Let's say, if Mother rejected the advances of that Benny without any apparent reason, and a year later we returned to the Pomegranate Branches Hotel to celebrate my sixth birthday and met my father there – however, life bursts out in its own order, and the truth is that the dramatic meeting with my father did not take place on my sixth birthday or on any birthday. After that northern vacation, I had to continue to worry in regard to Dafna's father for three whole months.

What would happen if Mother met with Benny, Dafna's father, time after time, and they became a couple in the end? The usual assumption is that I would eventually get used to it. I find this hard to believe. In my previous incarnation, I was a bear cub curled up in winter slumber. The thought about one girl, who would take from us the calm, sleepy waiting, and bring summer too early and force upon us shared meals and trips and all the rest, terrified me. When the threat to our future family cell was finally lifted, there was much more than a hint of relief.

It was not easily lifted. Because that Benny did indeed call. After and perhaps before everything, my mother was Darya, the girl of the moon dances, and that was not even in her previous incarnation. The thread connecting us was now long enough to allow her to turn around in circles, even to dance. My shocked body from the very thought of being tossed about like this managed to develop the flu, accompanied by shivering and dizziness. (The first winds of autumn had already begun to blow, a clueless social worker heard that I was absent from school and called to ask if we had money for heating.) Their date was postponed by a full week, but eventually took place and troubled me very much. It was also because, for the first time, she told me with whom she was meeting, which indicated her intentions. And, in particular, it was because the internal camera caught her straightening an earring with a look in her eyes or perhaps a scent that someone who was once her body itself recognized as meaning one thing: That's it. She did not plan to wait any longer.

Some would say that it was inconceivable that she had waited till now – for some reason, people tend to believe that no one else would come to terms with what they themselves are capable of. I cannot deny that she would get dressed sometimes and go out in the evening to dance or to drink something. Mika stayed to look after me on at least some of the nights. But one thing I know with certainty: No man crossed our doorstep and stayed long enough to step out of the characters he and she created and become the people they really are. As long as there were no signs of non-sterile love on the horizon – tears and moods and the shirt from yesterday – I was relaxed. The voracious scent now did not signify a casual conquest of the body, but worse than that. The autumn winds did not help. The poisonous voices whispered that it did not matter with whom, the main thing was to finally enter the home, take off the shoes, hang up the coat, and snuggle. I hoped that I was the only one hearing them.

But in the end there was no need for the flu – Benny pulled himself back on his own. Since he was an adult with no moon education, he did not know how to touch Mother in those places that blur pointed noses or nasal voices to make them seem not as bad as they really are. Thus, he missed the opportunity that came his way. He did not even invite her to dance. On their first date, and also on the second and third, he took her to three different and very expensive restaurants. The scent gradually faded and finally disappeared at exactly the right time. A car with a remote control wrapped in aluminum foil did indeed make it all the way from the Dead Sea and now waited on the refrigerator for the right time, but the man who is my father was not about to wait another whole year until we came again to the Dead Sea on the annual vacation – from the moment he decided, he was drawn to fatherhood just as strongly as he had recoiled from it at the beginning. As I reached the age of five and three months, he was about to fulfill his educational duty and teach me a first lesson in disappointment.

And this was preceded by expectation, of course. There was a certain amount of injustice in the fact that the three telephone conversations of Father with Mother-Darya took place while I was sleeping or in kindergarten. It took him three months to gather the courage to pull out the piece of paper with the Pomegranate Branches Hotel logo on which Mimi had jotted down the number in her neat handwriting. (Did he really need a note from her in order to locate the phone number? Probably not. And still, you can pick a flower for yourself, but the one that is picked for you has a driving force of its own.)

"Darya," he said, "it's me." A sentence that could spring from anyone. Still, she was happy to hear that it was him. If she were someone else, perhaps her voiced would have been mixed, even unintentionally, with accusation and pain and bitterness, even if in varying amounts. But Darya was Darya. Even now I smile proudly as I remember that she simply was happy to hear him. Her joy was sincere, without any tones of past and future, so light that it easily fluttered via the new thread and the words passed over my head like carrier pigeons that were diverted from their path by an earthquake. The awareness that we were traveling to the SaltySea to meet Father hit me by surprise. Why did they choose this distant location? I suppose that every child psychologist would advise Darya not to bring the man called my father into our small home, at least not at the beginning. The social worker would surely be horrified to think about the tragedy that was about to befall me and warn her not to endanger my childlike soul with premature promises. But, of course, Darya did not think of consulting with any of them and, in any case, I was the main reason for the meeting. But even I understood – first of all, it was a meeting of two. In order for me to have a father and mother, they first of all need to meet. Since they already had met, the time had come to follow the trail of breadcrumbs, to collect the abandoned heart strings from their place. It was the only place where it was possible to believe that time had been preserved in salt or at least its speed had been slowed.

We were traveling to the SaltySea. The road looked different in this season of the year, and we too were differently dressed in long-sleeve clothes. The words between us were words of winter (don't leave the heater on, we need to buy boots for you). They do not usually go together with the warm trip. Just the car was the same car and even it was groaning. The foggy landscape forced it to open its headlights wide.

During this season of the year, autumn crocuses are in bloom on the road to the Dead Sea – a rather ugly flower that succeeded in being rare. People who are exhausted from the road take pictures with them and then spread blankets for a picnic, just so the autumn sun can mock them and move an inch to the side, leaving them in the middle of a dark and abandoned spot. We were in a hurry, of course, and did not stop to look at the crocuses, but sufficed with glancing from the window at fields of wheat that had already been harvested. I showered Mother with dozens of questions: What does Father look like? What color eyes does he have? Is he strong? Why did he come back? What time will we meet him? Mother answered as best she could (beautiful eyes, green. Very strong. Because he missed you. In the afternoon).

The sea looked like it was opening its eye to us. A blue pool came into view through the window in silent amazement. There is a sort of protest in the water's lack of movement, as if it were trying to say that our late arrival would not atone so quickly for the abandonment. I felt a bit guilty that I did not have a birthday. And as if to demonstrate the fact that this was not just another regular vacation at the Pomegranate Branches Hotel, when we finally entered the hotel, exhausted and excited, we were received by an unfamiliar receptionist. It was an unfortunate case of a very smiling young woman – one of those who apparently were once told one by someone that if they just smile and stand up straight, the world will smile at them, and thus their natural gentleness was robbed, creating a smiling and erect creature infused with rigidity. She smiled an excessively broad smile at us and asked, "Yes, may I help you?" I glanced at her from the height of the table and considered whether to tell her that I'm going to meet my father. In the end, I decided that the prohibition on speaking to strangers also applies to receptionists at the familiar hotel. And besides – it is **my** father. This possessiveness was new and pleasant to me. I scowled at her.

Mother spoke with the receptionist and explained the circumstances of our arrival to her, which do not require a room charge. (It turns out that I was still the child of the hotel.) The receptionist was still smiling, but her eyes reflected the dread of having to make a decision. She said: "Just a moment, did you arrange this with

Mimi? Let's call her, she'll be here in a few minutes," and she dialed on the internal phone. We waited.

After no more than five minutes, rapid steps approached. My wonderful father was pushed aside in favor of the here and now. Yes, there was no doubt about it, it was our Mimi! A broad smile in exactly the correct proportion, a white starched shirt and, nonetheless, something was different about her.

"Don't charge them," she said to the young woman at the counter and walked straight toward me to give me an emotional hug. "Look who's here!" She asked me, radiantly: "Do you have an important guest today?"

So, it turns out that she was up-to-date. I was too old for this type of hugging, I nodded. "My father will come in the afternoon," I told her. Mimi was not a stranger. While she and Mother were talking about Mimi's new position (and avoiding with casual and discrete wisdom any mention of the meeting that was slated to occur), I broke away from them and placed my nose on the glass door at the hotel entrance. I will recognize him – green eyes, very strong and it was already almost afternoon. Five years and three months passed quickly, but I could hardly bear the minutes remaining until the meeting.

And Father did not come.

That is, not at the appointed hour, and also not an hour later. For five years, I had cultivated a perfect father. My real father already managed to instill in me disappointment and abandonment and distrust on the first day of our acquaintance.

"When will he come already?" I asked Mother. She made sure not to wear a white dress, but she looked very beautiful. Her blue dress was soft and full of cloth and rustled small waves. Was she imagining horrible accidents, being crushed under the wheels of a car and loss of memory forever? I don't think so because even here, even now, she gave me the same answer.

"He'll come when he's ready."

Minutes passed. Mimi had left some time ago, the smiling receptionist was busy with her affairs and Father was not ready. "Call him," I demanded.

"I called. There's no answer at home, he's apparently on his way. If he doesn't arrive by the evening, we'll call again. Come, let's go up to the room." She gave me her hand and I trudged after her to the elevator, dragging behind me a flimsy bag. In the room, we turned on the television. The afternoon passed, courtesy of "The Bold and the Beautiful."

For the first time in my life, I was facing two possibilities I had never imagined: Mother was wrong and Father was not coming. A cold caress of sudden orphanhood swept over me. Mother, on her part, looked excited (though, of course, a bit worried). After six years of waiting, the time of reckoning had come.

At eight o'clock in the evening, the blue dress was already tired from the graceful movements. It lay almost motionless on the bed. I was already washed and in pajamas. The shattering of routine, on the one hand, and the illusions, on the other hand, sent me running restlessly around the room.

I am the king of outer space. A ridiculous plastic shower cap is my crown. I forbid the human spaceships to enter my domain. Whoever crosses over is destroyed in a torrent of fire. The curtain, the dresser and the television – all of them are enemy spaceships in a dizzying battle that I win over and over and over, and do not ask questions. All of this lasts for an eternity, even after my bedtime.

What time was it when I fell asleep, arms spread across the double bed? As usual, all of the interesting things happened while I slept. A soft knock, a look and an explanation, I had to imagine all this. When Mother placed a gentle hand on my shoulder, I mistakenly thought it was morning, but only darkness winked through the unfamiliar window. In fact, I slept for perhaps two hours. When she said, "Yonatan, say hello to your father," I peeked at his face, a sleep-struck king in pajamas. His eyes were green like they promised. After a delay of five years and three months, I awarded him a first cry.

*   *   *

The way back home is an exact science of time and circumstances. An ill-timed arrival leads to a final fading of the vague memory and is liable to entail many tragedies – for example, returning to your childhood home after too many years and discovering that you flinch from using the toilet. On the other hand, returning too early might blur the memory of leaving and cause everything to start anew. It is almost impossible to simply pick up from the point where you left off. In Mimi's case, her success can be attributed to the Judean hills and cotton fields, which cushioned her final trip back from Tel Aviv to the South with the obedient, obvious and heartwarming thought – nothing has changed here.

A mistaken thought, of course. In fact, quite a bit had changed at the Pomegranate Branches Hotel and in the Southern region during the year that Mimi lived in Tel Aviv. Usually, the secret changes in the provinces you have abandoned are uncovered gradually – a store sign that changed, a stand that closed, hard-working ants under the mountains relocate the grains of sand. The body's skin cells peel off and are renewed every fourteen days, so actually all of the familiar people you meet will now have a different face.

Shlomo, for example. Soon after Mimi left, Shlomo signed up for a management workshop, one of those personal empowerment workshops in which the participants hope to transform their lives till now into a distant dough called "before." Accustomed to provide service, he did not want to disappoint the instructor, who really believed in him. He defined an objective (to set out on a long trip with his new fiancé), made a decision (to take a year off) and executed a mobilizing conversation (he called Mimi and suggested that she fill in for him). He received a lot of applause when he told about this at the concluding session.

And Michael, of course. He looked different. The greatest fear of returning lovers is a justified fear – Michael definitely changed during the past year and Mimi was glad to find that he was more familiar, happier, some missing piece had finally slid into place. As part of the changes Shlomo instituted at the hotel, he gave Michael free rein to expand the spa rooms. He was now managing a sort of small health club within the hotel and already had some regular clients (and primarily female clients). The fact that Mimi finally returned from central Israel to the place where just one young man was waiting for her, reached his face, perhaps around the forehead, via a sort of underground current. There was some turnover in the small staff of chambermaids. Joining the chef was a new apprentice – a skinny youth who followed him like a shadow and displayed a slightly exaggerated tendency to use herbs.

The mix of guests had also changed a bit – a change that only someone who was very familiar with the hotel would be able to detect. It seems that this year a relatively surprising number of young couples were staying at the hotel, a fact that was perhaps attributable to Michael's state-of-the-art spa. There was even a honeymoon couple, which stirred great excitement in the hotel. A festive announcement appeared that day in the newspaper: "The newspaper's editorial staff congratulates Yuval and Neta on their wedding. We wish them every happiness."

There were also some changes among the regular guests: The Morgenstern couple did not come this year. (Avi Morgenstern was now managing the construction of a huge chain of malls in Europe.) The writer who would come every year for a full month disappeared. (There was a tragedy in his family the previous year. It was before the holidays and one of his regular readers was in the midst of sculpting pomegranates. When she read about the tragedy, she was overcome by a desire to console him. In the end, she sent him a gift of three red pomegranates made of clay, now displayed in his living room. In this way, she distinguished herself from the amorphous body of readers and he found himself writing for her. But he had no idea what she wanted to read, and so he did not succeed in writing anything at all that year. Mimi, of course, could not have known all this – she saved his favorite room for him until the very last moment.) Teresa Holstein canceled her regular reservation, though not her arrival – she now stays in Elisha's vacation unit.

And of course, Darya Cohen and the child of the hotel. They were also scheduled to take advantage of their annual vacation, but in no way could it be said that this would be a routine vacation.

And Mimi. The changes that occurred in her were clearly evident, of course. Was it the trip to Tel Aviv that caused all this or perhaps there are periods in life in which time moves more rapidly? She was managing the hotel now. She was a substitute manager (salaries and payments to the various suppliers were arranged in advance), and still, after a month-long orientation period, Shlomo festively told her "I feel happy to leave the hotel in your hands." This sentiment partly derived from the fact that he had just married and was about to set off on vacation for a year. Nonetheless, several months had passed and it was already possible to confidently say: The hotel was definitely flourishing under Mimi's management. She did not realize the dream of a single color for all of the rooms (she lacked the authority for this and, besides, this suddenly seemed boring to her), but she was definitely refreshing the pictures in the lobby, consulting with the chef about new menus and there was a buzz in the air. She was energetic and responsible and fair and the staff was small enough to accept her. She was especially fond of the young receptionist.

Not only had the job position changed. In addition to the official clothes she became accustomed to wearing, small suits and high heels and stockings, another change was now shining naturally on her finger.

From Mimi's point of view, the question of what led to what is just as insignificant as the question of whether the serenity resting upon the hills of the South is imaginary or real. The story of her life was written in clear and easy-to-describe facts: She, Mimi, grew up in the South, left for the center for awhile and discovered that she was drawn to the landscapes of her childhood and the man she left behind. Now she was the acting manager of a hotel where she had started to work as a chambermaid and then as a receptionist, and soon she will marry Michael. It is a simple story, without letters in secret code between the lines. This is what she will tell the girl whose eyes are Mimi eyes. Leave if you want to, I also left, and I will always be here if you want to return. She and Michael looked for a place, now there are about to be one. They will be the first couple of the Pomegranate Branches Hotel. From her place in the lobby, she noticed a line starting to build up in front of the receptionist and frowned: She, Mimi, would never have allowed this to happen. She got up and walked briskly to the reception desk.

*   *   *

On my sixth birthday, the road to the Dead Sea was again padded with the abandoned clouds of cotton of the end of the sabbatical year. This was a year in which slaves and fruits and vegetables return to their original form of conduct, debts are erased and people who did not plow or harvest or plant for seven years could enter any field and pick the ripe fruit. And still, there is justice in this. The earth becomes accustomed to its vacation like a school pupil – at first, the body maintains some alertness out of habit, and with each passing day it relaxes a bit more. Now, before the end of the year, the fields are abandoned, satiated and full of expectation.

The landscape of cotton gradually changed and became a hilly desert just as the car passed the impossible sigh: "Sea Level." The light hills looked like the curves of a large woman and did not raise an eyebrow when encountering the simple picture we drew for her – a father, a mother and a child on the way to the Dead Sea for the annual vacation, despite the fact that we only officially met for the first time a few months earlier.

The memory of the first meeting is definitely sweet – I, the enthusiastic, excited, fortunate child, sat with Father at breakfast in the hotel and asked all those questions: What did you do in Australia? Why did you return? Do you want to live with us? What do you like to eat? And I filled a bowl with cornflakes and flooded it with rivers of honey. After that initial meeting, it was decided that I would spend time with him twice a week (the social worker would certainly be pleased). But he was interested in the whole package – a woman and a child. On the days when we were not scheduled to spend time together he would come to Darya, so in practice I saw him nearly every day. The moment this realization was stitched on my skin, it began to take on new life, but the stitches gradually fell off and the ride to the Dead Sea was still very long. Though I was excited at the beginning of the trip, I later sunk into the back seat and searched for a solution that would relieve the boredom.

"One-hundred apples on the tree, one falls down on a bumblebee. Ninety-nine apples on the tree, one falls down on a bumblebee. Ninety-eight apples..." We sang the silly, pointless song with dry throats. I was the one who taught them the song – I learned the words at day camp in the summer. They repeated after me obediently and displayed surprising skill. It is very possible that they already sang this once, perhaps even in this incarnation.

The first day of the vacation was my birthday. After several short stops on the way, we arrived at the hotel around noon, exhausted. The regular receptionist was no longer standing behind the reception desk. She welcomed us with a warm handshake and a dark suit (now she is the acting manager of the hotel. I was actually much more impressed by the other change that had occurred in her). "Here's our child of the hotel," she beamed at me.

Birthday presents: "The Young Archeologist" series of books (from Grandfather and Grandmother) and a knight's castle (from Father and Mother). They sang "Happy Birthday to You" in two voices, and I examined the new treasures with excitement. When I finished spreading the books out on the bed, I expected that Mother would go into the bathroom and would emerge from it as Darya with a bathing suit peeking out from under her dress. Instead, she asked: "Do want Father to take you to see a movie?" I liked this offer – most of my life I did not have a father and a mother. Ploys aimed at sending off children for an hour or two were still new to me. And in any case, one could speak of extenuating circumstances – in truth, they ultimately had not had much time to be alone. We went down to the children's room, where Mimi was waiting for us. It was not surprising that the audience consisted of me and one little girl.

"You can come back in an hour and a half," Mimi smiled at Father over my head. Father patted my shoulder (his movements were not natural yet, he had watched too many American movies) and he returned to the room.

Six years and eight months after the night of the flickering light bulb, the man who is my father stood facing the woman who is my mother and looked at her. In his imagination, her eyes turned sad and accusatory and haunting. Then he remembered that, in fact, they also had reflected the same serenity back then. Was he disappointed to discover that despite everything we were happy? I, of course, had always wanted my father. But we still had been happy with our lot, a clown fish and a sea anemone, protected on both sides.

I am not saying, of course, that to abandon a young woman after a night of love is the recommended course of action. Nonetheless, how wonderful. Her skin was still smooth (it was not the smoothness of adolescence), her eyes were shining. The white dress was replaced by a buttoned cotton dress. He opened one button, then another, and she was there. How many people in this world have had the privilege of exposing the still unfamiliar body of a young and beautiful woman, whose hidden breast, secret and ready to burst, was the place from which your son, your only child, suckled his first milk? The man who is my father ran an excited finger along the throbbing skin, the skin of the young moonlight woman. The unfamiliar woman, the love of his youth, a beautiful girl, the mother of his lost son. A symphony of contradictory emotions threatened to overwhelm him.

Carpe diem, what a sweet here and now.

And just like it was then, a few minutes later, embraced in his arms, she felt my steps approaching her, sensing my very existence.

"The movie ended!" I opened the door without knocking and entered the room. In some ways, a two-person cell is very convenient. Father and Mother stared at me from the depths of the blanket, initially dumbfounded in coping with the consequences of their actions. You lie with a woman, and then a child arrives. This time, my experienced father chose to smile at me. "But they didn't close the promenade. Give us a moment to get dressed and then we'll go down. I want to show you something."

A few moments later, we left the room and walked toward the elevator. I gave him a hand – the novelty had not worn off, my arm swung his arm proudly. This is my father. A new title in preparation for the anticipated loss of the exclusivity of my old title. On the way out of the elevator, we met Mimi who greeted us cheerfully as usual. "Is everything okay?" she asked. Her hand moved over her belly, caressing someone who has a pretty good chance of finally becoming the second child of the hotel.

This is not the only change I found at the hotel. I see it now through the lens of a six-year-old boy, but there were also other differences: On the wall welcoming those entering the hotel, on the short way to the reception desk, there now hung a series of pictures of flowering pomegranate trees against the backdrop of a silent blue sea, for example. The glass cabinet displaying tempting cakes (if we ignore the fact that they are the same cakes that have been on display there for seven full years already) was replaced, or perhaps thoroughly cleaned. And the mirrors were removed from the entrance wall, where they used to assault the guests before they had time to arrange their body into the desired shape. The deep bordeaux-colored chairs remained as they were. Under the velvet upholstery, one could see a light wrinkle of an additional sequoia ring.

But basically the place remained as it was – the entrance door still revolved and next to one of the tables in the lobby Elisha and Teresa were sitting. (Were they holding hands?) And I tried to remember whether their hair had always been so gray, I decided it had. They recognized me, of course – everyone knows the hotel's good luck charm. And Teresa and I go back a long way. Now she was smiling at me, "How are you Yonatan? It's wonderful to see you." I smiled at her too. The response was sufficient for both of us, but when Father said, "Don't you want to answer her?" I quickly stifled one thought (He has just arrived, why is he already telling me what to do?) and nonetheless answered: "Fine. This is my father."

"Very nice to meet you, very nice to meet you," Teresa and Elisha said. Their eyes reflected a shared and almost amused understanding – they apparently knew quite well who the man with the green eyes was. "So are you going for a walk in the area?" Elisha asked and Father nodded, a bit embarrassed.

"Well, it might not appear so, but there's a lot to see here. Riverbeds, caves, you know," Elisha gave me a serious look. "Not far from here, there's a cave called the Qumran Cave. They once found a real treasure there."

Father did not know Elisha. An electric current of concern streamed from his hand to mine – is this bearded man, this strange person, about to insist on joining us? Don't worry, my hand rested securely in his hand, we can trust him.

"Elisha studies the Qumran Caves," Teresa told Father. There was a new pride in her voice, a proprietary pride – as if to say, "We are studying the Qumran Caves." The new togetherness somehow also links her to Mother, who was sleeping in the room. Teresa did not ask where she was. Judging by her smile, it seemed to me that she had guessed that Darya was sleeping now alone, rocking in the thought of a father-son outing and the memory of the past hour, and there was not a more satisfied woman in the whole world. We said goodbye with a promise to go on a hike with Elisha the next morning. In the caves, he promised, there is a walking path and they show a film about the Community Rule group. I guessed it would be very boring. Meanwhile, my father and I went out for a walk.

How many times had my father raised his eyes to the night sky and introduced them with a father's enthusiasm to an imaginary child? Australia is very far, but still under the very same sky I stood and received my star lesson from Efi, Mika's husband. My first look of discovery I dedicated to him, it was him I admired. The simple truth is that I was happy.

I did not tell this to Father, of course. At age six, I finally developed some intuition. Even though I knew everything about stars (I have a solar system on the ceiling of my room), I let him lead me outside to the promenade and I enthusiastically followed his finger as it sketched bears and dippers. We were a cliché of a very sweet father-son.

But we were not without some cracks. A few moments later, I saw a kiosk that was open and asked for ice cream. Father looked at me for a moment – was it possible that Darya had already told him that I was not supposed to eat sweets before dinner, or perhaps he also had started to feel the healthy buds of the very same intuition that evening? In any case, when he finally bought me the ice cream, we looked at each other with understanding. It was nice to swing on the seam line, but there has to be order.

The next day we went down to the shore. Darya wore sunglasses and browsed a paperback in English. The internal camera caught a lazy finger turning a page, brow furrowed a bit, entirely focused on everything that is truly important. This is the picture I will pull out of the drawers of my mind when one day I want to look back and remember what type of woman my mother was. In her young face you could still see a puppyish quality that children cannot detect; you could see that before there was Darya there was Doris, and before that – the girl Dorit, who would pick the wood sorrels that always grew in the fields of clover. Whether or not she found a four-leaf clover, the shining yellow bouquets were immediate and sufficient compensation for her. There was nothing heroic about this lounging at the seashore in a remote hilly region, but still I knew that the picture would fill me with pride.

This vacation also featured a real and sophisticated camera – pieces of life captured eating popsicles, floating with arms spread in blue-green water, one child crying. Father bought a digital camera as part of the accelerated process of fatherhood and couplehood. He also took a lot of pictures of the scenery – the white island of salt, the mountains beyond the sea, the row of orphaned chairs that the morning bathers had dragged into the water. The vacation offered him many moments of the type that make people want to take photographs or paint or capture the moment in any way other than memory. Inexperienced as he was, he was yet to learn that scenery does not lend its soul to the camera. The fate of the boring pictures was doomed from the start. The Dead Sea looked at him patiently.

They say that an oyster always returns home. It makes no difference how far away you put it, the oyster will cross the ocean, mucous-like and lumbering, and ultimately return to the starting point. The first time I heard this, I planned to find an oyster and place it on a bench on the promenade in Tel Aviv. I thought, what could it do now? Take a bus? Go by foot? I imagined it lethargically boarding a boat at the port. One thing I can say for sure: The moment it arrives, it forgets. Hundreds, millions of years of journeying throughout the ocean suddenly become a hazy memory.

What does the future hold? Who knows. Maybe I will travel to India, like everyone. There I will learn for the first time about mysterious teachings, about the magic of the moment, about the tranquility in letting go, and about the power of hope. I hate clichés, but still. Something will be hiding there for me, a point of light. One that will draw me to it with a warm sense of déjà vu.